Jessie bent to his touch, molded to his body, gave herself to his kiss. It was so good to see him, to have him touch her, to feel his hard, masculine body against her. His mouth parted her lips and gave her a kiss that set her on fire, that drew out her soul and made it his own.

She had never been handled in this fashion by a man before. He nibbled at her lips, whispered magic into her ears in a voice that sent shivers down her spine. He taught her in those moments what he wanted from her, and guided by emotion and a startling wantonness, she responded and found a lust in her heart she had never realized she was capable of feeling.

He took her through a doorway towards his enormous four-poster bed. She marveled at his strength, at his grace. She could not think. She only responded to the ache in her limbs, thrilled to the excitement of his fingers. She saw only his eyes, felt only their united desire as he gently removed the remaining confines of clothing.

She felt herself falling. . . .

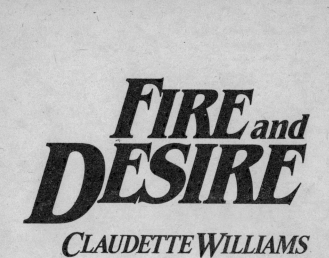

FIRE and DESIRE

CLAUDETTE WILLIAMS

FAWCETT GOLD MEDAL • NEW YORK

A Fawcett Gold Medal Book
Published by Ballantine Books

Library of Congress Catalog Card Number: 84-90920

ISBN 0-449-12775-3

Manufactured in the United States of America

First Edition: January 1985

Prologue

There was a quiet over the San Jacinto Estancia, for it was a sultry morning and noon was drawing near. It would soon be so hot that even the best of the gauchos would feel lazy as they prepared to enjoy their midday meal and then take on their individual responsibilities at the rancho.

Doña Rose gazed idly from beneath the wide-brimmed leather hat she wore to protect her from the sun's rays and stopped short as she saw him. He stood in the double doorway of the stable, and the sight of him took her breath away.

There was something about him that ignited the very air she inhaled. Rose, she berated herself, what is this nonsense? Rose, you must stop—you are married, you are a Cesares, you have a son! Her heart shouted rebellion. Love . . . he is love. . . .

Look at him! Arrogant gaucho! Standing there, leaning his hard broad shoulder against the doorjamb as he surveyed his underlings at various tasks. Just who does he think he is? He is *señor de nada!*—lord of nothing—and you, Rose, you are wife to Don José Cesares! She was English and gently bred. She was the daughter of an English squire, mistress of this great rancho. She was

1

the mother of Rodrigo, and yet she was lusting after this *señor de nada*.

What was she going to do? The answer brought hot blood to her cheeks. No. She hadn't given in to her secret desire, and she wouldn't . . . couldn't. So Rose Cesares looked at him and sighed. He was like no other gaucho. He didn't wear the colorful cottons and billowing pants that all the gauchos wore like a uniform. Not he. He wore a black shirt, its sleeves always rolled up to the elbows. He wore a dark rough buckskin pair of chaps that were silver-studded down the sides, beneath which he wore tight-fitting pants. His hair gleamed in black waves beneath his high-crowned wide-brimmed leather hat, and his eyes were black gems alive with fiery lights. His name was Facón. It meant knife, and it was what he carried always tucked in at the small of his back in the leather of his wide belt.

Facón looked across the green spread of rich lawn and found Doña Rose standing by the paddock gate. His black eyes glinted and his heart moved. She was a beauty with her long fair hair tied at the nape of her neck and blowing in the light breeze. Her body was curved in womanly lines beneath the summerweight riding habit she wore. She was Don José's wife, yet he saw only the woman standing before him, and he wanted her!

This was impossible, but he couldn't, wouldn't, look away as he should. He was all too aware of her, all too aware that she was feeling the same. He tipped his hat in her direction and she lowered her eyes. He could almost feel the blush that was burning her body, and he went toward her before she could run away as she always did. In English he gave her a greeting.

"Good day to you, Doña Rose." His voice was low and charged, even though he had not intended it so.

She looked up and met those gleaming black eyes of his and felt her nerve ends tingle. "Thank you, Facón." It was scarcely an audible sound.

He laughed easily. "Why do you thank me? It was not I who brought the soft breeze, the sunshine . . . the fragrance. . . ." Then before she could answer this and before he could stop himself, he added, "Though, for *you*, I feel that I could do such things."

She blushed hotly. How this man could make her feel! He raised her to heights she had never experienced before. Without touching her, he had touched her. "Facón, *you* are the only man I know that could accomplish such feats!" She smiled and felt like a schoolgirl again.

They were talking in riddles, but their meaning was clear to each other. His desire for her prompted him into further boldness.

"And what of your husband? Can he not make the earth move and the waters part?"

She should stop him now. How dare he take such a step! Why did she not put him in his place? She was Don José's wife. He worked for Don José . . . José, who was a good man. She lowered her gaze to the turf and said softly, "My husband's magic is of a different kind."

"And it is enough for you?" Facón could not keep the growl out of his voice. For too long now he had allowed himself to be teased by this woman's charms. He wanted her and she wanted him. He would have her admit it!

They had been walking slowly as they talked and they had reached the end of the stone path that led to the gardener's shed. She stopped then and looked at him full. "Not anymore . . ."

That was all that was needed. He had her arm in his hold as he pulled her off the path and put her back against the weathered shed. "Rose, I want you," he whispered before he bent and found the sweetness of her inviting mouth. He was too charged for tenderness in that moment, and his kiss was near violent as his hand immediately explored the shapeliness of her form.

She received his kiss and responded as his tongue explored and exploded the real world out of existence.

There was only the two of them. There was only the moment and the sensations they were creating in each other's heart. Never before had Rose discovered the meaning of passion. She felt wanton and wicked and couldn't give it up. She wanted Facón and she whispered this as he covered her face with his kisses.

"Yes, yes, my Rose . . . but not here, not now." He took both her hands and put them to his lips. "When can you get away?"

She hesitated. What was she doing? She couldn't do this. He pressed her for an answer. "Rose . . ." he insisted, "my Doña Rose." It was a caress, her name on his lips, and it won him a look. He hypnotized her with his gleaming black eyes. "You will listen to me. You will ride out on your horse later this afternoon. I will be returning from town, but instead of coming back here I will meet you at the peak. It is where you always go. I know; I have watched you." Again he was kissing her fingers, bringing up his eyes from her hands to stare hard and purposefully at her.

"Yes . . . yes . . ." she breathed, and then he was letting her go, walking away, not looking back. She watched his retreating form and asked herself, "Faith! What have I done?" And such was their beginning.

Rodrigo was thirteen. He was heir to the great San Jacinto Estancia. He was the only child of Don José and Doña Rose. His father had instilled in him a sense of responsibility, a sense of order, a need to rule. His mother had given him a love of life. He considered himself a man and, indeed, he was even at the age of thirteen showing signs of becoming an exceptional one. His hair was black and thick and fell in waves around his good-looking countenance. His eyes were so dark they could hold one spellbound, for deep in their depths there was a mesmerizing fire. His height was already above the average, and his shoulders promised an athlete's form, but more than that, he was nearly a man because he considered himself so.

Thus it was that he watched his mother and frowned. He saw her change of moods. He saw her daydreaming. He saw her attend to her appearance with a new enthusiasm. He saw her look at Facón! And this he saw all too often. As the months passed he began to understand what it all meant and he felt his heart gripped with his conflicting emotions. He was pulled by his loyalties. There was his father, whom he loved, respected, and honored. There was his mother, whom he adored and needed.

He was aware that this was part of life. Men and women of his class married for convenience and found their pleasures elsewhere. Yet he knew his father to be very much in love with the woman he had brought back from England, and until recently he had always thought . . . but then, there had never been that sparkle in her eyes, that schoolgirl quality in her laugh.

What to do? The question came up maddeningly, because he and his dearest friend, Varjona, were riding as outriders for Doña Rose. Her driver took her in the closed carriage to town, and as they put the hacienda behind them he could see Facón ahead on his roan. Facón! He was a gaucho. How could his mother give her love to a gaucho? He looked at Varjona, also a gaucho. Did he not love his friend in spite of the fact that their stations in life were so far removed? Hadn't he even taken measures to raise Var's station by insisting that he receive an education? He loved his gaucho friend, admired him; perhaps he had inherited that from his mother. He watched Facón nod to them, tip his hat to his mother; he heard her invite him to ride within the carriage and give her company. He heard their laughter as Facón joined her within the confines of the carriage, and Rodrigo was sickened.

Var called to him then and Rodrigo snapped a reply, hating Var at that moment, hating everyone. His father for not keeping his wife happy. Facón for being the rakehell man he was. Var for a reason he could not name. Himself for being helpless.

And so, time passed.

Facón looked at the soft English woman he had taken to his heart and frowned. "Don't look back, Rose. That life is gone."

She caught a sob in her throat, and her voice was scarcely audible as she dived into his arms. "It is for Rodrigo I grieve, Facón. He will be so hurt. And I—I will not be there to watch him become a man."

Facón touched her cheek. "He is already a man, and when he has added a few years to himself he will understand." Then he grinned. "As to the rest, you will have our sons to watch and touch and bring to manhood."

She still could not smile. She had left Don José in the quiet of the night. He knew she would do this one day, for he knew about her and Facón. Don José would weather it in his fashion, but Rodrigo? Oh, no, it would leave her boy bitter. He would feel deserted. She hoped the letter she had left him would balm his wound, but she knew well what he would feel when he read it.

Facón was urging her along. "Come, we must ride if we are to make camp by nightfall. Come, Rose."

Thus she left with her gaucho to enter a new world, leaving her family in the old. . . .

She had not been wrong in thinking Don José would be able to handle the hurt of her leaving. He was in his quiet, good-hearted fashion able to understand her motives, her needs, her weakness. He sighed for her and indeed, in the loneliness of his room, he cried for her, but he was able to take the blow.

It was not so simple for Rodrigo. He was only thirteen, and though he had found it possible to forgive his mother her love for Facón, he could not forgive her desertion.

She had left him. It beat at his brain and his heart and he would not cry. She had been softness and laughter. She had been the pulse, the lifeblood, at the rancho. She had presided over their lives with music and merriment, and she was gone . . . by choice!

She would not be there for Christmas, for his fourteenth birthday, for . . . anything. She was his mother, and she had chosen Facón over him! The truth trampled his feelings and gave him a bitter taste. He looked at his best friend, Varjona, a gaucho, and saw Facón, and could only turn away.

Doña Rose. Her name touched his heart and he fought it off. No! He would not understand. *No!* He would not forgive. She had left him. Such treachery was a woman— at least an English woman!

Part One

"*We are such stuff*
as dreams are made on, and our little life
Is rounded with a sleep."

—THE TEMPEST

Chapter 1

Vauxhall Gardens. Its two hundred years of existence had not affected its popularity in the least. It was still the fashionable place to go during the London Season, and the *haute ton* flocked there with hedonistic designs.

Its gardens were laid out for various pleasures, and these were as varied as the crowds the gardens attracted. Vauxhall's famous rotunda, nestled within beautifully landscaped lawns, was considered top on its list of attractions. In the rotunda's canopied balcony this night, with a full orchestra at her back, was Madame Weichsel. Her voice and her selection of song were very nearly as lovely as she was herself. The crowd below the balcony sat (or stood as the case allowed), watching and listening in raptured sighs of contentment.

Lady Jessica Stafford looked about at the assembled audience and smiled to herself. It was obvious to this young but knowing miss that the fashionable *beau monde* around her was receiving Madame with varying degrees of appreciation. There were the aristocratic Englishmen who leered and ogled Madame's provocative movements in her clinging and very nearly transparent gown of silver flimsy. This they did in rare style and with quizzing glasses held high. A ribald remark was passed now and then, accompanied by low chuckles. There were the noblewomen who whispered and gossiped behind fans about Madame's off-stage activities and gave one another meaningful glances in that regard. And then there were some who were even there to enjoy Madame's talent for song.

Lady Jessica was there enjoying everything. She was just nineteen, and this was her first London Season. Until this spring she had been safely tucked away at a select girls' seminary. She glanced at her uncle, who sat beside her, and noted that he was raptly involved with Madame's performance. She steadied herself and restrained the giggle that tickled her throat, for it was very nearly common knowledge that her uncle, the Earl of Redcliff, Admiral Thomas Stafford, was Madame's latest flame.

"She is very good, isn't she, Uncle Thomas?" said Jessie, for her sense of humor nearly always prompted her to tease.

He was forty-nine years old and quite an attractive bachelor, though he had a tendency to portliness. He caught the bantering of her tone and cast her a disapproving eye. "I think, my dear," he said depressingly, "that she is accounted a veritable nightingale."

"Quite right," returned Lady Jessica, dimpling, and shading her violet eyes with her dark lashes.

He was generally amused by his audacious and outspoken niece. She was not the usual sort of miss one was forever having to endure among his noble class. Under his breath, in a firm but affectionate tone, he said, "*Sauce-box!*"

This seemed to please Lady Jessica, for her lips parted in a happy smile. She set herself to hear Madame's next tune when someone caught her eye and her attention. Lady Jessica sat up in her seat, for she was a petite miss, and her violet eyes appraised this new and interesting object of intrigue.

He was a man in his late twenties. He was tall and well built. His hair was a raven shade of black and swept across his forehead in glistening waves. Its silky lengths were luxuriant and fell in layered waves to his neck, framing a lean and attractively chiseled countenance. His brows were slightly winged, his lashes dark, and, she thought, even longer than her own.

He stood in amicable conversation with his group of friends, young men all, and they took up much space in the narrow aisle. She could not help but notice that he was the center of their attention, that their talk was lively and their laughter catching the eye and ear of more than one disapproving dowager. She smiled to herself over this fact, noticing, too, that his own smile was disarmingly attractive. Perhaps she stared, yes, she admitted to herself, she was most certainly staring and was just about to look away when something (the buttercup hue of her sun-drenched curls, no doubt,) caught his dark, roving eye.

It was too late. He had observed her open scrutiny. Color flooded her cheeks, but faith, it was his own open look that drew the breath right out of her lungs! How dare he? How could he? What did he think, that she was some doxy to be audaciously ogled?

Honesty compelled her to admit that he did no more than she had done, but somehow his appraisal was different. Oh, he discovered to some inward satisfaction that an English beauty with golden curls haloing her well-shaped head and heart-shaped face was closely looking him over. This did not surprise him; he was quite used to this attention from females of all classes. Further inquiry, however, elicited the facts that her eyes of violet were framed in marvelously arched dark brows and long dark lashes, that her nose was pert, her lips full and inviting, and that she made quite a delectable piece. He was compelled to acknowledge her look for look, and tilted his head and hat in her direction.

Oh! She breathed hard, unable to believe his audacity! This was not how a gentleman treated a lady, and his smile? Why, it had changed into something of a sneer.

Who, just who, did he think he was? Up went her chin and away went her eyes. What? What was that her uncle was saying? Absently she answered him and then gave her attention to Madame's song. However, she managed to steal a glance toward the aisle sometime later, and with a touch of wistfulness she noted that he and his friends were gone.

The evening progressed famously, for her uncle's slew of friends descended upon them as soon as Madame's repertoire of music had been completed, and Lady Jessica found herself being much admired. Her uncle patted her hand.

"You see, my Jess, you will be hailed the "incomparable" before you have even been officially presented at your ball." This seemed to please him.

She sighed. "But Uncle, must I have a ball? Couldn't I just casually make my entrance . . . as I am doing tonight?"

"Certainly not!" His jaw set. "I may have been lax in other matters, what with my always being at sea, and don't think I haven't suffered pangs of guilt on your behalf, my girl."

She laughed and interrupted him. "Oh, now that is a corker!"

"Hush, Jess." He put up a finger. "Where have you ever learned such language?"

She dimpled. "From you, dearest, and you have never had to feel one moment of guilt, for if ever there was a happier girl, I should like to see her!"

He tweaked her nose. "Puss. Lovable puss, but don't think I don't know I've neglected you sadly, and a ball is due to the niece of an earl, and well I know it." He put up his hand to still any further argument. "I see Lady Jersey coming our way . . . and look . . . that is Sir Warren not far behind her. I fancy you might like him. All the petticoats do."

She was twinkling at him. "*All* the petticoats, Uncle?"

He eyed her savagly, but it was belied by the affection

in his voice. "Now, that will do, puss, and so I warn you!" He shook his head. "You can't go about quoting me. It ain't the thing, for the sad truth is me tongue has been ruled by the sea too long for me to change." He sighed over the problem. "I'm no fit company for you, child. What you need is a duenna, and that you shall have before I go off again."

She squeezed his arm. "I can think of no better company, Uncle, and I don't want some staid old dowager riding roughshod over me."

He snorted. "I'd like to see the woman who could cow *your* spirits!" Again he shook his head, but this time it was quite evident he felt some reluctant admiration for his niece's lively disposition.

She laughed with pleasure. "Oh, now, Uncle, you are thinking of all the dreadful tales you've had from the headmistress."

He tapped her nose. "No, no, I ain't. I'm remembering some of your antics I was privileged to witness firsthand!" He looked up to find Lady Jersey was indeed descending on them. "Mind now, the Jersey is a high stickler, and you'll be needing her approbation for a voucher to Almacks."

Lady Jessica's head went up almost immediately at that, and there was the glint of defiance in her deep violet eyes. "Really, Uncle, must I enact the simpering miss then?"

"Oh, take a damper!" he returned at once, as though he were speaking to a playful youth instead of a nineteen-year-old maid. "Just be yourself and you'll do just fine."

Lady Jersey's regal stature and her haughty air of self-assurance and aristocracy were characteristics enough to intimidate a green miss. However, Lady Jessica's entrance into society was something that maid was taking on with casual indifference, and she was not yet impressed enough to be easily quaked. Therefore, she met Lady Jersey with easy, light conversation, and within moments of their introduction the famous London hostess found herself exchanging bantering quips with Jessica.

"Thomas, your niece is delightful!" Lady Jersey exclaimed as she gave his cheek a tender rap with her black lace fan. She heard her escort coming up behind her and turned. "Darling, look, here is Thomas home from sea, and he has his lovely niece with him." She eyed Sir Warren as he passed a greeting with the admiral and turned to bend over Lady Jessica's hand, for the Jersey was already introducing them. "No, no, my dear," the Jersey was saying lightly to Jess. "Don't even think it! Sir Warren is a confirmed bachelor and a heartbreaker. He has absolutely no rules and no sensibility for what we poor weaker sex suffer when we gaze at his handsome face." She was laughing loudly, for Sir Warren was casting her a rueful glance.

"Even at the risk of incurring Lady Jersey's displeasure, I must beg you to believe that she jests," put in Sir Warren quickly as he came up from Lady Jessica's gloved knuckles to discover that the hue of her violet eyes was like nothing he had ever seen before.

"Does she?" returned Jess ingenuously. "But then, 'tis what my uncle was saying about you only a moment ago."

Lady Jersey's ready mirth was very near indecent at this, and Sir Warren, not in the least abashed, gave over a mocking groan and said, "I see my reputation precedes and withers me in your estimation, my lady."

"It precedes you, yes, but *I* didn't say it has withered you. I am afraid I am one of those who will not be swayed by any but my own experiences."

"Then I am saved, for I declare myself your most humble servant, my Lady Jess, and mean to do naught but win favor in your eyes and in your heart."

Words indeed to set a young miss dreaming. Here was Sir Warren Woodfall, an intriguing flirt who spent a good remainder of the evening doing his utmost to charm her. His hair was a fair shade of yellow and styled in a mass of Brutus curls. His brows were thick and straight, his lashes just a shade darker, his eyes blue, his nose strictly masculine, and his lips thin and sensuous. All this was on a body whose lines were tall, lean, and athletic. And if this was not enough to tease Jessie into sweet dreams, there was the pleasant fact that he had set himself to amuse and enchant her with an engaging deftness all his own.

Right then, why should any other man make his way into her dreams? Why indeed, and no other took up her conscious thoughts, but just as she slipped into the hypnotic pleasure of fantasy, a pair of dark, flashing eyes suddenly intruded. Odd. A chiseled, devilishly handsome face clearly was there against the darkness of her dream and the touch of a sneer, a mocking smile, disturbed the sweetness of her dreams.

What was she doing, thinking of that arrogant rogue? He had been dashingly good-looking—it was true—but he had annoyed her with his flippant behavior in her regard. Even so, she wondered who he was as she drifted off into peaceful slumber and had the rather dubious pleasure of having him haunt her dreams as she waltzed in them with Sir Warren.

Chapter 2

The next two weeks took Lady Jessica into late April
and a hectic turmoil of getting ready for her coming-out
ball. The dowager, Lady Wilton (an elderly aunt of the
admiral's), was installed at Stafford House to play duenna for Lady Jessica and hostess for her more-often-
absent-than-not nephew. This she did with great zeal,
expertise, and affection. She stood now (and there was
little more than five feet of her), finger pursed to brightly
colored lips, studying her great-niece's form in the ball
gown of white and silver.

"Stunning! I saw five daughters married, m'girl, and
you outdo 'em all! I swear you do." Her faded gray eyes
flashed with appreciation. "It's plain as pikestaff you
haven't a notion what it means to look as you do, have
the background you have, and the fortune to go with it!"
She clucked her tongue. "Every fortune hunter in London will be vying for your hand, and it will be up to me
to chase 'em off, for that damnable uncle of yours will
be gone to sea again and much he'll do about it!"

Lady Jessica was gazing at herself in the long looking
glass. Indeed, she rather liked the pearls and white lace
flowers entwined with her long buttercup curls and the
straight lines of filmy white material that hung closely to
her well-shaped body. She liked, too, the way the short,

frothy sleeves swagged over her slender arms, though the low cut of the heart-shaped bodice brought high color to her cheeks. However, at Lady Wilton's words she broke into a musical giggle and chided her great-aunt. "And what of me, Aunt Charlotte? Shan't I have the sense to send such fools off?"

"Humph! Not if they look like that Sir Warren, you won't!"

"Now, that is too bad of you," returned Lady Jessica, rallying her. "I am persuaded that you cannot truly believe Sir Warren to be a fortune hunter."

"Absurd child! Though he might end on that road the way he sits a table."

Jessie's fine brow went up. "Never say, Sir Warren gambles?"

"Well, what sort of a question is that? What London beau does not?" She shook her head. "The difference is that he don't know when to get up, and larger fortunes than his have been exchanged over a gaming table in White's, let me tell you."

There was a knock at Lady Jessica's door at this point, which interrupted Lady Wilton, and she called out an irritable welcome. Lady Jessica's young maid peeped in and said fearfully that the admiral was demanding their presence downstairs at once. "Says he won't be left to greet his guests on his own."

Lady Wilton's head of gray curls came up. She gave herself a once-over in the mirror, adjusted the gold feather around her ear, tugged at a wiry curl, smoothed her gold satin dress, and said with some exasperation that no one expected his lordship, the admiral, to do any such thing. She turned to her great-niece and wagged a finger. "Mind now, *you* are *not* to come down until I have sent that silly chit up to you to say you are wanted, for I mean for you to make a grand entrance."

"Must I?" groaned Lady Jessica. "Can't I just come down with you and make up one of the reception committee?" There was a twinkle in her eye, a plea in her voice, and the sure knowledge in her head that this was not possible.

Lady Wilton did not bother to answer more than a "Try not to fuss over yourself while you are waiting. And don't sit down, for you will wrinkle your dress!"

"Oh!" cried Lady Jess, half on a laugh, half in earnest. "I have a good mind to foil all your marvelous plans, throw off my fineries, and make for the stables!"

This (if she heard it) was not acknowledged by the dowager, for she was snapping off orders to idle servants as she made her way downstairs to join her nephew and prepare to greet their guests.

The ballroom was alight with wax candles. The scent of spring came in on a soft night breeze. Flowers touched the senses, for they were everywhere, as were lackeys with glasses of champagne and trays of delectables.

Don Rodrigo flirted silently with a tall beauty as she was waltzed past him, saying in an undervoice and in perfect English, "Simon, will you tell me, please, *what* we are doing here?" There was a touch of impatience in his voice.

Simon Bolivar looked up at his tall friend and sighed. They were both from South America. They were both hot young patriots working toward a similar goal. However, Don Rodrigo did not believe, as did Simon and San Martin, that they might enlist British aid. It was Bolivar's new bride that answered Don Rodrigo. She stamped her foot and said in Spanish, "Don't be disagreeable, Rodrigo. It does not become you. We are at Stafford House because we must pursue our friendships with the people in power, and the people in power attend these functions. Besides, this Stafford girl, she is much talked about. They say she is the new English beauty, and I would like to see her."

He pinched her nose affectionately. "Then, dear heart, I have no other wish but to remain here for your pleasure." He smiled as she patted his hand. "You see how hard I try always to please you. It is a mystery why you remain with this—"

"Hush, now," she interrupted. "I won't have you insulting my poor Simon. You are a great dashing cavalier, but your soul is hidden. My Simon is naught but a pure-hearted gaucho whose heart is bared to me." She dimpled at him. "There, I have said something to make you frown."

He laughed. "Have you? *Madre de dios,* woman! You throw me over for this miserable *perro* and you wonder at my frown."

"Enough," said the lady's husband. "I would talk with Rodrigo." He waited a moment to see if his lady would adhere to his wish, and, with the surprise he always felt when he found her complacent, he proceeded. "What I do not understand, Rodrigo, is your . . . disenchantment with these British. After all, your own mother was English."

"I am not disenchanted with them. I know them. Therein lies the difference, and remember that my mother's nationality has naught to do with my personal politics."

"Yes, but surely you—"

Don Rodrigo cut in impatiently. "We have been over this more times than I care to recount, Simon. I was educated here. I went to Eton with these men. I studied at Cambridge with them. Believe me, if they do agree to assist us in our revolution, it will be for one reason only and that, you know very well, would be to get a foothold. . . ."

The grand staircase of Stafford House was a spectacular construction of ornate ivory and gold woodwork. Its rich color of highly polished steps took a circular route from the second landing to the first. There the staircase met a darkly veined white marble floor. One was therefore given a full view of this magnificent structure from several angles, and one angle in particular could be seen nicely from the open double doorway of the ballroom. Of course, the dowager, Lady Wilton, knew just what she was doing when she collected her guests in the ballroom before sending word for Lady Jessica to join them there.

Jessie's descent was perfectly timed, and the sight of her floating down the staircase quite took one's breath away. She was a vision. How could she be anything else? Her waist-length hair of gold had been collected into Grecian splendor, touched throughout with silver and white lace flowers. Her gown of white organza sparkled with its silver embroidery and clung to her provocative figure as she moved. Her violet eyes glittered with amusement as she caught her uncle's expression of wonder, and then suddenly she froze, for she could see the crowd straining their necks to have a look at her.

She felt the hush that came over the assembled company, and it very nearly frightened her into reticent shyness, but the dowager very wisely pinched her nephew's elbow and said below her breath, "Fool! Go quickly and give her your arm."

It served to preserve the moment into the next. The admiral, looking very fine in his black velvet, went forward immediately and bent his arm toward his niece. "Confound it, girl!" He winked. "For a moment there I thought I was looking at your mother. You are just like her, you know."

Jessie's recollection of her parents was very vague, but this compliment pleased her into forgetting her shyness. "Am I? Oh, that does please me, for I am certain I have heard you say how lovely she was."

"Lovely? There were none to compare to her. Quite broke my heart when she chose me brother over me."

"Why, Uncle, I never knew that," she said on a note of surprise, all the while walking beside him to the ballroom. Hearing the music filtering through the now buzzing crowd, marveling silently at the glory of fashion spread out before her and amazed at her uncle's disclosure, she was a piquant picture indeed.

It had been Jessie's arrival on the scene that had cut off Don Rodrigo's sentence. He stood transfixed as he watched her entrance. It flitted through his mind that she looked familiar. Where had he seen her before? He stood watching as her uncle began introducing her around. He heard his friends commenting on her beauty and then Lady Jersey was playing with the waves of hair at his neck; he turned a smile to her and caught her hand, for they were old friends.

"Ah, my love, where have you been?" He was kissing the wrist above the lace glove she wore, allowing his black eyes to travel from her red-painted lips down the slender throat to the full bosom and then back to her eyes.

"Spanish devil!" she bantered. She saw his dark eyes flicker toward Lady Jessica, now doing a country dance with Sir Warren. "No, Rod, she is not in your style."

"Isn't she?" he returned, his dark brow up.

"Now, don't bristle up with me. I meant only that I rather think she is too sweet and innocent for your volcanic passions."

"No doubt you are very right, and therefore there is but one solution, sweetheart," he countered at once. "Come home with me and assuage my . . . er . . . volcanic needs."

She laughed and ran a lingering finger over his lips. "I am persuaded that might be most pleasant and just a bit dangerous. Prinny would not like it, you know, for he believes me, and rightly so, faithful to . . . his interests."

Don Rodrigo frowned. "Ah, and since my friends and I will soon be requiring the prince's influence, it would not do to displease him." He gave her hand a squeeze and sighed. "Very wise." Again he was looking toward

Lady Jessica. "A favor, then, Sarah. Introduce me to this little buttercup and sanction a waltz."

"Outrageous! The waltz is not yet approved in this country, Don Rodrigo, and it may be that she does not even know its steps."

"Then I will teach it to her." He was urging Lady Jersey along, for the country dance had ended. Deftly he managed the crowd and brought the Jersey up to Jessie.

"La, child!" ejaculated Lady Jersey, casting a rueful look at Don Rodrigo. "Here is a Spanish rogue demanding to be introduced to you, and as he is here all the way from Argentina, I suppose I must favor him with that much, after which I strongly suggest you send him on his way!"

Lady Jessica's smile was very nearly and quite ludicrously wiped off her face as she turned around and found the handsome devil of Vauxhall Gardens looking down at her. She heard Lady Jersey's introductions, felt him take her hand, and saw him bow low over her knuckles. She met his black eyes look for look and realized he had not remembered her from that night at Vauxhall. Well, why should he? It was amazing, she thought, that she should remember him so vividly, but more than that, faith, why was his presence so intimidating? It was a fact that irritated her sense of self. Then all at once he was leading her toward the orchestra and asking for a waltz. She objected. "Oh, I don't think . . ."

"It is quite all right. Lady Jersey has sanctioned it," he answered.

His hand went to her waist, and she felt herself shiver. Quickly she glanced toward the Jersey, who nodded gravely. Mercy! She had never waltzed with a man before. They had been taught the steps at school, but she had only practiced it with her schoolmates. Here was an experienced man—and such a man.

"Even so—" she attempted to object still.

Again he cut her off. "Hush, buttercup, and just let me guide you." he said softly. He liked the feel of her in his hands and brought her a touch closer than was the mode. Others had joined them on the dance floor by now, but even so, they were much looked after, for they made quite an arresting sight.

"You are very sure of yourself." Her chin was up, for his arrogance annoyed her.

He threw back his head and laughed. "At times," he answered shortly.

"You will say, no doubt, that we poor, adoring females have given you enough reason?" she baited, her violet eyes sparkling.

His brow went up. "You are angry with me? Why, I wonder."

"Of course not. Why should I be angry with you?" she returned. "We have never before encountered each other."

All at once it came back to him! Perhaps it was the sparkle in her violet eyes, for it was that now which brought back the memory of her face in the crowd at Vauxhall. She had been appraising him, and he had returned her appraisal with a survey of his own! "Of a certainty we have, my lovely!" he answered, and his smile was caressing as his dark eyes became shaded. It was a trick of his own, seductive in nature, for he seemed intent on the study of her lips as his voice lowered. "Did you think I could forget having seen you at Vauxhall? Indeed, I have dreamed of you every night since." He lied beautifully, gallantly.

She was a green miss and still would not have believed him, had he not said it with such sincerity, had he not mentioned Vauxhall, had *she* not dreamed of him in the two weeks since she had first seen him. Jessie's cheeks took on heightened color and she managed to counter, "Fie, Don Rodrigo, I thought only rakes and rogues went after green girls like me."

It was in her day a most bold way of speaking. She knew this, but she had never been missish, and therefore more often than not found herself speaking her mind.

He threw back his head and laughed out loud. He was amused, though he thought her behavior just a touch jaded and did not totally approve. The girl was already like most of her kind, and since he had good cause to be cynical about females, this was not complimentary. "But I admit it freely. I am a rogue, a Spanish devil!"

She smiled. "Good. We understand each other, then, for I have always been accused of being a rogue myself." She didn't realize how he was taking this. She frowned. "You have hardly any accent at all, you know. One could almost take you for English."

"That is because I spent most of my youth here in England getting an education. Also . . . my mother was English and always insisted we converse in her native tongue." Suddenly the memory of his mother and the shame she had brought his family name darkened his expression.

Lady Jess noticed this abrupt change in him, but the waltz had ended and already she was surrounded by young men soliciting her hand for the next cotillion. She saw him recede, and saw, too, that he had managed to closet himself in a corner with Prime Minister Pitt. Her brow went up with interest. Now, what, she mused silently, would a South American have to do with an English prime minister? However, as she found herself besieged by dandies and rakes alike, the evening wore on in high style and she had little time to find an answer to this question.

As it chanced, though, she looked up some forty minutes later and found Don Rodrigo with the prime minister beside him taking leave of her great-aunt and her uncle. Her brow went up. No casual meeting, then? They did not have the look of men out purely for each other's company. They did not have the look of men out for sport; besides, what would a rogue of Don Rodrigo's stamp have to do with the staid and portly Pitt? Curiously she mentioned it to her uncle when he chanced to approach her some minutes later. "And so, my dearest admiral, what is toward?" she rallied, her violet eyes twinkling.

He eyed her for a long moment and said carefully, "Eh, puss?"

"Oh, please, Uncle. I may be a female, but that does not make me blind."

"Haven't a notion what you are talking about," he answered, looking at no one in particular as he produced his snuff box and flipped open its lid.

"Haven't you? Well, to be plain and open about it, then, what interest can our prime minister have for the likes of Don Rodrigo Cesares?"

"Impudent kitten" is all she received in way of reply.

"Uncle?" she pursued.

"Have a head for politics, eh? Lady Hester, Pitt's niece, does as well . . ."

"Uncle?" she prodded.

"Have a notion you'll suit," he said in answer to this.

She opened her violet eyes wide. "What?" she asked dubiously. "Lady Hester and me? I have never had the pleasure of her acquaintance, and besides—"

"No, no, no," he cut her off. "You and Sir Warren. You'll make him an excellent political hostess. That's what he'll be needing, for he means to make a name for himself in Parliament. Mark me."

"Sir Warren?" she returned sharply. "Whatever do you mean?"

"Oh, just a hunch I have, girl. Seen the way he looks at you. . . ."

"Indeed. I have seen the way he looks at a great many women." She laughed.

"Absurd chit. All men with red blood in their veins eye the pretties. That's normal, you know, but he does look at you differently. Besides, never knew him before to pay any attention to a marriageable chit."

"Oh, do stop," she said, now blushing.

"Wouldn't you like it, Jess?" He was now serious, for he sincerely believed that given time, Sir Warren might come up to scratch.

She thought about this. Sir Warren was good-looking. Indeed, his fairness of face and form was nearly godlike. He was certainly charming, amusing, and there was that about him she found most desirable. Yes, he was attractive, and she had even dreamed of finding herself in his arms. She had wondered what it would be like to have him kiss her, but marry him? She didn't know. How could she?

"I . . . oh, Uncle, I haven't known any man long enough to know if I want to spend the rest of my life with him."

He pinched her cheek and agreed before he moved off, and it wasn't until afterward that she realized how effectively he had turned her off from her initial inquiry.

Later that night when she was trying to sleep (a thing she found strangely impossible), she thought about Sir Warren. He had behaved most markedly this evening. He had whispered flattery in her ear and had even placed a lingering kiss upon her cheek. She sighed. Everything about him was seductive, and it was most exciting, but love? How could she know what love was?

At school last season, all the girls had imagined themselves in love with their music professor. He was young and attractive and terribly thrilling to be near. He had done the forbidden. He had kissed her. The first time had been on her birthday. She had turned eighteen and they had given her a wonderful party. Somehow she had found herself alone with him in the schoolroom and he was kissing her. It had been her first real kiss from a man, and she had allowed it. A day later he had managed to get her alone again, and his kiss had become more intense. She was infatuated, intrigued, thrilled, and then she had seen him making sweet and affectionate love to her French teacher. A moment of reckoning, understanding, hurt pride, and reality had infused her with a certain insight. Such things happened in life. Her disposition was such that she was not resentful, and it never occurred to her to judge all men by the action of one. However, she did begin to open her eyes and watch their antics whenever the opportunity arose. She noted with interest that they were for the most part fickle creatures given to selfish pursuits. Her uncle provided a perfect example of this. She adored him but was not blind to his faults.

He was the Earl of Stafford, and his fortune made it totally unnecessary for him to take on a career that would leave her forever at school. It was something he had to do; it was what he enjoyed. So, smilingly, she remained a year longer at school. She accepted it, but her eyes were opened a bit wider all the same.

She sighed now in her bed, for she was feeling a restlessness of spirit she had never experienced before. What was it? What was love? Her professor had certainly whispered such words into her youthful ear, but he could not have meant it. And she could not have really been in love. After all, she was not devastated by the betrayal.

Don Rodrigo's flashing dark eyes came to mind. Faith, he was such a man! Wildly, sensually captivating. What would his kiss be like? She felt herself go hot in the darkness of her room. Dreadful girl, she chastised herself. What are you thinking? He is a rake who would use you if he could! Forget him!

Chapter 3

Sedately now, Jess! Calm yourself, Jess. One does not gallop wildly through Hyde Park. It isn't the thing. Do you want Lady Jersey refusing you a voucher to Almacks? Lady Jessica was attempting to get the better of herself as she trotted down the wide bridle path through the park. At her back, her groom kept his cob at a respectful distance, and as Lady Jess remembered the uncompromising manner of her uncle's tone when he had sent the groom after her, she bit her lip. This was irritating beyond endurance. Oh, God! She was clothed in the finest velvet riding habit. The emerald green with its matching top hat displayed to advantage the exquisiteness of her fair beauty. In the morning sun her buttercup-hued tresses gleamed brightly, and Lady Jess should have been pleased. However, she cared very little for such finery. She would have preferred to have her hair down and tied at her neck with a simple ribbon. She would have been more comfortable and certainly happier in a pair of old britches riding astride, and she wanted a gallop. Oh, faith, how she wanted a gallop!

She surveyed the long path stretching out before her. It was early yet, not a fashionable soul about. She glanced behind her and noted that the elderly groom was ambling slowly in her wake. He seemed half asleep. Perhaps she should wake him up. Her mare could get away with her. . . . A terrible admission, but it could be said. A glint came into her violet eyes. A gurgle of laughter tickled her lovely lips into a smile, and before she could talk herself out of her fancy she urged her horse forward and into motion! The mare was pleased to run and extended herself with enthusiasm. Jessie laughed out loud, for she hadn't had a gallop in over a month.

Oh, but it was good to feel the morning wind against her cheeks! She cooed to her mare, urging her faster. How she wished she could discard some of her years, don her old britches, and ride astride across the fields. Nineteen! She was all of nineteen, on the marriage mart, and . . . missing her youth. How simple life had been only months ago. What had happened?

As these thoughts flitted through her mind, she could hear her groom yelping at her back for her to slow down. Oh, this was beyond everything! It wasn't fair of Uncle to send the groom along—and just as she sighed and thought to bring her horse into her hands, something happened.

So quickly that there was scarcely a moment for thought, a toddler escaped his nurse's circle and, wildly gurgling, his pudgy arms up and waving, he toddled on his toes onto the bridle path. Lady Jessie's mare saw a flash of small color thrashing its arms in high glee, and for all the horse cared, it could have been a giant. The mare's ears alertly flickered at this new danger and shied abruptly.

Lady Jessica's sidesaddle seat was a newly acquired skill, and she should have been more firmly in her saddle. Her horse's pop and swerve to the right sharply unsettled her relaxed position, and the next thing she knew she was traveling in the air, marveling at how long it took to get to the ground.

An interminable length of time took her vaulting through the air while she saw whizzing past blurred faces and various shades of green. All this while she dreaded the inevitable meeting of earth and body. It came forcefully. She landed on her chest with a hard thump. Her top hat of elegant green velvet bumped with her nose and rolled some distance, and then she thought she heard the nursemaid exclaim in broad cockney that the "poor loidy" must be dead!

She groaned, and as she attempted to rise and reassure the hysterical nursemaid that she was very much alive, she realized that she was winded. She stayed put a moment and set herself to regaining the air in her lungs when she heard a familiar and firm male voice in her ear.

"Lady Jessica, can you hear me?"

Her groom? No, she could hear her groom wailing in the background that it wasn't his fault and what would the admiral say. Faith! What *would* the admiral say? She groaned again, but the familiar male voice insisted on more.

"Lady Jessica, I don't want to move you until you have answered me as to your condition. Can you hear me? Is there, do you think, anything broken?"

Broken? Good God! Her mare! Where was her mare? She managed to turn her head around and was surprised to find that her voice was scarcely audible even to her own ears. "My mare? Princess?"

"She is fine, and your groom has her in hand. Now, if you will"—his voice was demanding yet strangely gentle—"do you think you are able to sit up?"

In answer to this Jess propped herself onto one open palm and recalled herself to her surroundings. Her cheeks were bright with color, and she was all too aware of her overwhelming embarrassment. Of all the men in the world, why did this one, this rakehell Don Rodrigo Cesares, have to be the one to witness her fall?

"My lady," he asked softly, "are you feeling faint?" He had seen her close her eyes, watched as her hand flitted to her forehead.

She heard his voice calling her to order. How could

she face him? Boldly! Was she some child to be intimidated by a handsome rogue? No, she was not! Her violet eyes opened and discovered his black eyes appraising her from head to foot. Faith! It was enough to stir her blood and lower her eyes again. "No . . . no, thank you." She started to rise. Her buttercup curls were a tumble of silken confusion all over her shoulders. Her riding habit had been dirtied and torn in several places. There was a smudge of dirt across one cheek and a dot of blood trickling down her ear from a minor scratch at her forehead, but other than that she had sustained no major injury. She would mount her horse and return home. She was on her feet and suddenly tottering as she moved to take a step toward her groom and horse.

His arm had never left her and supported her now around her trim waist. "What, my lady, do you think you are doing?" He expected no reply. "You have been badly winded by your fall, so don't think I mean to let you remount your horse just yet." He shook his head. "My man has hailed us a hackney, and yours will see your animal back to its stable."

"Nonsense!" came her quick, clipped, and intense reply. Why she should feel threatened by this man was more (at that moment) than she could understand, but she was determined to overcome this sensation. "I am perfectly capable of riding home, and while I thank you for your concern, I do assure you, 'tis not in the least bit necessary for you to put yourself out."

His brow went up. He had spent enough years in England to know a spoiled English noblewoman when he saw one, and he had learned the knack of handling such creatures. However, he was in the mood to taunt this particular one. "Really? I don't wish to offend you, my dear, but my witnessing of your handling of the reins leaves me with an entirely different opinion."

She nearly choked on her own breath, so acute was her rising heat. Her violet eyes blazed, and he was all too conscious of her beauty even in her state of disarray, and he found himself thoroughly involved with her response; her chin was up. "I have been riding all my life, sir, and somehow I seemed to have managed well enough without your opinions!"

He laughed, and she bristled still further. "Your luck is to be marveled at, my dear, for how you can have done so with your reins as loose as they were and your seat as relaxed as it was. . . ."

"Ooooh!" she squeaked, for her rage had constricted all words. How dare he speak to her like this? The fact that she had not paid attention to her seat, her reins, or her surroundings with any horse sense was all the more irritating. "How—how dare you!" she released. "I will have you know that I have as a child hunted the Quorn and assisted as a whipperin. I—I—I . . ." At this point she found herself being scooped unceremoniously into his arms and suspended the lecture she was about to read him in order to demand in wrathful, outraged accents, "What the devil do you think you are doing?" Unladylike terms, but the situation seemed to call for it. "Put me down! Do you hear? You . . . you . . . arrogant beast!"

He laughed again, for her hot temper had adorably flushed her cheeks and drawn on something within him. Perhaps it was only the momentary desire to train a wild thing, but subdue and conquer her in this round he meant to do. "May I suggest that you calm yourself, my lady. You have already drawn more of a crowd than I am persuaded is seemly. I am delivering you, willy-nilly, since you haven't the sense to come quietly, to the waiting hack, then I mean to see you home. I believe that upon further reflection you will agree it would not do you or your good uncle credit for you to be seen riding through the park with your riding habit soiled and torn, your hair a mass of disarray, and your pretty nose smudged with dirt." So saying, he was pleased to find the lady speechless as he deposited her upon the seat of the waiting coach. He closed the hack door, gave her address to its driver, walked around, and entered its confines from street side. So doing, he relaxed into its corner and smiled to see Jess avoiding his eye, much in a pucker but attending now to her appearance with a tug to her riding jacket and a pat to her hair.

His dark lashes partially shaded his piercing black eyes as he regarded her. He was used to different, quite different behavior from the females of her class. After all, he was something of a catch on the marriage mart and was therefore accustomed to misses and maids putting out lures. His was a noble line of blood, and added to this was the fact that he came from money. Of course, the English aristocracy were wont to raise eyebrows at foreigners, but his wealth even more than his bloodline expunged this consideration from all but the highest sticklers. He could see that Lady Jess didn't like him, but more interesting than that was his observation that she wasn't giving his above-mentioned qualities any thought. Odd, that! Just a bit piqued, he meant to see if he could attract a better response.

She exploded the silence, though, with a sudden turn to openly regard him and in accents of sarcasm. "I suppose you actually expect me to thank you for your high-handedness?"

He repressed his amusement and said gravely, "Indeed, *I* expect no thanks. However, I was always under the belief that it is a courteous thing to do, and as my experience with the English has led me to observe that most of you *perform* the courtesies, I find myself a bit surprised. However, if my action, which you must know was to do no more than take you away from curious eyes and would-be scandalmongers, has displeased you, please forgive me."

He was poking fun at her. She knew this and, even so, fell right into his trap. What could she do? She lowered her eyes and, in a subdued tone, replied, "For that, I do thank you. . . ."

He laughed out loud. She was in many ways a veritable child, yet the woman in her could not be denied, and it was a most alluring combination. Damn, but he might derive some pleasure and take this to the bedroom. He watched her a moment and then deftly he moved with gentle art, taking her into his arms as though it were the most natural and expected thing for him to do. "Then thank me properly, little spitfire." His mouth was on hers, easily taking, sweetly giving, and as he kissed her, something that had started out for fun turned into a sudden, low-keyed hunger. Her supple, provocative, and youthful body stirred his desire as he felt her against him, and in spite of the fact that she had raised a fist to push away, he sensed a response in her and it further intrigued his blood.

Jessie was startled. This was, of course, not happening, was it? Lord, yes, it was. Absurd. This was absurd. He was a self-assured rogue. He was a taker of hearts, and he was daring to play with hers. How rash of him to take such a liberty—and then she felt herself bend to his touch. What was she doing? His move had taken her by surprise. Her response left her breathless and bewildered, but she blamed it on his kiss. His kiss. It was like no other. It was the kiss of an experienced and talented lover and it thrilled her. Of course it would, she silently explained to herself. After all, you have always been a romantic. Stop, Jess, she told herself as she gave herself over to that kiss. He is a womanizer, but, oh, the sensation his kiss aroused. No, Jess, he will break your heart if you let him.

Breeding and logic came to the rescue and she pushed hard against him. "Let me go. How—how dare you take advantage of me in this manner? My uncle will have your blood for this!"

He chuckled and set her away, still holding her shoulders. He scanned her outraged countenance, but her hand was pressed firmly to his chest. He grinned with open amusement. "It would be a fair price to pay, but then, if it's my blood you want, I think I shall have another kiss. . . ."

"Stop, oh, please. . . ." she cried out in alarm.

He threw back his head with his open laugh. "If you wish." His hands dropped and he settled back into his corner to appraise her as he spoke. "Jessica," he said softly, and, when she would not look at him, said again, "Jessica . . ." This time she turned to give him her full look. "You do know that I would not have kissed you had you really not wanted me to."

She frowned and retreated into her corner. Was that true? Was he turning things around, putting the blame on her? Was it possible that she had somehow teased him into that kiss? He read her confusion and repressed another laugh. Instead, he took pity on the child in her. "Ah, Jess, don't be afraid of me. I shan't eat you, and unless you will it, I shan't kiss you again—now."

"You won't kiss me again ever!" she snapped.

They had reached her uncle's establishment in Grosvenor Square and the hack had pulled up to the curbing. Don Rodrigo's black eyes were once again shaded by his thick lashes as he responded to this direct challenge. "Don't you think so, my beauty? But then, perhaps I won't wish to." So saying, he was out of the hack, coming around and opening the door to offer his hand.

She ignored it as she gracefully, lightly stepped down, brushed past him, and took the slated steps to her front doors. At her back she heard his low laugh and felt herself go rigid with indignation. Oh, God, but she wanted to slap the smile off his face. Not want to kiss her? Indeed! If she had the means, she would make it his every wish and then . . . and then she would make very certain it would be something he would never achieve!

Chapter 4

Lady Jessica's moods were strange over the next four days. She found herself fluctuating between high spirits and fevered irritation. She would dress for a rout in great anticipation, taking care with her looks, making certain her style of gown and its color were exceptionally suited to her. However, if she meant to dazzle Don Rodrigo, she hadn't the opportunity, for he was nowhere to be seen. Why she should feel frustrated over this, she could not tell, but she was aware that she did feel this way.

It was nearing midnight, and her violet eyes had ceased scanning the room to look up at Sir Warren in question. "What's that you say, Sir Warren? I *am* sorry, but I didn't quite hear you."

Egad, but she was lovely, was the thought that came to Sir Warren's calculating mind. He had been wondering, marveling, at the lack of interest Lady Jessica was showing for his suit. He meant to have her, and it was a new experience to find that the lady didn't give a fig for his studied courting. "I was saying that the stars you are gazing at this evening are nothing next to your eyes."

She shot him an amused glance. "You do that so well, one might imagine you mean it." She was bantering. His was a practiced art, and she was not about to let him think she was green enough to be taken in by his flirting.

"Wounded to the quick." He bowed in mock dismay. "Is it that you don't believe what I say to you, or that you are not aware just how your beautiful eyes glisten?"

They were standing by the French glass doors of Lady Rombout's ballroom. Jessie turned away from the bright room and smiled as she shook her pretty head of buttercup curls. "Now, just how should I answer you, Sir Warren?" But then all thought stopped and zeroed into irrational emotion as something caught her eye.

Perhaps it was the elegant line of the black velvet Don Rodrigo wore. Perhaps it was the height of the man, or the width of his shoulders. Indeed, perhaps it was the handsome profile, chiseled in lean lines. Her violet eyes found him and watched as he stood in the ballroom archway speaking jovially with their hostess. And then he turned and across the room his eyes found Lady Jess.

Damn, he cursed silently. Was it possible to feel this rushing of blood just from the sight of her? Had he been this hungry to see her again? His business in England had taken him into the country with his friends, but all the while this English wench was on his mind. Inconspicuously he made his way through the crowd of fashionables. He did this with such charm, passing a jest here, a smile there, a greeting to still another.

She watched his progress with admiration. Oh, faith, he was coming her way! She must stop looking at him. She should not be standing here looking at his every move. Was he coming? (This because he had stopped to chat a moment with a group of friends.) Yes, yes, he was. What was she to do with Sir Warren hovering possessively at her side?

She turned a smile to Sir Warren, who had been repeating the latest gossip about the Prince. "Sir Warren . . ." She surprised him by interrupting. "I think I am beginning to feel the heat in this room. Indeed, would I be imposing on your good nature if I asked . . ."

She did not have to finish the question. Gallantly he offered before she could ask, "Of course, my love. I shall fetch you a glass of negus immediately. It will make you feel much more the thing." He bowed and was off. She looked after him anxiously, watching him vanish in the thick of the crowd around the punch bowl.

"White becomes you." It was softly spoken, but it had the power to lift her off the ground. She found herself looking into flashing black eyes. He was taking her bare slender arm; he was lifting the white lace shawl to her bare shoulders; he was leading her outdoors to the terrace with its brilliant torches lighting the still spring night air. "The fresh air will do you good," he said in way of explanation. Hell and brimstone! What was it about this English chit that got up his blood and set him to aching? He was certain she was untried, a virgin, and it had always been his policy to leave the innocents alone. Here perhaps was the one exception, for damn if she didn't ask for his touch with her eyes.

She went with him, gliding along beside him as though she were moving in a dream. This was ridiculous. She attempted to regain control. "Where do you think you are taking me?" The words came out softly, almost huskily, and she was surprised by her tone. She had meant to give him a set-down. She had meant to speak harshly.

He brought up her gloved hand and pressed a kiss to her knuckles, and she was certain she could feel the heat burn right through the white material. It served to silence her. It served to set her blood to circulating. His answer to her question was a low chuckle.

"Be patient, little one. I only mean to make you comfortable."

Was she under some spell? she asked herself as she allowed him to lead her into the dark recesses of the garden walk. What was she doing? Here was a rake of the first rank, and she was actually going outside alone with him! It was absurd, and how dare he just show up out of nowhere and expect her to . . . to . . . to do just what she was doing! She felt her cheeks go hot with the truth behind this thought and was grateful to the cool night's breeze. Her heart? Yes, it was there and beating so loud, she was sure he would hear it.

He stopped at a stone bench that was conveniently wedged between two pyramid yews and he looked at her a moment with the moon brightly glowing and the torch flame at her back. She was breathtaking, and he wanted her. Damn, but he wanted her. His passion was tickled by the defiance in her deep violet eyes, and his good sense was shoved aside by the urges of spring. Still, he underwent a conflict as he sought to dally with her, for undoubtedly she was an innocent and he was breaking his own rule.

His black eyes caressed her face and his words came softly as he gently seated her with him on the stone bench. "And now you will tell me, Lady Jess. Have you missed me?"

Bold! Was there ever such? She tempered her words and returned glibly, "Missed you, Don Rodrigo? La, but have you been away?"

He threw back his head of glistening black waves and released a robust laugh, and then he was taking up her gloved hands in his, raising them to his lips as he bent his head, catching her eyes with his own, softly rewarding her for her courage. No ordinary miss here. No, indeed. "Well met, spitfire! And now that I have been summarily taken to task for having kissed you and vanished, answer me truly. Have you missed me?"

She bristled and her temper flew to her face, to her lips, before she could restrain herself. "Devil! Missed you? Answer you truly? Take you to task? Why, I haven't the time or the inclination to waste my breath on you!"

"And so I am crushed," he said, but his chuckle belied his words. He released her hands and put on a fine dejected countenance. "There, I thought to leave you with the memory of our kiss, and not only do you forget it, but you do not even realize I have not called on you in three days."

"Four," she answered tartly, "and I think it very ungentlemanly of you to keep referring to . . . to something you forced on me." However, at this she found herself being taken into his hands, his black eyes alight with excitement, with amusement, as he laughed low and huskily.

"So, my spitfire *has* counted the days. Damnation, woman, do you know how magnificent you are when you are angry?"

"How dare you touch me!" she threw at him, for he had her firmly by the shoulders and was somehow bending her to him in the most irresistible fashion. She schooled herself to lean away from him, but it didn't seem to work.

"I dare," he whispered, "what you invite."

He was going to kiss her if she didn't stop him. She put up her hand to his chest and pushed. "Stop this nonsense!" she heard herself breathe in a voice she did not recognize and was certain was not at all convincing enough for this roué.

He chuckled again, for she was right; her voice did not at all put him off. "Oh-ho! So my lady says me nay. A fine challenge, spitfire, and I do accept it." Imperceptibly he had managed to bring her into his full embrace. With some skill his hand found her trim waist and he allowed her to know that had he wanted to, he could have taken her kisses. However, having taken her into his hold, he made a show of letting her go, dropping his arms, and moving back from her.

"There, you see how I acquiesce?" His gloved fingers flicked her pert nose. "There will be a time, my Lady Jess, when you will want me to touch you . . . kiss you. . . ." He was getting to his feet, pulling her gently to hers. "And then perhaps it will be too late, for I may no longer be here." Before she could answer this he bent his arm. "And now if you will, I shall escort you back to poor Sir Warren, who, I am certain, is searching you out with great concern. After all, you did send him for your negus, didn't you?"

She was very nearly certain that had she a bat, she might have tried to land a blow to his head. She wasn't sure she could breathe, her anger was so high, so lung-filling. He had brought her to the very edge of madness. She rather thought she hated him. He had insulted her in every single way imaginable—and why? Why? She had never given him cause to treat her in this manner. Had she? Of course not.

She did not take his proffered arm, but looked first at him and then at it with great contempt before she swept past him in a grand style. Swiftly she made her way to the ballroom, where, thankfully, she found Sir Warren coming toward her.

Sir Warren's blue eyes considered her as he handed her the glass of negus and looked past her to discover Don Rodrigo entering the ballroom in her wake. Now, Sir Warren was no fool. It flitted through his mind that although he was himself quite a catch, and that Lady Jess seemed interested, this Latin also seemed to have caught her attention. Was the South American having a go with the lovely heiress? Was he playing deep? He and Don Rodrigo had been at Cambridge together. They were near the same age, but they had never been friends. Each had been too competitive, and they had often found themselves on opposite sides. Well, well, he wasn't about to let Don Rodrigo win Lady Jess, and, from the looks of it, the Latin had managed to get off to a reprehensible start. Fine.

Lady Jess took a long sip of the cool drink, set it down on a sideboard table, and cried out merrily, "A country dance, Sir Warren. Come, lead me off." Bold. She knew she was bold, but she had to do something.

"With the greatest of pleasure," he answered promptly, and regarded her from blue eyes meant to be tender.

They were, and they won a shy response from Jessie before he led her out. Here was an excellent man, she told herself. He, too, was a flirt, to be sure, but she rather sensed he was in earnest in her regard. He was not like the Spanish devil . . . only playing.

The tattlemongers and dowagers of better breeding looked at the pair on the dance floor and nodded to one another. Here was a match of the season. The unattainable Sir Warren had, to all observances, cast his cap in Lady Jessie's way. A suitable match, indeed.

Lady Jess did not give a fig for what was being said. She did her utmost to display to Don Rodrigo that she was in good humor. She bounced from country dance to cotillion. She pranced, she bubbled, she glided in adorable style among her friends and the many bachelors who sought her out. She jested, she laughed, she teased. She was her usual lively self, but she knew there was something lacking. She knew, but she would never let *him* know. That would never do. So she danced with every eligible bachelor presentable enough to impress Don Rodrigo and was pleased to discover the South American rake taking note of her machinations.

Sir Warren headed her list of admirers, and it was with him that she spent most of the evening flirting outrageously. She appeared very gay, very happy, and though some dowagers' brows went up at her bold behavior, the decided opinion was that she was a "diamond," and "incomparable!"

She schooled herself during the course of the evening to keep her eyes from seeking out Don Rodrigo. Why should she care what he was doing? It would be a very good thing indeed if she never saw him again. Still, it was most gratifying to discover his dark eyes surveying her as she flitted about. Was he jealous? He certainly looked somber. Even as this thought came to mind, her violet eyes were held by his black gaze, and what must he do but raise his champagne glass to her in a silent toast?

Truth was that Don Rodrigo was amused. Here was this wondrous English chit enacting quite a scene for him. He was no fool, and she was a green girl determined to show him that she didn't give a fig for him. Well, well, her behavior displayed just the opposite to him, for he had some experience with maids of all ages and styles. Even so, there was something about her, about the way she moved, the sound of her infectious laughter, the tilt of her head, that kept his interest tickled. And then he watched her with Sir Warren, and his dark brows drew together sternly.

Here was a serious suitor, and Lady Jessica seemed genuinely interested in this particular blade. Ah, why should that concern him? It shouldn't. Therefore he made up his mind to forget the Lady Jess, and when next he met her glance he raised his glass to her.

Her reaction very nearly bowled him over. Her violet eyes grew dark with rage. Her bosom heaved; she uttered an exclamation he could only guess at, and with something of uncontrolled rage she stamped her foot at him! He stood staring after her in some amusement, some surprise, and felt himself all the more captivated. He chuckled to himself, for here was certainly a woman-child in delightful form.

Lady Jess's foot came down hard before she could stop herself. She reacted emotionally, physically, to his silent toast. He was maddening! Infuriating! She rather thought she hated him. Her nerves were on end, all because of his outrageous behavior. He had set her head on fire and she couldn't think. Then suddenly she was watching him take his leave of his hostess.

Why the sudden feeling of vague loss? Was it because he had made her feel beneath him somehow? Yes, yes, that was it. He walked away a victor in this battle, and it was uncomfortable to think he had seen her act like a child. Ooooh! She had to show him, and then he was once again looking her way, his sensuous lips curving, his hand tilting his top hat as he left the ballroom, his walking stick in hand. He was gone. He was gone, and she felt all at once deflated.

There was no time for more, as her uncle was coming her way, his cloak draped over his arm. He touched her chin as he reached her.

"My dear, I have to leave you, but Sir Warren has been kind enough to offer to escort you home."

She frowned. "What is it? Where are you off to, Uncle?" He laughed. "Inquisitive puss. Business, m'dear."

"No, oh, Uncle, I saw you in a corner with Pitt. Never say he means to send you off again?"

"Not a chance." He winked, and a moment later he was gone.

It entered her mind that Lady Hester, the prime minister's niece, had said something earlier about the need for the good admiral at sea. Oh, no, please, not so soon! Would Prime Minister Pitt be sending her uncle out to sea already? Was that what this late-night meeting was about? Drat Napoleon! Drat the Third Coalition! Her uncle was retired . . . he had promised . . . and she wanted a life at home with him so badly.

A sigh must have escaped her lips, for Sir Warren bent low over her hand. "And I flattered myself that the lady would be pleased enough to have me escort her home?"

She threw him a half smile and inclined her head. "And the lady is pleased and most proud to have such a notable gallant at her side." She had not been able to keep a sardonic gleam from her look.

"Ho! Why do I take there something of a reprimand?" He was leading her to their hostess and doing it quite adroitly through the squeeze of people around them.

"Reprimand?" She laughed. "I wouldn't dream of taking on such a task."

"Again I am wounded to the quick! We will quickly make our good-byes, but in the carriage I will demand an explanation." He pinched her cheek.

True to his word, he scarcely waited for his driver to urge his neat barouche forward before he turned to Jessica and called her to order. "Well, my beauty, do you think me so puffed up in my own consequence that I would not bear the brunt of criticism?"

She laughed, and it was a low sound of amusement that tantalized him. "Sir, it is simply not my place. . . ."

"Here and now I declare to you, my love, that it will always be your place. . . ." His jolly tone of voice had lowered into a soft caress as he bent to take the chin he held in his fingers. He uplifted her face and gently, tenderly touched a kiss upon her cherry lips and felt his body stir with desire.

She had known he meant to kiss her. This wasn't exactly proper, but she decided to let him. After all, he was a suitor for her hand, and she rather wanted him to kiss her, if only to experience another man's art. Nothing. His lips met hers and nothing. In fact, her mind wandered for that brief moment and thought of a pair of black eyes glinting.

Later that night, when she lay against her pillows and thought about Sir Warren, it was with a sigh. Perhaps it was the style of his kiss. Perhaps it was too gentle. There had been no passion in it. That was it, of course. Yet, tonight in the garden, Don Rodrigo had not even kissed her, but he made her blood bubble and rush about madly in her veins. His touch had made her head spin and her thoughts blast about in her mind without essence. She had felt a desire she had never known herself capable of experiencing.

This was no good! No good at all. She turned on her side, pounded her pillow, tightly shut her eyes, and determined that somehow she would forget Don Rodrigo and his hell-bent eyes! She had to. She simply had to!

Chapter 5

Charles Fox stood, his hands clasped behind his back as he rocked himself to and fro on his heels. Here were these Argentines, these radicals, asking for his help. His help? Damn, but he would give it if he could. Lord knew he stood for freedom. . . .

Don Rodrigo frowned as he leaned against a sideboard table, his muscular arms folded across his chest, his legs crossed at his ankles. "I don't understand why you hesitate. You were friend to the American colonies in their fight; you have always defended the French Revolution when all your kind shouted it down. . . ."

Fox put up one pudgy hand, and his smile was soft, whimsical, his faded eyes darting openly between Don Rodrigo and his high-strung comrade, Simon Bolivar. He was sympathetic to their cause, but he was, at this time in life, all too realistic. "Steady, lads, steady. I haven't said I ain't with you, now, have I?"

"Nor have you said you mean to help," put in Bolivar, his hand playing havoc with his dark curls.

"Simon," reproached Don Rodrigo gently, "allow Mr. Fox to speak."

"I beg your pardon," answered Simon, at once hanging his head. "Do go on."

"You, Don Rodrigo, have spent enough years in England to know something of our politics." He pursed his lips again. "Therefore, you will understand when I tell you that at the moment you would be better served by enlisting the help of a Tory, not a Whig."

Don Rodrigo's black eyes narrowed as he answered thoughtfully, "No doubt, you are referring to Prime Minister Pitt's present power over Parliament?"

Fox inclined his head. "Though in truth he seems to care for nothing but the success of his Third Coalition—"

"Which will collapse before the year is out," returned Rodrigo impatiently.

Fox smiled. "How clear it is to all but the Prime Minister." He shook his head. "However, we digress. Pitt and I have too often crossed swords. Ours is a bitter rivalry, and it would not serve you if he were to become cognizant of the fact that you applied first to me."

"Yes, but . . ." Bolivar was standing up now. He had been alternating his position between standing and sitting, unable to keep still with his impatience. "It is rumored that you will be England's next Secretary of Foreign Affairs."

Fox released a short laugh. "Is it indeed? Yet I repeat, go to Pitt with your propositions. Watch him. Take his reaction in silence, and then return to me."

"That is all very well," started Bolivar irritably, "but we waste precious time with these diplomatic maneuvers. The time is now! Now, can't you see?"

"I see very well," answered Fox quietly. "France quarrels with Portugal and Spain, which makes it feasible for South America to revolt. Pitt will ask you how England will benefit by lending its aid to your cause."

"It will benefit by diverting its trade," answered Don Rodrigo gravely. "You need timber for your vessels. Canada cannot meet all your demands. Your stocks in your naval dockyards need to be replenished. South America is the answer." His sharp eyes took on an intense expression as he watched Fox's reaction. Yes, yes, he had hit home and he knew it.

Fox conceded it at once. "An excellent argument, my friend." Fox smiled and put a hand on the younger man's broad shoulder. "Present it to the prime minister just as you have presented it to me, and I doubt it could fail to sway him."

"So I shall," responded Don Rodrigo immediately. "We need both Pitt's support and the Whig support."

"I don't know that the Tories will be sympathetic to your cause, lad. They don't believe in the revolution theory and won't as a rule lend aid in that direction. However, convince Pitt that helping you will be advantageous to England and you'll have him neatly won. He is many things, but above all others he is faithful to what he thinks will benefit our Albion Isle." He grew suddenly thoughtful at these words and mulled them over a bit while Don Rodrigo and Bolivar exchanged quick, clipped conversation.

It was Don Rodrigo who took the initiative to leave, urging his friend along by grasping Bolivar by the elbow. "I thank you, Charles Fox, and when we have negotiated with Pitt I mean to return with those negotiations to you, for while the prime minister is faithful to his country, that still leaves *my* country in danger." So saying, he inclined his head and was gone.

Fox stood for a long moment before sighing and ringing for his servant. That was a thought. Just what would Pitt do with Don Rodrigo's proposition?

Lady Jessica felt the atmosphere subtly altered in her uncle's London town house as the week progressed. What was going on, she could not tell, but that it was of a political nature, she was very nearly certain. Whigs and Tories alike came and went, and though they all pinched her cheek, patted her lovely arms, and managed to convey the address of normalcy, Jess knew better.

This she sensed in the quiet air that hung about her uncle's head whenever he had not set himself to entertain her and from the meaningful glances she noticed being exchanged between the political set during dinner parties. She found it whenever she happened to enter her uncle's study to discover him closeted with Lord Sidmouth of the Home Office, Lord Windham, or the prime minister, Pitt, himself. Just what was going on, she could not say, but she kept her eyes and ears open, for she was full of natural curiosity.

Then it was Wednesday evening and they were entering Almacks with all of London's *beau monde* excited and in a fever because Admiral Nelson was in town and was expected to make his appearance at the famous club. Lady Hamilton was present, and all eyes were on Admiral Nelson's lovely mistress as she waltzed with her tolerant husband, Sir William Hamilton. The woman's eyes flitted in the direction of the entranceway every now and then as she braced herself for Nelson's arrival. Few knew that she and her lover had already had the pleaure of each other's company when he had first put into port.

Lady Jessica listened as the group of girls surrounding her giggled and gossiped about the famous couple. It was a curious thing, Admiral Nelson and Lady Hamilton, and it tickled her mind, touched her with questions, when the sound of a familiar youthful male voice, light, chuckling, and full with banter made her spin around and exclaim, "Pauly . . . oh, Pauly . . ." with which she dived toward the young gentleman answering this appellation.

With a grimace he halted her progress by catching her bare shoulders and holding her at arm's length. "Hold there, m'girl! Where do you think we are? Lord, but ain't that just like you? Rough and tumble. That's what you have always been. That's what you will always be if you don't mind your ways. Don't think that white sparkly frippery thing you are wearing is fooling me, coz I tell you plainly, it isn't!"

She managed to dislodge his hands and throw herself at his chest, laughing all the while and not in the least abashed at his stricture. "Pauly, oh, you miserable beast! Where have you been? You promised to be in town for my ball and you weren't, though I never expected you would be, for you have never kept one promise you ever made to me, and isn't that just like you not to notice what a wonderfully grown-up woman I have become!"

"Woman? Woman, is it? Well, let's have a look." He again set her apart, all this beneath the gaping eyes of Lady Jessica's crowd of young friends.

They examined the young man with growing admiration, for the young viscount Paul Bellamy was worthy of their fluttering hearts. He was tall; he was lean; he was (though rather carelessly) fashionably dressed. His eyes were an interesting shade of blue. His long, windswept locks were waves of silky golden brown lengths that fell across his forehead, over his ears, and curled around his neck. All in all, he cut quite a figure, and more than one of Lady Jessica's circle of friends found themselves blushing behind their fans and hoping to catch his eye.

The viscount was not in the petticoat line. In all his twenty-two years he had always found himself more interested in the legs of his horses, the running of his vast estates (left to him with the title when he was still in knickers), and the breeding of his foxhounds. He was forever careening over the countryside with his following of friends, for he was a popular fellow, but it was always in the pursuit of sport, and females did not rate high on this list! Jessica had caught his interest when they were children because of her willingness to climb trees in his wake, her keenness in the hunting field, her skill in assisting him as whipper-in with the hounds, and her tomgirl propensities. The fact that her uncle's estates and her summer holidays put her in his way as they attained their adulthood was enough to foster their friendship.

It had been nearly a year since he had seen her, though they had exchanged some letters. When last he had visited her, she had been at school with her style of hair and dress fit for a schoolgirl. Now, here she was, with her buttercup curls piled high on her well-shaped head, and a froth of white cut low over her full breasts and tightly clinging to her small, trim waist. Indeed, she was a woman, and he mused over this fact, his finger at his pursed lips as he chucked her beneath her chin and said lightly, "Well, you are parading as a woman. I'll give you that. Come on the dance floor and we'll discuss it further, shall we?" So saying, he had her gloved hand and led her forth.

She laughed. "Oh, Pauly, it is so good to see you. Now you can tell me all the things I'm eating my heart out to know."

"Can I indeed?" He put up a brow.

"Beast! Don't come on the gentleman to me; I know better," she countered.

"Come on the gentleman, you little minx!" he riposted. "Just what, then, do you think I am?"

"Shall I tell ye, darlin'?" she returned coyly.

"Just try, and I'll whelp your—" he cut himself off. "Whoops, can't do that anymore, can I?"

She laughed happily. "Thank the gods, you cannot." She sighed contentedly. It was good, so good, to have someone she could banter with comfortably. It was what she had been needing. "Now, tell me, Pauly. Is it really true that Lady Hamilton and Nelson have a child?"

He cast her a sharp eye but answered her, " 'Tis true, though why you should be sticking your little nose in that direction . . ."

"Just curious," she answered him quickly. "Doesn't Sir William . . . mind?"

"Why should he? 'Tis done, you know." He looked at her sideways. "Well, *you* wouldn't know, not having a mother to put you in the ways of things. Look, Jess, marriages are arranged. We, well, people of our rank and birth . . . don't ordinarily find ourselves marrying for . . . well . . ."

"We don't as a rule have love matches," she supplied.

"That's the ticket." He breathed a sigh of relief. "So if a man or woman finds herself . . . in love . . . with someone other than her . . . or his spouse, well, naturally . . . if they are discreet . . ."

"But Lady Hamilton and Lord Nelson can't have been very discreet, for the whole world seems to know. . . ."

"Right, well, theirs is . . . of a long-standing duration, you see, and they are quite devoted to each other. It was bound to become, well . . ." He shook his head. "Damnation, girl, why have you got your head all wrapped up in it?"

She frowned. "Pauly, I'm expected to make a . . . brilliant match."

"Sauce-box." He grinned. "So I've heard. They say you are the 'incomparable.' Heard your name toasted at White's, you know."

She pulled a face. "Do you think I give a monkey for such things?" Then, not waiting for his reply, she said, "It isn't that my uncle would force me to marry anyone I held in . . . in dislike, but, oh, Pauly, I don't seem to want to marry anyone—anyone at all."

He snapped his fingers as he twirled in the steps of the country dance. "You will. Don't worry your pretty little head about it." He felt his shoulder suddenly caught, firmly yet politely, and turned to discover a tall, rakehell of a man whom he judged to be nearer thirty than twenty.

Lady Jessica's heartbeat was attacked. Her violet eyes widened to take in the full measure of the man cutting in on her young viscount's dance. She was irritated and excited by the move all at once. She wanted the safety of Pauly's presence, yet something in her wanted the encounter with Don Rodrigo. She hadn't seen him in days, and all at once it seemed to matter. She felt rather than saw Pauly bend politely, wink at her, and back off, giving her into Don Rodrigo's capable hands.

"*God's life!*" Don Rodrigo breathed on a low note.

"Do you have any idea how deep your eyes slash into a man's heart?" He had her gloved hand held tightly (unorthodox in the measure of the dance) to his heart, as though he meant her to examine the truth of his claim, however, before she was able to answer, he brought up her fingers to his lips and kissed them, his long lashes shading his eyes during the act.

She dug deep and managed to gain some control over herself. She was able to give him a short, mocking laugh and an answer. "Consider yourself safe from such a danger, Don Rodrigo. Yours is too deeply buried to be reached."

He was surprised, but he came back determined to conquer. "You cut me to the quick, sweetings, and why? What have I done to displease you?"

"You have interrupted a dance I was having with my . . ." She was about to say friend, but she changed it after a moment's hesitation. "Very favorite beau."

He felt himself stiffen, his pride, of course, interfering with his good sense. "Then it will be an object of mine to reunite you with him." He was now whirling her off the dance floor toward a corner of the large ballroom, for he could see the young man in question surrounded by a pack of swells, all sipping champagne and all in spirits. Jess could see it, too, and knew that Pauly would not appreciate an intrusion now.

"That, Don Rodrigo, is not necessary. The viscount will find me when it is convenient . . . to us both," she was able to answer, her chin well up.

Don Rodrigo grinned and held her close as he bent to whisper into her delicate ear, "Do you know, my little spitfire, we were meant for each other's arms, and one day . . . soon . . . that is precisely where we will find ourselves."

She pushed away and still she was nearer to him than she wanted to be. Couples were already forming for the next country dance, but he had her firmly in his hold, and there was just no getting away without creating a scene. She wanted to slap his face, put him out of countenance. Her voice was low, charged with her hot temper. "*Señor*, I am a great believer in the fates, but if I thought they meant to put me in *your* direction, I would move Heaven and Earth to fight them." So saying, she was able to break out of his hold and turn on her crystal heel.

He was a passionate man, and he had been aroused by her challenge. He meant to teach her, this mere woman-child, just whom she was choosing to wage war with. He caught her bare arm and brought her against his hard, lean body. His voice, when it came, was full, husky, and meant for seduction. She excited every nerve in his body to potency, and he meant to have her one way or another. Forgotten was the fact that they were at Almacks with all the world about them. "Ah, sweetheart, those are brave words, but know this. You won't be fighting the fates only." He shook his head. "For in truth, I don't doubt your ability to defeat them. No, in this, you will have to fight me—and that, my lady Jess, is a fight *I* mean to win!"

Violet eyes burned into black as she sought within for a reply. Oddly enough, she was not grateful to Sir Warren, who, witnessing the irregular behavior of these two, came toward them, lightly calling Lady Jessica back to her surroundings. She did turn then, and she did take Sir Warren's arm and allow him to lead her away. Her mind was wildly racing as Sir Warren made glib conversation.

She was irritated beyond endurance with Don Rodrigo. How dare he? Early in the evening she had heard his name mentioned and lingered long enough to hear it said that all the world knew he had the actress Madame Keenen as mistress. He had installed the woman in his lodgings, and it was said that he was greatly enamored of her. No doubt he would have taken her for wife had she birth to go with her beauty.

It was a lowering thought for Jessie to believe that his

dalliance with her was only to wile away the hours, the hours during his time in society. No doubt he was itching to be with his actress right now . . . and so young Jessie surmised.

He was a rogue, a hell-bent flirt, and he would break her heart if she were not careful. He claimed to want her, but he had not even gone to the trouble of paying her a morning call at her uncle's establishment as her other suitors did. Now it was all so clear. His intentions were only to seduce her to his bed. She was a Stafford, and yet he would dare? Yes, so it would seem. He saw her as a woman, an Englishwoman he could leave behind after he had been amused. Well, she would just have to forget Don Rodrigo and his black eyes!

Chapter 6

What . . . just what in blazes was he doing? Don Rodrigo
Cesares searched his soul as the hired hack drove him
the distance from his leased lodgings in Kensington Square
to Lady Jessica's town house. The hack made a full
screeching stop as an accident in the crowded street
suddenly blocked the bustling traffic and created havoc.
For a moment Don Rodrigo's mind was diverted by the
driver of his hack, who felt it encumbent upon himself to
give his considered opinion on the scene and to express
this in broad cockney curses.

A pretty flower girl noticed Don Rodrigo's profile and
more from a desire to catch his eye than to sell her
wares she sidled boldly to his window and swung a hip
as she made her proposition. "Flowers, sir, for yer
loidy?"

He discovered her round blue eyes and smiled, took
out a coin, and put it in her hand. She beamed as she
handed him the posy. He took it up, brushed it with a
light kiss and handed it back to her. "They aren't half as
pretty as your eyes, sweetheart." His carriage lurched
forward, but he caught her look of longing before he
relaxed once more against the squabs of the seat, and he
grinned. A sweet child, and pretty too. That was it, of

course. What he needed was such a diversion, and then once again Lady Jessica's face appeared vividly before him and her violet eyes flashed, challenged him. Damn, why couldn't he get her out of his mind?

There was his mistress, June Keenen. She was certainly a beauty, and she had satisfied his needs these past few months quite nicely. Yet last evening, after his encounter with Lady Jessica, he had found himself oddly restless in June's company. Damn it, why? June was a beauty. Her amber-colored hair and her soft blue eyes were enough to keep a man staring endlessly. Her art of womanhood was such as to please the most exacting of men, and her disposition was bright enough, witty enough . . . hell! What was wrong with him? He was bored. That was it. Even here in England, where there was such a wide variety of women to choose from, he was dissatisfied with them all.

It was his protective shield. He was able to see all their faults. They were unable to touch his heart from where he stood. No, damn, he would not be caught with his shield down. Time and women had taught him well!

An answer, then? There had to be an answer. Why did he pursue this Lady Jessica? She was just an English chit who would one day marry, as did all her class, to please her relatives and establish herself creditably. Then? Then she would go from one affair to another, discreetly, of course. Quite discreetly.

He sighed. Who was he to judge? It was the way of the world. Young innocents really did not stand a chance. Eventually they must submit to life and lose their wide-eyed stares. Right then. What was he doing, paying a morning call on Lady Jessica? The hack had stopped at Grosvenor Square, and he hesitated as he looked up at the Stafford town house.

Lady Jessica played with a long strand of her buttercup hair and then threw it over her shoulder as she dropped down onto the lap of the viscount, Paul Bellamy, put her delicate arms around his neck, and declared him to be the greatest beast that ever walked the earth!

"Jessica!" scolded Lady Wilton with an accompanying shake of her small head of gray curls. "I will not have you dropping into Paul's arms like that. Do try and remember that you are both no longer children." This simply would not do. They behaved as though they were still babes romping together. The *beau monde* would never approve of such antics.

Jessica pouted at her great-aunt and made no move to rise. "But Aunt Charlie . . ." She saw her aunt laugh at the abomination of the name Charlotte, giggled, and proceeded. "Pauly says he won't take me to the Thames River Fair, and Uncle says I am to go only if Pauly is in attendance."

"Bless you, Jess. Crushing me new yellow pantaloons won't get me in a mood to please you," the viscount was moved to respond, with which he attempted to push her off his lap.

All this did was to get Jess to hold on tighter and to gurgle delightfully, "Please, Pauly, please . . ."

"No." He looked to Lady Wilton for help. "Tell her, Aunt Charlie, tell her the fair ain't the thing. She won't like seeing the abominations they've got over there."

"Trouble is, I think the dreadful child will enjoy it all immensely. Never did have any sensibility. Have only to think it might be a trifle exciting for her to run into raptures over a thing," mused Lady Wilton out loud, "and, blast it, boy, don't be calling me Charlie. I won't have it."

He pulled a mock face of shame. They had called her that from youth and knew very well that she would miss it if they didn't.

"Yes, but . . ." He made another attempt at reason, for he was well aware that taking Jess to a fair could only end in trouble. There was no saying what mischief she could get up there, and he would no doubt win the blame.

"Better take her and have done," summed up Lady Wilton.

"Oh, God!" groaned the young viscount.

"I adore you, Pauly," cried Lady Jessica in high glee as she gave her friend a bear hug and planted kisses around his forehead. "I knew you would never say me nay."

"But I have! I have said you nay."

The doors of the ivory and gold papered and decorated morning room opened to the announcement of "Don Rodrigo Cesares," at which the Stafford butler stepped aside to allow the gentleman in question to pass.

Lady Jessica was at that precise moment caught in the act of attempting to force a kiss of sorts upon the viscount's aquiline nose. Don Rodrigo's name was heard and she froze in place. Don Rodrigo? Here? Don Rodrigo? The question and then the answer his sweeping entrance made came like a thunderbolt through her mind. Don Rodrigo was here. He wore (in the latest style of Beau Brummell) a walking coat of fine dark blue. Its collar was precisely cut, as were the lines to its short waist, where a cummerbund of a darker shade could be seen. His shirt was cut in neat white lines and his cravat tied with expertise. His pantaloons were tailored in buff and displayed to advantage his height and his athletic form. His long, windswept black hair made a dramatic frame for his dashing good looks. His entrance very nearly devastated Jessica.

Lady Jess scarcely suppressed a gasp as she turned an interesting shade of crimson before she jumped to her dainty feet. As it happened, she was wearing a morning gown of white muslin dotted throughout with red velvet and tied at her trim waist with a wide ribbon of the same. It occurred to her life-long friend that her face matched her gown, and with something of a knee-slapping joviality he pointed his finger and exclaimed, "Slap me, Jess, if your cheeks ain't as bright as your . . ."

She managed to tread nicely on his foot. "Hush up,

you dolt!'' she whispered as she watched Don Rodrigo make his way across the room to her great-aunt.

Don Rodrigo had been strangely taken aback by the scene that met his black eyes. He may have expected many things to be happening in the earl's morning room, but *this* was not numbered among them. Who was this puppy? How did Lady Wilton allow such antics beneath her very nose? Was this . . . dandy of a lad Lady Jessica's intended? Could this boy be Lady Jessica's love? It was impossible! Yet she had been in his lap and behaving intimately with him. Well, well. Was an announcement in the air, and, if so, why the devil did such a thought irritate the hell out of him?

He made Lady Wilton his bow, wishing he had still his hat and cloak and was making his exit. Ah, well, nothing for it but to see it through. He dropped a perfunctory kiss upon her fingers as he listened to her rattle. ''How good to see you again, Don Rodrigo,'' she was saying lightly. ''Didn't have the opportunity to really talk to you the other night. Knew your mother, you know, nice gal. A bit light-headed, but a nice gal. Surprised us all when she married your father and went off to that godforsaken country of yours.'' She shook her head. ''Heard the fever took her.''

So, Lady Wilton had known his mother. How much did she know? ''I am afraid so. . . .'' he was saying. He never spoke about his mother, and he made no exception now. He turned to take a step toward his quarry, the reason for this visit. Damn, but she was beautiful with that golden hair falling around her shoulders, those violet eyes wide with surprise, those cherry lips pursed, expectant. She drew a reluctant smile from him as he bent over her hand. ''Lady Jessica,'' he said softly, ''my visit is, I see, inopportune. . . .''

Faith! What must he think of her?

''Oh, no, no, not at all. Lord Bellamy and I are old friends.''

''So I surmised,'' Don Rodrigo returned dryly.

The viscount had popped up by this time. He had heard a great deal about this Argentinian fellow. It was said that Don Rodrigo had beaten the *Nonesuch* in a race to Dover. It was said that Don Rodrigo could drive a high-perch phaeton to an inch and that he displayed himself to advantage in the ring with Gentleman Jackson. Here was a man after his own sporting heart. He laughed and went forward to introduce himself before Lady Wilton or Jessica thought to do so.

"Jess and I go back some years, so you mustn't think anything about what you just witnessed. Nothing in it, you know." He gave Don Rodrigo just about one second to digest this before diving into the subject that interested him most. "Heard tell you've taken Carstares's challenge and mean to drive a pair of grays against his bays to Brighton for time?"

Don Rodrigo smiled. "I am afraid that neither Carstares nor I was sober when we set that date, but as it's been posted in the betting book, it will have to be taken on."

"Well, I don't blame you for having second thoughts. His lordship's bays have never been beaten," said the young viscount.

"Oh, I haven't second thoughts. His bays don't stand a chance against my grays. It is just . . . the timing is not good for me. I have some business I really needed to conduct, and this race cuts into it."

Lady Wilton had been studying Don Rodrigo severely from her place on the sofa. She could see by the way his dark eyes moved over Lady Jessica that he was attracted to her great-niece. Hmm. Here was food for thought. Was she pleased? He was quite a catch. Yes, this was true. He had breeding and he had money, but he also had a reputation with women. There was a hardness in him that disturbed her. She glanced toward Jessica, and her fine gray brow went up thoughtfully. Now, there was no mistaking the fact that the girl was reacting emotionally to this rakehell. That could be trouble.

"Don Rodrigo?" Lady Wilton called his attention. "You will excuse Lady Jessica, I am sure. She has promised this scamp here to attend some frippery fair with him this morning and must now run up and change her gown."

Jessie turned to her aunt in some surprise. Now, what was this? The viscount, too, looked Lady Wilton's way, but of course neither youth would demur. Out of respect for her they kept silent, but Jess could not resist saying, "I don't need to change, Aunt Charlotte. I have a matching spencer and hat that will be fitting enough for the fair."

"Right then, better go along and fetch it, for I am certain Paul will be wanting to get on with it," said Lady Wilton, not in the least embarrassed by her high-handedness.

The viscount's face took on a sudden light. Here was an idea! He turned to his newfound friend and uttered in joyous accents, "I know what you will like!"

"Do you?" returned Don Rodrigo, his brow going up, his dark eyes twinkling and his lip curving.

"Right. I am promised to Jess here to take her to that blasted fair on the river. Well, no need for you to rush off alone. Make one of our party instead."

Lady Jessica's violet eyes opened wide, and she very nearly swatted the viscount. It was all she could do to keep her hands from pinching at him when she attempted to intercept this with "Oh, no, Pauly, Don Rodrigo doesn't want to go to some silly old fair." She kept her eyes averted from Don Rodrigo. "You must know he is not a tourist but has lived in England as a boy and attended Cambridge . . . during his youth." This last she added as an afterthought and was tickled to discover it irked him.

"Ah, silly fair, is it?" returned the viscount, momentarily distracted from his purpose. "If you think 'tis a silly affair, then why drag me to it?"

64

"Well, I would enjoy it, of course, but I don't imagine Don Rodrigo would—"

"Ah, but I would, my lady Jessica. Immensely," commented Don Rodrigo quietly.

"You would?" riposted the viscount, relieved. Here would be a steadying influence over Lady Jessica and a new acquaintance to discuss sporting cant with. "Right then, off you go to fetch your hat, Jess. We'll await you in the hall."

There was nothing for it. What could she do? Here was a muddle indeed. She didn't want Rodrigo with them—she didn't. So why this sudden exhilaration of feeling? As she opened the door and started to leave the room, she saw her great-aunt in the background and was surprised by the elderly woman's expression. Aunt Charlie did not look pleased.

Chapter 7

"Drink today, and drown all sorrow,
  You shall perhaps not do it tomorrow.
 Best, while you have it, use your breath;
  There is no drinking after death!"

sang a brightly costumed jester as he pranced on an open-air stage of no particular design and less beauty. He then found Lady Jessica's deep violet eyes twinkling and moved in her direction as he sang out the remainder of his song.

"Wine works the heart up, wakes the wit;
  There is no cure 'gainst age but it.
 It helps the headache, cough, and tisic,
  And is for all diseases physic."

He beamed then, for Lady Jessica giggled behind her gloved hand and stepped nearer to the viscount. "Pauly, isn't that the drollest verse?"

"Aye, and not fit for your ears, little girl." He turned to Don Rodrigo. "Ain't that so?" Then, not waiting for a reply, he proceeded with his lecture, feeling the weight of his job as chaperone. "Your aunt won't like you listening to such things. Come along." However, it was at this moment that he was diverted from his purpose and post, for he caught sight of a group of his cronies. They saw him just about at the same moment, and with a wild-sounding hail they moved across the busy thoroughfare to greet one another in fine style.

Lady Jessica found herself suddenly alone with Don Rodrigo and was all too aware of his nearness as he moved to take up her elbow. "It looks as if the viscount has met some of his friends," he said easily. "Why don't we signal for him to follow us at his leisure?"

What was she going to do? Here she was, virtually alone (the squeeze of people all around did not seem to count) as she found Don Rodrigo contemplating her with a show of amusement. She couldn't call Pauly away from his friends. No, she wasn't such a shrew as that. "Yes, of course," she answered, "if you can catch his attention."

Don Rodrigo caught the viscount's attention very well and the viscount's merry approval. "Yes, yes, Rod ol' boy, do take Jess along. I'll catch up with you two later."

Don Rodrigo had Lady Jessica's elbow in his firm and yet oddly gentle hold as he steered her away from a crowd he strongly felt was a touch too ribaldly enjoying themselves for a lady's eyes.

"I am told there will be fireworks at the riverside tavern in just about twenty minutes. Why don't we hire a small boat and get out of this squeeze?" he suggested softly.

She looked up at him consideringly. "I don't think that would be seemly, sir."

"Ah, the proprieties? And this atmosphere"—he waved his gloved hand eloquently—"in the very heat of dirty people and the stench of cheap liquors and bad tobacco, this is seemly?"

She smiled reluctantly, admitting the point. "Well, no, but . . ."

"Believe me, buttercup, you and your reputation are

safe with me on the river." There was a tease in his voice, a sparkle in his eyes, and it won a response.

She laughed amicably. "Very well, then, if you think you can handle the oars."

"Ah-ha! The lady challenges, and I am but her obedient servant." His black eyes caressed her as his hand moved down the length of her arm and found her hand.

She felt the pressure of his touch as his hand closed over hers. She was annoyed with herself, with her apparent susceptibility to his charms. He was again suavely taking a liberty with her, and it was sending a tingling sensation through her limbs. This was more than she could stand, and it had to stop!

He was amused, for he sensed her confusion. She was really quite enchanting. One moment enacting the sophisticated gentlewoman, and then suddenly retracting into the shy maiden. There was a playfulness about her that attracted him. There was a pride in the way she held her chin that made him want to bring her to her knees and make her bend to his will. There was a tease in her tone, a challenge in her eyes that made him want to win her for his own, and yet she seemed at times no more than a child. Enough of this nonsense! She was a woman and, as such, she was not to be trusted!

He pulled her along with him to the rough dockside overlooking the gray Thames River, and he felt her gloved fingers gently attempting to withdraw from his hand. He tightened his grip, and he smiled to himself. Then there was the matter of the rowboat, and the next few moments saw him haggling with the boatman over time and price. This done, he turned to Jessie, grinned boyishly, and said on a low note, "My lady, yonder awaits your yacht."

The boat had a weathered look to it, and Jess could see the glint of sunlight as it bounced off the puddles within the boat's confines. She pulled a comical look. "So I see, but will my captain know how to handle her?"

"He should, since he captains something larger than that when he is not on land."

She had heard that he had his own vessel docked in Southampton, but chose to tease him further. "Ah, but ordering a crew about is quite different from taking on the business yourself."

He shot her a rueful glance. "Well, then, necessity will teach me the knack," and then, pinching her pert nose, "Come along, brat." Suddenly he was scooping her up into his capable arms and carrying her over the damp flooring to place her gallantly on the wooden bench in the small boat.

She went pink with embarrassment, but inwardly felt a surge of satisfaction at his handling. The boat rocked as he entered it, and she occupied herself with steadying her position.

His black eyes twinkled as he watched her. He took up the oars, and a moment later he was rowing her out toward the tavern. The fireworks had already started, and there was quite an array of color filling the sky. "It is beautiful, isn't it?" he said at length, for she was staring round-eyed in innocent appreciation.

"Oh, yes . . ." she breathed, and then she caught his expression. "Faith, don't tell me you don't think so."

"Oh, but I do. I most certainly do," he said on a low note, and there was no mistaking his meaning.

She sighed. "Do you always play games?"

"Not always."

"Then tell me. What are you thinking now? Honestly."

"What could I be thinking? What could any man be thinking, sitting here, looking at you? Just as you appreciate the display of color in a darkening sky, so must I. Only for me, *you* are that color."

There didn't seem to be an easy response to this, so she countered by ignoring it and changing the subject. "Don Rodrigo, tell me about your country and your home. I have never heard you speak about it."

He had rowed out a distance. The question seemed to

sadden him, and he halted the steady motion of rowing, allowing the boat to drift as he considered giving her an answer. "My country is a child growing, seeking to better itself."

"Do you love it? Are you homesick?"

He nodded slightly. "Sometimes, but I am fortunate enough to have a great many friends in England, and a home is, after all, where one's friends and loved ones reside."

"Yet you consider Argentina your real home?" she pursued.

His expression suddenly changed and he got a far-away look in his eyes as he thought of home. His voice was soft when he spoke.

"My homeland is a wild and willful being, very vibrant, very full and many-faceted."

"You speak of it as though it were a woman." Her fine brow was up with curiosity.

He smiled. "She is as capricious as a woman, certainly."

"You sound homesick. Lonely for your friends and family?"

"As it happens, I have in England a great many friends, and family as well." He evaded her question skillfully.

"Really? I hadn't realized you had English relatives."

"Yes." His face grew stern.

She sighed. "How wonderful for you to be able to travel and to be at home in two worlds." She eyed him a moment. "For you seem very much at home here."

He agreed to it with a half smile. "Let us say that I enjoy England when I am here, but for me, there really is only one home—my Argentina, my ranch."

"Ranch? You have a ranch? Oh, how exciting. I have read about them. Your ranchers, the men who work for you, are called gauchos, aren't they?"

He was pleased with her genuine interest and inclined his head. "Yes, they are a breed unto themselves, hard-living, hard-working. Even our play is quite, quite dangerous."

"What play is that?" She leaned forward.

"We have a game, a test of skill. It is called *pato*, and there are some dowagers that dearly wish to outlaw it." He was frowning. "I suppose it is the monotony of the working day out on the plains, or the herding of the sheep, for a gaucho is a man who must always experience life to its fullest."

"What do you mean? What is it about this *pato* that makes it so exciting?"

He smiled patronizingly at her. "It cannot be easily explained, but it is very basic, very simple. We choose a field and at its length we place a ring. We choose even teams and for points we ride at a given pace with a six-handled ball, which we must attempt to place through that ring while on horseback. Each team member puts himself in jeopardy as he attempts to do this, you see, and it can be most dangerous."

"It sounds intriguing." She looked past him wistfully. "I would dearly love to see it played."

He laughed out loud and reached out to take her hand, which he brought to his lips. His kiss on her gloved fingers was most charmingly executed, and his black eyes slowly, lingeringly caressed her lips before he met her violet eyes. "It is my belief, little spitfire, that what you would dearly want is to actually play the game. Of course, your riding seat would soon find you on the ground." Again he laughed, and there was a tease in his voice.

She bridled, her shoulders moving back. "That is unfair. You cannot judge my seat by one observation."

"No, no, I cannot. So you will ride with me tomorrow and show me how accomplished you are."

She eyed him.

"It would be my pleasure to do just that!" she returned, and then sighed. "I do wish I could ride astride, but it is impossible in London. Aunt Charlie said it would be disastrous to my reputation."

"Then we will ride out of London. I will take you up

in my phaeton with our horses in tow. You may don whatever you deem fit and mount your horse astride."

She brightened. "Right then."

"And so I shall see if you are up to the rigors of my country, for in my opinion, you would melt beneath its sun."

"I don't know that I give a fig for your opinion of me. However, I have the feeling that your opinion extends itself to all Englishwomen, and perhaps that is why I am so set to prove you wrong," she said thoughtfully.

He leaned forward and suddenly had her chin, tilting her face up to very nearly touch his lips, and his voice was low and provocative.

"It will be delightful to watch you try."

She pulled away and he laughed softly. She was moved to reply on an angry note, "You are something of a rogue, Don Rodrigo."

"But of course, I most certainly am," and then looking toward shore, "Ah, I see the viscount waving to us from the dock. I must return you before the proprieties are indeed offended and your aunt bars me from your door."

"Then do, I beg of you, sir, keep me out here a bit longer," she said sweetly, folding her arms across her middle.

He threw his head back with the strength of his laugh, and when next he contemplated her, his smile was wide. "But then, my lady Jessica, you would miss the opportunity to score a hit for Englishwomen. And I am persuaded you don't really want to default on that particular challenge."

She bit her lip and looked away. He was insufferable. He was arrogant, hateful, puffed up in his own consequence, narrow-minded, and . . . and . . .

And what? No time to think, for, thank goodness, here was Paul giving her his hand and lifting her out of the boat as Don Rodrigo turned to settle up with the boatman.

Chapter 8

The sun glowed brightly in the morning's blue sky. The breeze was gentle and refreshingly cool as it came in quiet waves, bringing with it the scent of wildflowers and honeysuckle. A road of dark earth stretched out flatly for what seemed like miles. On either side of the road tall oaks separated it from lush green pastures.

Jessica contemplated her surroundings with a sense of growing uneasiness. Here she was, breaking all the rules of her society. But it really wasn't so very imprudent after all, she reasoned. There was Don Rodrigo's groom standing with the phaeton's horses at the side of the road. She was not, therefore, alone with the South American rake, was she? No. No, she was not.

Yes, but look at you with your riding skirt hiked up to your knees! Look at you, seated astride! Yes, but no one would have the opportunity to look at her, she answered herself. She was, after all, five miles outside of London, and the course she and Don Rodrigo would be taking would be over the fences through the farmlands that surrounded them.

She adjusted the wide brim of her Gypsy hat, touching the white scarf trailing from its crown to her back. Her long tresses of buttercup curls were neatly pinned away from her ears. Her gray mare pranced beneath her, eager for her run, and she leaned forward to pat the mare's neck. "Easy there, love, easy."

Don Rodrigo hoisted himself neatly onto the back of his black gelding and trotted up to her with a smile. "If you wish to withdraw now, my little one, I know a very nice inn we may repair to for nuncheon." He had seen the look of uneasiness in Jessie's eyes and meant only to give her a way out.

She bristled at once. "I am not so fainthearted, sir." She looked at his own frenzied steed and commented on a dry note, "Your gelding looks as though he may kill you, and if it is *you* who wish to forget our little wager . . ."

He laughed out loud, touched the tip of his dark beaver hat, and then gestured for her to move before him. There was only one way into the pasture. Jessie eyed the post and rail, its footing before and after, and guessed the line fence to be about three feet nine inches. She brought her horse under her, took a gentle feel of the mare's mouth, and urged her forward. The fence was taken neatly, the landing was managed easily, and Jessie felt the exhilaration of its successful completion as she turned to watch the black, his fores tucked beautifully, following her lead. She laughed out loud and moved forward as they had planned, taking the slope east and away from the road. She loved riding like this, unhampered by convention, at one with nature and nature's gifts.

They were approaching another line fence, this not much different from the one alongside the road, and she sat back, bringing her horse in, slowing the mare's pace, judging her distance. This time Don Rodrigo was beside her, and she could see him grin as they moved along, head 'n' head. Again they flew over the fence with perfect ease, but this time the tall grass before them stretched downward into a valley and she could feel the mare pick up speed. She shortened rein and called her mare to order as she slowed her pace. She could feel her own breath coming in spurts as they put turf behind them.

Don Rodrigo was touched with a reluctant admiration for Jessie's skill with the reins. She was certainly far more accomplished than he had hitherto believed. He could see at the bottom of the hill a fairly wide, deep stream, which sliced unevenly through the green field. Don Rodrigo's black eyes grew grim, for while he felt confident that his black, whose ability he had learned to respect, would easily and willingly take this obstacle clean, he was not so sure of Jessie's young mare. He knew already from their conversation during the carriage ride out here that Jessie's mare was just five and still quite green, and there was something in the change of Jess's expression that worried him.

He spurred his black forward and called over his shoulder to Jessica. "I will give you a lead over the bank. Ride her well, love. Don't trust her for a moment, for *she* does not appear to trust the water."

This (as it happened) was precisely what Jessie had been thinking, and had it not been for Don Rodrigo's evident sincerity in the matter, she would have bristled against him. Instead, she felt a wave of pleasure that he should care. However, there was no time for such fancies. She could feel her mare tense beneath her as the stream loomed in the distance. Oh-oh, here now was certain trouble. Her mare had balked during the hunting season, and Jessica had on several occasions very nearly lost her place in line when her green horse had refused water ditches. She prepared for this eventuality by producing her crop from out of her boot. It was neck or nothing or she would be shamed before Don Rodrigo once again. No, this was something she could not allow.

The mare saw the crop in her mistress's hand and felt the sudden determination that accompanied the squeeze she felt against her flanks. Her ears flickered and her head came up in her extreme tension. Ahead was some dark and glistening thing. She did not wish to approach it, and her movements beneath Jess became uneven as she attempted to waver. Jess had her very nearly cantering in place as she drove her on. No, thought the mare, no . . . not this dreadful dark wet stretch. But she felt the pressure of her lady's legs as Jess sat her saddle deep and pushed her into her hands, pacing her for the moment when they must needs spring.

Jessie timed it perfectly. She was vaguely aware of Don Rodrigo's encouragement as he took the stream flying, and landed easily on the other side. She brought the crop down on her boot, hard and loud, bringing her mare to attention as she spurred her forward, and then they were flying, beautifully, gracefully, with Jess giving her mare rein as soon as they left the ground.

In her supreme exhilaration Jess cried out merrily as they landed, "Bravo! Bravo, you marvelous dear thing, you!" with which she bent to pat her mare's neck.

"Good girl!" called Don Rodrigo proudly as he trotted forward. Proudly? Here was a marvelous, spirited woman-child who made him feel as no other ever had, and at that moment he was more determined than ever to have her. Before either one knew what he was about, he had reached over and lightly taken her neck in his gloved hand, deftly bending her to his will as he lowered his head and stole a kiss.

It was a light thing, full with the triumph of the moment, scarcely touching the passion she seemed always to arouse in his breast. He wanted to lift her off her horse, hold her to him, stroke her caressingly, but he felt her respond in easy, sudden friendship and knew just how to control himself and, thus, the relationship. Damn, but he meant to have her, and he knew that if he moved now it would be too soon. This one would take seducing. She was a virgin child, but he had to have her. It was all he knew, all he understood, when he was with her. He did not want to hurt her, yet his desire for her overrode conscience.

Jess was on a high. She had taken the stream, and,

what was more important, her mare had done it beautifully, with agility, with style. It was ineffably thrilling. It was an ego booster, and his kiss, she took as a compliment of the moment. Indeed, it brought the blush to her already heightened color, but she accepted his kiss with a laugh, for her mare moved off to graze, pulling her away from him and saving the moment.

"Well, buttercup, I admit myself fairly beaten and accept the loss of our wager. You have shown me that you are certainly a horsewoman of no mean caliber!"

She giggled. "Astride, that may be said, but I've never really been able to handle the reins as well when I'm riding sidesaddle." With this last she sighed. "I suppose I shall have to apply myself to the task."

"Didn't they require it of you at your girls' school?"

She twinkled. "Of course, but I have never been one who did what was required of me." With this, she urged her horse forward once more and laughed over her shoulder. "I do believe, sir, we have another fence or two waiting."

His black eyes gleamed and he was already passing her as they took the field and headed for a gate that would lead them onto a wooded forest trail. Forgotten, or, rather, put aside, were Don Rodrigo's intentions for this golden-haired beauty in the spirit of the ride they were both enjoying, and when she glanced at him, she was all too aware of a certain attraction for the boyish expression of his face.

This new kindred spirit put them at ease with each other and established a door for new emotions. She knew it and had the wisdom to worry over it, for she also knew he was not hers for the taking!

Sir Warren's blue eyes held a cold glint of disapproval as he took in Lady Wilton's words. What was this? How had Lady Wilton allowed Don Rodrigo to take Jessica off?

"You say Don Rodrigo has taken Lady Jessica for a

drive in the country?'' Clearly he showed his opinion of such permissiveness.

Lady Wilton's fine steel gray brow went up. She was no more pleased than he, but she would not permit him to be a judge of the matter. "Well, of course. I could have no objection. After all, Don Rodrigo had with him a groom, and besides, he advised me that he would be taking Jess to the Greenwich Inn, where they would be joined by his friends, Señor and Señora Bolivar.''

"Even so, considering Don Rodrigo's reputation, I should have thought *you* of all people would have found a way to—''

Lady Wilton interrupted him, and the frost of her voice made him aware that he had overstepped. "I know, Warren, that you have a vested interest in my great-niece. However, if you had any knowledge of her at all, you would realize that once she has a notion in her head, there is no use trying to stop her.''

He eyed Lady Wilton a moment, his brows knit in thought before he returned a question to this. "So what you are trying to tell me is, that Jess had a fancy to ride out with Don Rodrigo?''

Lady Wilton took pity on him. She wasn't sure that it was his heart that was involved here, but that Sir Warren Woodfall meant to make Jess an offer was a certainty. "She was certainly determined to do so, but not, I think, for the pleasure of his company.''

"For what, then?'' He was puzzled.

"She did not take me into her confidence, for she was ever one to keep her own council, but I rather think they had some argument that this ride was meant to settle.'' She shook her head. "I wouldn't concern myself too much over it. If I know Jess, she has proven whatever point was in question and will have no more of the scamp after today.''

"You underestimate his power with women. I am told he is quite a charmer, and from what I was able to observe the other night, his present sights seem to be set on our sweet Jess."

This gave Lady Wilton moment to pause, for it was her own fear.

"Do you think so? I was given to understand that he was not in the habit of playing with maids of quality."

"That may have been so in the past, but it is my belief that he is attracted to Lady Jessica, far too attracted to allow the principles that have guided him before to do so now."

Lady Wilton was herself concerned about this. She answered him thoughtfully. "Then perhaps, Sir Warren, we are wasting time."

"Precisely so, ma'am." He inclined his head of ginger waves. "It is my intention to ride out and intercept them—"

She cut him off. "Sir, you must know that would set up my Jessie's bristles. She would not like to feel manipulated by either of us. However, if you were in the neighborhood of the Greenwich . . . on your way home to London . . . it would not appear odd for you to stop by the inn for a spot of tea."

"You are most wise." Sir Warren was taking up her weathered hand, dropping low over it.

She watched him leave, adjusting her gray curls beneath the ivory lace of her mobcap. She wasn't quite sure that she had done the right thing in allowing Sir Warren to interfere in this matter, but she wasn't about to have this rogue Don Rodrigo seduce her Jess! It did not auger well, this constant attention the Latin was paying to young Jessica. He was not the sort that usually bothered with marriageable maids, but it had been evident to her the other day that he was certainly interested in her great-niece—and not for marriage.

There was Jessie's reaction to all this to be considered. Jess would not like it if Sir Warren took on a possessive air. Lady Wilton grimaced to herself; she hoped he would know better. Perhaps all this was unnecessary.

Perhaps Jess had not fallen victim to Don Rodrigo's charms. Indeed, she had had the impression that her Jess was rather put off by the Latin. Well, time would tell, only time.

Chapter 9

The path that led through the landscaped gardens of the elegant Greenwich Inn was a narrow, winding, and secluded one. It was flanked by full, tall evergreens, and its circular route touched a swiftly flowing, shallow rocky stream. Wildflowers bloomed in riotous color, and as Don Rodrigo led Jessie along, she exclaimed out loud about the fresh spring scent.

She was conscious of him, all too conscious of him. She should not be here walking alone with him. Why hadn't the Bolivars arrived yet? They had found a message awaiting them from the young couple saying only that they would be delayed. Had that been contrived? No, of course not. She was being silly, too suspicious.

Don Rodrigo walked slowly, and his own mind was a tumble of conflicting thoughts; his body was in battle, for his blood was on fire. He had quite made up his mind to leave the child be. She was a woman; she was a beauty and he wanted her, but he had decided at the close of their ride that he would not ruin her. He would adhere to his old, safe rule and keep his hands off her. Right. So what was he doing here with her now?

Her Gypsy bonnet she had left at the inn beside his beaver hat. Shyly she glanced at his profile. Faith, he was so handsome with his black silky waves blowing around his rugged face. She glanced quickly away and remarked on the beauty of the setting.

Why couldn't he breathe? Why did he feel he would choke if he spoke now? What was wrong with him? Her long golden hair flowed in full glistening and buoyant waves to her trim waist. Only a ribbon held it away from her face, and that face . . . .damn, but it was mischievously, tauntingly lovely, as were her lips, pursed, cherry, and teasing him to kiss.

"Sweet buttercup, do you realize what your eyes do to a man of my stamp?" His voice was low and husky as he took her shoulders suddenly and turned her to him.

She attempted banter to dispel the moment. "Now, how should I know that when I have never known a man of your stamp?" She spotted a squirrel holding a piece of food in its hand and cried winsomely, "Oh, look. . . ."

"I am. Ah, Jess, forgive me." He was drawing her into his embrace. He couldn't stop himself. This was not what he wanted to do, but hell, he just couldn't stop. She was in his arms and he was kissing her, taking her kiss, feeling as he had never felt before.

She could stop him. She could, but she didn't want to. She wanted him to kiss her and oh, oh, it felt so good. His lips touched and parted her own, and with gentle pressure she received him as he took her breath away. Her knees weakened and she was thankful for his arms as his tongue made its entrance and taught her new delights. Gently, tenderly, he took and she responded. Her hands went to his neck as she pressed herself to him and she felt his arms tighten.

Had he ever wanted a woman so much before? Had a woman pressing her body into his ever felt quite like this before? What was different? Why was he moved to a new dimension. Oh, hell, he had to have more, more. . . .

She felt his hand move to her rump, and she should have pulled away, but as he held, caressed, pressed her to him, she only knew she wanted him to go on. Stop!

An inner voice called her to order and she felt herself stiffen. Against him? No, in truth, she went rigid with shock at herself, at the abandonment she felt while in his arms. A sixth sense came to protect and remind her what was due to her as Lady Jessica, a Stafford of the house of Redcliff! As she silently berated herself for her wild behavior, she was able to put her hands against his chest and gently push at him.

"Don Devil!" called a male and merry voice.

Guiltily the two drew apart, and after one long look and the tender caress of her cheek, Rodrigo looked away and smiled at the sound of his friend's call. "Coming, *el perro*!" He took Jessie's gloved hand and pulled her along; thus the disquiet they may have felt was lost in the sudden face of realities.

Simon Bolivar grasped his taller friend's upper arms and greeted him warmly. "Well met . . ." He glanced toward Jessica and whistled softly as he turned fully and made her a flourishing bow. "*Madre de dios*, but now I see that you may be wishing me at the devil!"

Don Rodrigo gave his friend a withering glare and made the introductions. Simon declared himself enchanted and offered Lady Jessica his arm. "My lady, it will be my pleasure to rescue you from this miserable fellow and take you to my bride, where you will be more comfortable, I am sure."

"Simon . . ." called Rodrigo sweetly.

"*Si?*" answered Bolivar.

"Do go to Hades," he returned just as sweetly, which set the three to chuckles as they entered the inn through its garden doors and found a full-bodied and lovely dark-haired woman in Spanish raiment awaiting them.

Here, Jess had the irritation of watching Rodrigo go to the dark-eyed plump and pretty woman and plant a light kiss upon her lips. What was that she felt? Jealousy? Nonsense. It was absurd. Jessie looked away and attempted to give Simon Bolivar her full attention as he went about the business of introducing her to his wife.

However, no sooner had Simon made the introductions than Rodrigo began flirting outrageously with the Spanish lovely.

Simon intervened with a show of force. "Away, devil! Away, I say! God's death! Do you ignore me? Shall we meet on the dueling field, *amigo*? Eh?" He turned in mock rage to his wife. "My Beatrice, my love, tell him you will have none of him!"

"Oh." The pretty pouted. "Not even a little bit of him, my Simon? Ah, but I think you very cruel." Her dark eyes twinkled merrily.

He tweaked her nose, and his voice was a tender sound. "Many things you must have, but *he* is not one of them!" Pleased with the laughter that ensued, he clapped his hands together and exclaimed, "So, we are hungry, are we not? Come, let us see what these English can do for our appetites."

"Ah, I have found the English fare . . . most delectable," said Don Rodrigo softly as he took Lady Jessica's arm and gently steered her out of the garden room into a long, wide, and brightly lit hall.

It was here that they heard a male voice making an inquiry of the innkeeper, and Jessie's winged brow went up in some surprise, for she recognized the voice. Her suspicion was confirmed when they rounded the corner and entered the large, elegantly furnished dining room and found standing at the counter a tall, well-dressed buck in town riding clothes of blue. His ginger locks were windblown and his hazel eyes smiled as he discovered the person he sought. "Lady Jess!" he exclaimed in some marvelous show of surprise. "What good fortune"—he lowered his voice as he came toward her and took up both her hands—"to find you here when I have been thinking about you all day."

She was astonished to see him and not altogether pleased. However, she allowed him to kiss her gloved hands, and when he had straightened up she asked, "Why, Warren, whatever brings you here?"

He was nodding to Don Rodrigo and putting on his punctilious smile as he also included the Bolivars in his glance. He had met them on occasion in London and needed no introduction. He answered Jess on a glib note. "I was visiting friends not far from here and decided to stop by the Greenwich for a late lunch before traveling back to London. And you?"

It flickered through her mind that it was odd he had not taken lunch with his friends. However, she accepted this and turned as she answered his question to wave the Bolivars and Don Rodrigo into the conversation. "You know, of course, Señor and Señora Bolivar, and Don Rodrigo." She waited for him to acknowledge them, which he did in a polite and stylish air. She watched him curiously. There was something about his being here that disturbed her, but she couldn't quite fathom its meaning. She proceeded quietly. "We were just about to go in for lunch ourselves. . . ." She left the sentence hanging, for it was not her place to extend an invitation to Sir Warren to join them.

Don Rodrigo was not amused. He did not for one minute believe Sir Warren was with them by mere coincidence. He was too much a cynic and had immediately decided that this was a contrived meeting. It feathered his anger, and he found himself stiffening against Sir Warren and not at all disposed to extend an invitation to the man to join them.

Simon Bolivar coughed and glanced sideways at his volatile friend. This was awkward indeed, for he sensed Don Rodrigo's dislike for this Sir Warren. However, the amenities must be preserved, and he took it upon himself to uphold them. "Perhaps, Sir Warren, you would like to make one of our number at the table that has been laid out for our pleasure?"

"Why, that would be splendid," responded Sir Warren at his most cordial. "I would like that very much." He took Lady Jessica's hand and slipped it through his bent arm before leading her forward.

She was annoyed with his proprietary air. However, she did not wish to embarrass him and allowed it to pass. Don Rodrigo took a step forward with every intention of setting Sir Warren away from Jess, but Simon, well acquainted with Don Rodrigo's temper, had took the precaution of laying his hand upon his friend's arm.

"I think you will . . . reck not . . . eh, *amigo*?" Simon whispered.

It was an old English saying they had often used during their long-standing friendship. It served to appease Don Rodrigo's ill humor, and it put things in proper perspective. In fact, at this moment, he asked himself what the matter was. Why should he mind if Sir Warren flirted with Lady Jess? Hadn't he decided to leave the girl be?

At the blue and white plaid covered table, Don Rodrigo's eyes glinted as that resolve seemed to fade. Damn! If Sir Warren did not take his hand away from Jess's (which the Englishman was now patting as she related the adventure of her day), he thought he might take him by the throat and, damn, if he didn't do that right now, hang convention!

Beatrice Bolivar nudged her husband. "You must, I think, draw Rodrigo's fire, *sí*? He seems to wish to run this one though, eh?"

"*Sí*, my love, and you will, I think, manage him better than I," he whispered. "Bat your pretty lashes at him and see if he will not stop glaring at that one." He could feel Rodrigo's tenseness beside him.

Beatrice touched Rodrigo's chin. "So," she said jovially, "my Simon tells me you go to visit with Pitt tomorrow. It goes well, *sí*?"

Rodrigo glanced at her briefly and smiled. "You know exactly how it goes, my treasure." He knew she meant to divert him, and was slightly amused.

Sir Warren heard the prime minister's name mentioned and turned with some interest, for his ambitions were political. "What's this?" He was looking sharply at the two Latins, for he could see a glance pass between them. "Tell me Argentina means to join the fray against Bony?"

Simon Bolivar smiled ruefully. "No, I think not. We have enough to contend with at home." He inclined his head. "Though, I think, we may yet serve your country—if Pitt is amenable to our ideas."

"Really?" questioned Sir Warren, intrigued. "And how could Argentina possibly serve our needs?"

Simon was about to answer, for his pride rushed to his lips before he was able to judge the matter. However, Don Rodrigo cut him off.

"A silly notion," Don Rodrigo said sweetly. "How could our heathen country possibly exchange favors with your Albion." He took up the basket of sweet buns and looked at Lady Jessica's violet eyes as he offered them to her. She sat directly across from him, and as she took one up she gave him a thoughtful smile. None of the conversation had passed by her unnoticed. She had awaited the outcome of Sir Warren's curiosity and was all too aware that Don Rodrigo's answers had evaded the issue. Well, well. What were the Bolivars and Don Rodrigo up to? Cautiously she said, "I don't think it a silly notion for Argentina to apply to England now. Suppose, just suppose, the Argentines wanted their own government, wanted freedom from Spain's oppression, Spain's taxation. This would be a very good time to apply to England for help."

"I don't see that," replied Sir Warren, turning to her in some surprise. "We have enough to do with handling Bony."

Don Rodrigo's black brow was up with surprise. What did this little English flower know of politics? "Sir Warren is quite correct. What good would it do England to help Argentines to revolt against Spain?"

"Napoleon quarrels with Spain and Portugal; therefore, Spain can not easily squash a revolt all the way in South America when her forces are needed at home. Besides, she may join forces with France to put down the prime minister's hopes for the Third Coalition. It is said that Spain and France will fight us on the sea.'' She smiled. "So, would it not be wise to keep Spain occupied?''

Don Rodrigo inclined his head and raised his glass of wine to her. "Very wise, my buttercup. An excellent argument.''

"So,'' breathed Sir Warren, "that *is* why you are here? To enlist our help against Spain.''

"Do you think so?'' returned Don Rodrigo. "I rather thought all this was merely hypothetical.''

"Really?'' returned Sir Warren sarcastically. "Then why this meeting with Pitt?''

Don Rodrigo's brow went up. "Lady Hester is a friend . . . and has invited us to tea.''

"Ah,'' said Señora Bolivar with a sigh of relief. "They bring our meal, for I am sure I am quite famished, you infamous beast.'' This last she directed at her husband. "For you kept me waiting forever at that terrible place with all the cattle and pigs.''

Lady Jessica took pity on her new friend and helped her to change the direction of the conversation. She released a short and quite lovely laugh. "Cattle and pigs? Whatever were you doing with such divergent livestock?''

"Ah, this boor of a husband hears that there is a remarkable cow for breeding, *sí*? Well, what must he do but cart me off this morning to have a look.''

"But why?'' asked Jess incredulously.

"Ah, for our Estancia Aguay, our ranch, you see.'' She looked to Don Rodrigo. "You here, you have lands, farms. We have very large ranches . . . you know?''

"I've heard a little but never firsthand. Please, do tell me all about it.''

This was well, for the next hour was pleasantly spent with the two women chattering away and allowing their gentlemen a word only, and that here and there.

*   *   *

Lady Jessica sighed as she relaxed in her seat and watched the passing scenery. Beside her Don Rodrigo handled the reins in fine, deft form. At their back, ready to pay the toll, which they were fast approaching, was Rodrigo's small Spanish groom. Oddly enough, and although it had been Sir Warren's intention to ride beside the open phaeton, he was nowhere to be seen.

"I do not understand how that can have happened," said Jess, eyeing Don Rodrigo sideways.

"It is not unusual for a horse to throw a shoe," returned Rodrigo easily, "and on such a rutted road, one would not wish to risk his animal."

"Yes, but two shoes?" riposted Jess, not to be put off.

He threw back his uncovered head of black hair and released a hearty laugh. "Ah, so I am found out."

"*You* did it, then!" She was wide-eyed. "I thought so, but I couldn't believe it!"

"It is the perversity of my disposition, I suppose," he said on a long and mocking sigh.

"Oh, stop, you . . . you villain!" But the lady was laughing. "Why two shoes? Wouldn't one suffice?"

"No, I thought I would be certain. You see, he seemed so determined to accompany us." He shook his head with a sudden frown. "I only regret that it put upon Simon and Beatrice to remain with him."

"Ha! You don't give a fig about that. In fact, you—"

"In fact, I wished to see you home myself," he said softly, his black eyes suddenly growing serious.

She attempted to change the mood. "When did you do it?"

"It was an easy thing," he said lightly with a shrug of his broad shoulders. "A quiet word to my man—he was very clever about it, don't you think? Leaving one shoe partially on . . ."

"Amazing that the ostler did not see him."

"A coin does much when offered to a poor boy. He looked the other way."

"Oh, that is quite horrid," she said on a frown.

He laughed and tweaked her nose. "He is your beau? Are you missing him so badly?"

"No, he is not my beau, and, no, I am not missing him so badly, because I rather think my great-aunt put him up to this, and I don't like anyone trying to manipulate me."

"I don't think he was put up to it by any other than himself." He watched her for a reaction. "In truth, little Jessica, I think he means to marry you."

"Do you?" Her bristles and her pride were up.

He laughed. "Will you have him?"

She was hurting now. He didn't care that she might marry another man. He took her kisses, but didn't care that she might offer them elsewhere. She must remember always that his were the charms of a rake. A libertine who would flirt, who would wean away a kiss, who would charm and then leave her heart damaged. She could not allow that, so she answered thoughtfully, "I care for him, but I am not ready to get married—just yet."

He eyed her. "Wise little puss. See if you can get a duke, then."

"You are without scruples, sir." She shook her head. "But not everyone is. I don't mean to marry for any but one reason."

"Love?" he scoffed. "You are too smart. Love is a fleeting thing. Find a better reason."

She was serious suddenly. What kind of man was this Don Rodrigo? She looked at him intently. "Truly, is that what you believe? Don't be flippant with me, sir. Answer me as a friend."

He looked at her long. "From my experience, and I have much, it is what I believe." His eyes still stroked her. "There is much I would teach you, my lovely buttercup, but the word *forever*"—he shook his head—"is a lie."

"What of Simon and Beatrice? They are so in love," she countered.

This was something that was true. His answer was a harsh one. "They are newlyweds, my dear. Ask me if they are in love five years hence."

"Oh, that is so very cynical."

"And you will marry your Sir Warren," he answered. "He is a determined man."

"Perhaps," she answered. "If I fall in love with him."

"And could you?"

She looked at Don Rodrigo for a long time and answered lightly, "In time I think any woman could fall in love with him. Sir Warren is handsome, charming, gallant." She saw him pull a face and added quickly, "And I don't think he will break my heart."

"No, he won't do that, but neither will he bring it to life," Don Rodrigo said on a low, harsh note.

There didn't seem to be anything adequate to say to this without putting herself forward, so she allowed the subject to die in silence before she brought them around to a safer topic.

Chapter 10

Sir Warren stood in a corner of Lady Jersey's ballroom and through narrowed, hostile, and jealous eyes watched Lady Jessica go through the steps of the quadrille with Don Rodrigo. The emotions he was experiencing took the hazel color of his orbs and darkened their hue, hid their luster, and dispelled his habitual air of aloofness. He appeared to his intimates to be a man rubbed to the point of abrasiveness.

All this because of a woman! Sir Warren, you see, had quite made up his mind to have the lady Jessica and her ample fortune. She was in his estimation just the sort of female who could provide him with an heir, aid his political ambitions, and enhance his bed. Her lineage was not to be faulted, her money was greatly needed, and there was something more than her beauty that attracted his eye and brought his passion into play. He had made his decision, and it had never entered his mind that the lady might not fall in with his plans! After all, he thought bitterly now, she had not given him any indication that she might be adverse to his courtship. Quite the contrary, she had appeared flattered and intrigued.

What had happened, then? Don Rodrigo was what happened! The chit seemed unable to see anyone else when the man was present, and when the Latin was not present, she seemed always restless, discontent. This was intolerable. The rogue meant to have her . . . but not as a wife! Did she not see that? No, she was a girl infatuated with an exotic rake, and he would have to open her eyes and make her see. How?

A difficult problem to be handled with great delicacy. Don Rodrigo could be dangerous when crossed, and it was plain as a pikestaff that the Latin would not easily allow himself to be cut out with Lady Jessica. A cautious and thorough scheme would be needed. A half-truth, turgid and full-force enough to make Lady Jessica's anger take over long enough to oust the Latin from her dreams. No doubt she believed at present that her charms were enough to elicit a marriage proposal out of him.

Well, he would just have to show her how wrong she was, and that should be easy enough.

"Deep in thought, eh, scamp?" This from Lady Wilton, who had been watching him. She wasn't quite sure she wanted Sir Warren to have her sweet Jess, but she knew that Don Rodrigo would hurt the child if she did not do something soon. Sir Warren was the only answer she could come up with.

He smiled, pleased to have Lady Wilton on his side.

"Yes, and over that darling of yours." He shook his head. "I fear she has stars in her eyes."

"That's right. She does, and what we need to do is blast them out of the way so that she can see again."

"Precisely so, but one does not wish to break her spirit . . . bring her low. Besides, I don't think she would listen," he said on a frown.

"He is a devilishly handsome man, hot-blooded, and I was given to understand he satisfies that blood with a well-known actress," Lady Wilton returned softly. She was now looking away from the ginger-haired man at her side, smiling at a passing acquaintance.

He studied her for a long moment. "Indeed . . . but what is that to anything?"

"An acquaintance with my Jessica should answer you.

She will not share her heart with anyone who plays her false.''

"Yes, but she knows enough of the world to know that a man will—''

"Ha!'' laughed Lady Wilton. "What she knows in the abstract is quite different with what she will allow in the man she means to have!'' Her chin pointed at Don Rodrigo derisively. "He woos her in such a fine form that she may think he cares for no other. Her jealousy might rule the moment if she were to discover otherwise. I am not saying it would do more than cause a rift, but a rift could be used as the first step in severing a relationship that I believe will only bring her heartache.''

Sir Warren looked at her long before a slow smile began spreading across his face. "Dearest heart,'' he said on a low whistle. "Allow me to tell you that you are brilliant.''

"And so must you be in this matter. . . .''

"Yes, yes, it will take some very cunning handling,'' he said thoughtfully.

"Then, indeed, I have no fear that it will be manipulated in prime form,'' she answered, and moved away.

Sir Warren's smile grew, and even the sight of Don Rodrigo leading Lady Jessica out of the ballroom did not dispel the curve to his lips. That's right, my devil Latin, he thought viciously. Enjoy yourself, for you'll not have her on your arm after this night.

With this, he turned abruptly and went in search of his hostess, for he meant to begin the wheels turning immediately and there was much to accomplish, and when he was done, he would make the little bitch pay for the trouble she had put him to!

Stars in her eyes? Indeed, there were stars in her eyes, rockets blasting in her head, bubbling blood in her veins, and overwhelming emotions as confusing as they were uncontrollable in her heart. He felt for her; she was sure of it. Now, if only she could channel his feelings, bring them to life, make him admit to them, and draw him out of himself and into her world!

Unfortunately it was Don Rodrigo's very resolve not to deflower Lady Jessica that was now bringing about her downfall. This because in spite of the fact that he was resolved to leave England without taking her to his bed, he was not ready to discontinue his friendship with her. Her company brought him too much laughter; it brought him a pleasure he found he did not wish to forgo. She was an amusing child full of lively spirits, pranks, and easy, open manners. He rather liked her, and saw no reason why he should not enjoy himself.

"I will beat you at your gull-catching, so don't try your games with me, brat!" he advised her as she pulled him along, for it was not he who was leading them away from the ballroom, but she.

"Now, how can you be so unkind?" she bantered, and then laughed adorably. "Anyway, I don't mean to play my prank on you, but on Pauly, who deserves much more for the awful trick he served me this afternoon!"

Don Rodrigo chuckled. "Now, what can that puppy have done?"

"Ah, and when I tell you, see if you don't think hanging enough for the villain. What must I find this morning but a note at my breakfast table written in hideous scrawl and signed by Pauly. 'Dearest friend,' quoth he, 'take my cousin off my hands today and forever will I be in your debt.' Right, what must I do, fool that I am, but agree with but one very small stipulation. Return by high tea and relieve the tedium of the day by escorting said cousin and myself to this coffee house in Covent Garden that I have been wanting so badly to see. Never mind. 'Yes, dearest friend,' promised he, by four o'clock, promised he!

"Did he return to do this little thing? No, he did not . . . and this cousin of his, who must she turn out to be but Gertrude!"

"Dare I ask who this Gertrude might be?" He was grinning wide.

"Well you might ask, for she is that little pot of giggles and stupidity that was hovering around us all evening!"

"Ah, Miss Bigfoot, for never have I had my toes trod upon more in one cotillion and by such a small creature," he said, his brow going up. "But as I recall, *you* used your wiles to encourage me to take her on the dance floor."

"Yes, well . . ." started Jess, relenting with a sigh. "Poor little thing, she was just standing about, you know." Then she discovered the viscount to be exactly where she had believed he would be, at a card table in a pleasurable game of whist. "Ah! There he is."

Don Rodrigo laughed out loud and took her by the shoulders in his attempt to put a halt to her attack. "No, my pet, you cannot, in all good sense, charge down upon the lad in front of all his friends."

She stopped and considered this. "Hmmm" was her response, for she was wise enough to check her temper. Then she glanced toward Pauly's card table and remembered instead the boredom of the afternoon and his broken promise. "Oh, but don't you think I can put better use than he to that glass of champagne at his elbow, Rodrigo?" Although it was sweetly said, there could be no mistaking her meaning.

He chuckled, and his ungloved hand went to her chin as he felt an overwhelming desire to hug her to him, to brush her lips with his, to kiss her nose, her hands, the lovely swell of her breasts above the low cut of her blue silk bodice. "I am certain that you can, but, again, would that prove anything but that you are a temperamental female?"

She stiffened. "Is that what you think?" He was leading her out of the card room, crossing the marbeled hall to a pair of heavily molded oak doors. These he opened, ushered her through, and then closed the door at his back. She turned around, to find him staring oddly at her. They were in a book room whose garden doors had been opened to allow the circulation of fresh air, and they were alone. She did not heed it, but persisted. "Well, you haven't answered me. Am I like all my kind? A temperamental female?"

He found his eyes taking in every detail of her appearance, from the top of her flaxen curls to the tip of her blue silk slippers. She was incredibly alluring in the clinging gown, and he found his pulse racing, his body aching, as he discovered a sudden hungry need to touch her. His voice, when it came, was low and fringed with huskiness. "You are certainly temperamental, sweetheart, but not at all like most of your kind." He flicked the tip of her nose in an attempt to remind himself that she was young and a virgin.

"I—I don't know whether you are flattering me or insulting me," she returned on a short, nervous laugh. She was all too aware of his nearness and the glint of his black eyes, so full with their desire, and it made her knees weak.

"I am doing neither, pet, for I am only stating a fact." There, he couldn't bear it any longer. Her violet eyes taunted him to take, as did her full, youthful breasts heaving with her breath. Damn, but her cherry lips, full and inviting, were made for a man to kiss, and he couldn't, just couldn't, think logically anymore. All he knew was that he had to kiss her! Before either one realized what he was doing, before either one could summon the will-power to stop it from happening, he had her in his arms and his sensuous mouth was taking hers in passion. His kiss plunged them into sensation as his hand found her breast and released it from the confines of her gown. Her body was soft, pliable, and oh, so good to touch. A sweet fragrance enveloped and tantalized him as he bent his head to suckle at her rosy nipple and he teased it into pertness.

She couldn't believe this was happening. She was on

fire. Her body moved to his touch, her will was no longer her own, and as her legs buckled beneath her, she clung to him for support. Oh, faith! She loved the aroma of his nearness, reveled in the caress of his hands, and closed her eyes against the blast of rockets that dispelled all thought. She was in heat, and her heart pounded out only one name—*Rodrigo, Rodrigo, Rodrigo!*

She felt him lowering her to the sofa. Yes, yes, she wanted him to, but no, she couldn't, mustn't. She had to stop herself from allowing this. "Rod—no . . ." she heard herself whisper and was sure she only half meant it.

He couldn't think. He burned for her, needed her now in his arms, responding as she was to his ardor, but he heard her soft objection. He kissed her still, but as he did he schooled himself into control. He hugged her to him in his effort to put an end to his lovemaking and take it no further. His sigh was long and nearly violent. "Run from me, my lady Jessica. Run from me and don't look back, for I will end in destroying you if you allow it."

The words stung, for they told her openly his affection was purely physical, that he was not in love with her. She managed to pull out of his arms, and though she was stunned by the hardness behind the words, she managed to pull on her pride. "Oh, you could not do that, sir. I, too, do only what I wish to do, and a moment before it was my object to be—amused."

She was pulling up her gown, attempting to hide her burning cheek with a show of sangfroid. Her words played with his temper, bristled him into stiffness, and he inclined his head. "Very good, my lady. It seems I was incorrect in assuming that you are not like all your kind."

This, too, stabbed to the heart in a quick, very nearly blinding blow. She gathered her courage to smile at him and get to her feet. "It is fitting, I think, for we are, then, well met!"

He laughed and it was a harsh, clipped sound. "Touché! Your tongue neatly puts me in the place I deserve, for I am the cad, am I not?" He was rising to his feet, wondering how much of what she was saying was truth, for indeed, did he see hurt in those violet eyes? Was she a wounded child striking a pose for the sake of pride, or was she in truth like all her kind?

"Again, we find ourselves in accord," she said as she took his bent arm and allowed him to lead her out of the room. She was at her best, for she couldn't let him see, couldn't let him know, what she now knew beyond all hope—that she loved him totally, fully, and with every fiber of her soul!

He was irritated with himself for having allowed his attraction for her to override his principles. What was this? He did not tamper with marriageable maids! "Ah, here is your aunt and Sir Warren, both looking for you," he whispered. "I bid you good night, sweetheart, but you may be certain I will make myself present for further lashings tomorrow." So saying, he kissed her hand and backed off. She turned and found herself flanked by her aunt and Sir Warren, and there was no time to think, for both needed her attention, which she was happy to give. Indeed, she had no wish to think or to remember. All she knew was that she loved him, and he . . . he did not love her.

Later that night as she lay in her bed, she remembered all too well and all too vividly the touch of his hand, the feel of his hard, lean body, the look in his black eyes, and his kiss, his kiss . . . oh, God! How could she give him up? What choice did she have? He did not want her.

She said it out loud, just in case hearing it might trigger a thought to prove this wrong. "He does not love me. He would rather forgo his passion than take me as his wife." There, it was reverberated through the air, and still she could not find the lie in the words. It was true. He was attracted to her . . . *only that*!

And she? She loved him with every measure of her young, lively body! There was something in his eyes. If she did not avoid looking into his eyes, she would be fairly caught by him always and unable to control the emotions he raised within her breast. She loved him. How had she let it go that far?

Love? It was a hurting thing. Devil take her for a fool. Fools always ended in hell, and that was where she was. Why? How did it happen? He had aroused her in a way that had brought her entire being to life and then—oh, praise be . . . there was no "and then." How had she allowed it to happen?

It was him! All week Don Rodrigo had played the gallant. He had charmed her; he had flirted with her audaciously, sweetly, boyishly. He had teased her with those black eyes of his, and he had never overstepped, never attempted even to hold her hand. He had delighted her spirit, awakened her imagination, and turned her heart over with his deft handling. So she had forgotten that he was Don Rodrigo, the devil rake! She had forgotten that he was Don Rodrigo, the libertine, the womanizer, the heartless rogue, the—the beast!

Ah, Jess, you've done your poor heart in, you have, and for what? For a man who will leave England and never even remember your name! But there was a heart there; she had sensed it, felt it, knew it was there. Why, why would he have played this game with her if he didn't care?

Because he *is* the devil rake and can't help himself. 'Tis his ego, you know. It must be fed and you are a fine morsel. Better turn to Sir Warren, who will make you a good husband and love you well.

"I don't love Sir Warren," she told her dark room. There was no answer, but the sound of her heart and its beat was simple and repetitive. "And Rodrigo doesn't love you . . . doesn't love you. . . ."

She was a fighter by nature, and she didn't buckle beneath the blow. Instead, she drew strength and answered the challenge. "Not yet, he doesn't, but he could. I could make him; after all, he does want me . . . and . . . oh, God, with just a little bit of good sense, perhaps I can win that hard heart of his yet!"

And it was with this resolution that Lady Jess finally fell asleep, not that it was a peaceful sleep, but sleep it was. Don Rodrigo was not so lucky. He found himself tossing and turning fitfully. He had left Lady Jersey's with every intention of going into White's and passing an hour or two at the gaming table, but no sooner had he stepped out onto the street than he felt suddenly blue-deviled. He walked, discovered himself in front of his lodgings, and in a convulsion of irritation damned all women and stomped up the slated stairs to his front doors to let himself in. A session with a very good bottle of brandy lulled him into thought that served only to bring Jessica very clearly to mind. Odd, that; considering the quantity of brandy he had imbibed, one might have thought her image would be a hazy one. Not so. Too forcefully he could see her violet eyes, feel her soft skin, the swell of her high, firm breasts. He cursed and began pacing the Oriental carpet beneath his feet. There was only one thing to do under such circumstances. He should pay a visit to June.

Why not? Damn, but it had been nearly two weeks since he had bedded June. Hell and fire, what did she look like? June, lovely, professional, more than adequate. What color eyes did she have? Hair? Yellow. Yes, amber lit, that was it, with eyes of blue. Tall and graceful. He would visit with June and let her satisfy his needs. That was the ticket!

Chapter 11

June Keenen stood at her bedroom window and gazed out at the dimly lit street. Her curved amber brows were drawn over her small, thin nose. Her lips were pursed in a pout, her hand was on her slender hip, and one long white leg was on display as she turned to pace the floor of her bedroom.

Her black lace negligee trailed in a long line from her neat waist and did little to hide her curvaceous and womanly charms. She surveyed her room with dissatisfaction, but it was not the blue and gold decor that displeased. It was the fact that she was alone.

Where was he? Why hadn't Don Rodrigo come by to visit her? Ten days had passed and she had not even received a note from him. Why? He still continued to pay her bills, and in the last two days she had done her utmost to run these up if only that he should raise a brow and come by to see her about them. It was beneath her to send him an epistle requesting his company. After all, she had her pride.

Plague take the man! How dare he treat her in this fashion? There were others very willing to see to her comforts *and* her pleasures! Why hadn't he been by? Another woman? Her pale blue eyes darkened over this possibility. She was a possessive woman and wanted the men she had in her life to display an aura of adoration for her. It was true that she had never been able to get Don Rodrigo to behave thus, and it was also true that she had never before wanted a man the way she wanted Rodrigo.

She drew on a long breath of air, closed her eyes, and gently swung her head of waved amber hair from side to side to undo the kinks in her neck. It had been a grueling night at the theater, and her performance had taken its toll on her nerves. The audience had been coarse and vulgar. Afterward she had been besieged by men, all wanting one thing of her and some, yes, some, she might have been interested in seeing.

But no, in the back of her mind she had hoped Don Rodrigo would be coming to the lodgings he had established for her. She had returned here to wait for him. Plague take his soul! She needed someone; she needed the attention of a man. . . .

A knock sounded at her door and a small young maid in a dark frock, white apron, and white mobcap bobbed an inexperienced curtsy.

"There be a gentleman downstairs wishful of seeing ye, ma'am. Oi told 'im ye wouldn't want to be disturbed 'n' all, but 'e be ever so bold."

June Keenen's blue eyes narrowed; one arched brow rose. "What is this gentleman's name?"

The little maid went forward and stuck out her hand, in it she held a calling card which she offered to her mistress. June Keenen took it and studied the name. Sir Warren? Well, well. How very interesting, to be sure. Everyone knew that Sir Warren was hanging out after the Stafford wench. He no longer kept a mistress, it was said, and he meant to move ahead in Parliament. What was he doing here at this hour? She knew him only by a flirtatious remark passed here and there, though it had crossed her mind that it might prove enjoyable to get to know him better.

"You may send Sir Warren up," June Keenen said at

last, and as she watched the young maid leave, she tapped her hand with Sir Warren's card before dropping it on a nearby table. Don Rodrigo would not be pleased to find out she had entertained another man in her bedroom. Yes, but she could handle Don Rodrigo, and this encounter might prove amusing.

Her chamber door opened and Sir Warren came through, the door lightly held in his ungloved hand. Each appraised the other for a moment. June's blue eyes discovered a tall, well-built, and desirable male. Warren's hazel orbs found a match, and both smiled as he came forward to bow over her white hand. Slowly he came up from that bow to discover along the way that her breasts, though small, were high, firm, and nicely adorned with pert rosy nipples. He made no secret that this was discernible through her black lace and he openly lingered before he brought himself up. She was a tall woman whose inches brought her very nearly to his aquiline nose, yet there was a femininity about her that was most alluring.

With timely grace she moved only a stride away, giving him her back for a moment, but allowing her large gold and blue covered bed to serve as a backdrop as she turned to face him. "Now what, sir"—there was a hint of an invitation—"can I do for you?"

He laughed and wagged his finger as he went forward to take up hers and put it to his lips. "Now that, my beauty, is a dangerous question."

"Is it?" She was smiling coyly. "But then, I do so like to live dangerously."

He smiled appreciatively. "Now that, my dear, is a statement that could send most men reeling into fantasy!" He was here to discuss business. He had to remember that and put aside all other considerations—for the moment. But here was Rodrigo's mistress openly enticing him. Interesting. An ego builder at the very least.

"Most men, eh, but not *you*?" she answered, piqued.

He first answered silently by allowing his hazel eyes

to slowly scan her lips, travel the length of her throat to the wide scoop of her open neckline. His tone was tantalizing when he answered, "I have always dealt in reality. . . ."

He managed to arouse her, and her laugh was quick, husky. "And I, because I am an actress, deal in fantasy, but have it your way, Sir Warren. What reality are you here to, er, play with?"

"One that might benefit us both," he answered, taking her chin and lifting it ever so slightly as he bent his head to drop a kiss upon her lips.

She pressed herself against him, hoping to fever him, for she was now feeling the heat of desire and wanted him in the same state. Her hand undid the ribbon at the bodice of her negligee and allowed the flimsy thing to drop around her ankles. She returned his kiss, teasing him with her body, rotating her hips against him until she felt he was ready for more. He didn't seem easy. He was attempting to control himself, and it irritated her that he was still attempting to resist her charms. It furthered her determination to seduce him, and she found herself taking his hand, putting it over her small breast as her tongue moved to his ear.

Damn, but she was all woman! He wasn't here for this, but this quick, heady encounter was scintillating. Throwing all else to the winds, he gave himself over to the thrill of holding, touching, her soft body.

Don Rodrigo had his own key to June Keenen's lodgings, and he chose now to let himself in. However, the young maid had heard him and stuck her head into the hall. She very nearly gasped audibly when she saw it was Don Rodrigo with his foot upon the first step. She rushed out.

"Sir, how nice it is to see ye, sir." She had to stall him. Perhaps her mistress could be sent a message if she were first able to detain him downstairs.

He smiled and gave her cheek a tweak. "Thank you."

He started for the stairs once more and found his arm clutched. With his brow up he turned and looked with some surprise at the child. She blushed furiously. Here was the man who was responsible for her wages, but more than that motivated her, for she had a girl's infatuation for him. In her innocence she imagined him in love with the woman abovestairs and wished to spare him the sight of that woman's betrayal.

She dropped her hold on his arm and lowered her eyes. What could she do? "Would ye be wanting some refreshment, sir?" she asked softly, searching her mind for a way out of this dilemma.

He had no idea what was wrong with the girl but that she was taken with him, he very naturally assumed. He grinned and said lightly, "Indeed, why don't you bring us up a bottle of that very fine cognac I had sent over some weeks ago?"

This was no good! That was not what she wanted to do. How could she keep him here? On a heavy sigh she stalled for time. "Ay, then you wouldn't be wanting a bite to eat. There is some very lovely game pie cook set aside. Oi would be that pleased to set you a plate in the dining room, sir."

This was very odd. He frowned and considered her for a long moment before dawning lit in his dark eyes. So, his pretty mistress was not alone upstairs? Why hadn't he realized sooner? He was touched by a wave of irritation more than anger and very little disappointment. It was, after all, what he expected of all women—treachery!

"Do you know, little girl, it has suddenly occurred to me that your mistress might be . . . tired after her long night on stage. Why don't I give you a moment or two to rouse her, for as it happens, I must speak with her." It was quietly said, leaving no doubt that he knew what was afoot.

She blushed hot pink, dropped a curtsy, mumbled something incoherent, and rushed up the stairs. He was left to turn on his heel and make his way to the front parlor. He stood there for a long time while his fingers tapped at his sensuous lips and rubbed his square jaw. He was not in love with June Keenen, but his pride was piqued by her infidelity. They had enjoyed an erotic and adult relationship these last few months, and he could find no immediate reason why she should serve him such a trick. It had been part of their agreement, yes (he remembered how well he had drilled this point), that she would not share her favors while accepting his protection. Well, well, here was yet another female very much like all her kind!

June Keenen's maid rushed the bedroom like a wild girl. She didn't bother to knock, for she was flustered and anxious and so she found her mistress standing naked in Sir Warren's arms. Immediately she averted her eyes and lowered her head.

"Ma'am, oh, ma'am," she managed to breathe in spite of the fact that terror had played havoc with her vocal cords. "'E . . . Don Rodrigo . . . 'e is 'ere. Lord 'ave mercy on us, oi don't know 'ow oi kept 'im downstairs, but thot's where 'e is, though oi jest don't know 'ow long 'e'll stay there."

June Keenen froze. She was not ready to lose Rodrigo. Quickly she gathered her wits and her negligee around her. "Take Sir Warren out the back way. I trust you have his coat and hat near."

"Oi, that oi do. Oh, do 'urry, sir," she urged, looking to Sir Warren.

Sir Warren was amused. All this haste. He wasn't in the least concerned and rather enjoyed cutting Don Rodrigo out with Madame Keenen. However, nothing could be served by antagonizing June, who did seem put about by the news of Rodrigo's arrival. He dropped a kiss upon her lips. "We shall have to conclude our business—tomorrow." It was a statement made without any doubts.

"Yes, yes, of course, only do go quickly," she answered as she scanned the room, making certain there was no evidence of his visit.

"So I shall, but with your promise to meet me at the Bell Tavern in King Street tomorrow at noon." There was no question of her refusing.

She frowned, uncertain as to her plans for the following day.

"I shall try. . . ."

He turned on this, and his expression was arresting. "Don't try, my sweet; *be there*." It was very carefully said, and his tone indicated something near a threat.

She responded to it in the only way she knew how. "Yes, of course I will meet you." She had fought to get where she was. She had used her beauty and she had used men, but she had long ago learned to be chary of men such as Sir Warren. He had something on his mind, and it would not do to balk him!

Belowstairs in the front parlor, Don Rodrigo pulled away the rich dark brown damask drape and stood in the darkness of its protruding, squared lead-paned window. Here he had an excellent view of the small town house's front court and of the dimly lit street. He watched as Sir Warren came around the house and made for the curbing. As he realized who June's caller was, he was filled with surprise and supreme annoyance. He felt a sudden urge to pull the expensive hangings down and fling them to the flames. Sir Warren? Damnation, June, Sir Warren?

Madre de dios! Sir Warren, who wanted his Jess, was here with his mistress! May the devil take him! What was this? And then a question entered to stop all others. Why had he thought of Jess as his? She was not; she never would be.

He had come here to June to prove how little he needed Jessica. He had come to prove how well he could do with another's body in his arms, but what must he find, Sir Warren! Oddly enough, he was not outraged.

He told himself he should be, and certainly he was very irritated, but more than this he could not muster from his heart. His heart? He told himself it was dead to all feeling, which, he also told himself, was a very good thing, for otherwise he might now be hurting.

He sighed in the darkness. He would have to go up to June, demand an explanation and . . . and . . . damn if — he would! What he would do was a simple thing. He moved to the fireplace and took up a long candle, lit it, put it in its holder, and went to the desk. There he sat for a moment and hurriedly composed a note. The door of the parlor opened and June's maid came in. "Madame Keenen is awake, Don Rodrigo, and would be ever so pleased to 'ave ye visit wit 'er."

"I find that I haven't the time after all," he said, getting to his feet and reaching out to hand her the letter he had just folded in half. "Would you see that your mistress gets this?" So saying, he tweaked one stray curl peeping out from her cap and leisurely made his way to the hall and its front door.

Some moments later, June Keenen read, her blue eyes narrowing into slits of wrath:

Querida:

There is a saying you English are fond of. I find it most appropriate now. "That in your teeth, my lass."

All other words would be wasted. I have no quarrel with the decision you made tonight. It was time.

The house you may continue to enjoy for another three months, at which time its lease will terminate. All receipts accumulated to this date, I will be pleased to defray. However, all others after today's date you shall have to present elsewhere.

Vaya con dios, querida,
Rodrigo

June Keenen had never been a good loser. She was not one of those people who could chalk it up and move on. She did not see the other player's point of view. Her first reaction was to break everything in sight. Her second was to steady her temper. She took up the note and dropped it in the fire. There was still tomorrow. She would be sure to go to the dressmaker's and have at least five gowns ordered. Of course, she would have the receipts dated in her favor.

This decision enabled her to feel a bit better about the whole thing, and so it was she was finally able to lay her head down and get to sleep.

Chapter 12

Lady Jessica, a beauty in pale green silk, moved her hand expressively toward the window before she returned an outraged countenance to the young man standing some five feet from her.

"And now will you look, Pauly. It's raining!"

He pulled a face. "And what is a little rain to us, pray?" He shook his head. "I don't see what all the fuss is about, Jess. I have already said I will take you to that blasted inn today!" He was definitely on the defensive and just a little bit wary as he watched her pick up a Sevres vase full of hothouse flowers. He breathed easier when he watched her absently put it back down, and he watched her still as she walked restlessly about the room. Something was wrong with her, and he had a feeling there was more to it than she was saying. "Good God, girl, Gerty might be dull-witted, but you are the same age, and you must have found something to do together?"

She glared at him angrily and he had no doubt that he was still on her black list. "Scoundrel! Gerty is not only dull-witted, but she is a shrew who must have her own way, which is . . ." She searched her mind for an adjective to amply describe the tediousness of the girl's company. ". . . Well, suffice it to say that her notion of a lively time was to spend the hours at needlepoint! Pauly?'' She sought his sympathy and understanding. *''Needlepoint!''*

''Damn strange thing to do, but then, she *is* a girl, and that's what you're supposed to do.'' But before she could call down a heavy stream of curses upon his head, he quickly amended this very unwise statement. ''Though I ain't saying it's what *you* would like. Anyone who ain't addlebrained could see it's just the sort of thing to set up your bristles and having you clawing to go out.'' He considered the vision of Jess sitting demurely with his cousin and snapped, ''Good God! It's no wonder you want to pull my hair out.''

''Yes,'' she answered with a sniff, ''though I would have forgiven you, had you kept your promise.''

He went to her with a laugh and put a strong arm about her petite shoulders. ''That's a love, for you will forgive me now.''

Oddly enough, this and his easy manner totally undid Jessie, and she found herself bursting into uncontrollable tears. She dived into Pauly's chest to hide her face and made unintelligible sounds between the sobs.

The young viscount was horrified. He had not seen Jessie cry like this since they had been children and she had been unable to get her pony over a fence. ''Jess?'' he called, wide-eyed. ''Jess, what is it? What did I say?''

''Not . . . not . . . you . . .'' she sobbed. ''Me. Must be . . . me . . .'' How could she explain what she did not understand herself? She pulled his linen handkerchief out of his pocket and made nice work of it. ''Don't . . . pay . . . any attention. . . .'' She offered his handkerchief back to him.

He grimaced at the thing and told her to keep it. ''I tell you what,'' he said, recovering. ''You are bluedeviled. That's all. Been gadding about London Town, spent a tedious afternoon yesterday, you miss some of your old friends''—he nodded knowingly—''that's it.

way, Lady Jess." he returned severely, watching to see if he had depressed her levity, which he thought had taken a dangerous turn. Females could, after all, take on the strangest notions and then be forever plaguing one. While Jess had never before displayed any romantic interest in him, he had enough of an opinion of himself to think that there was no saying that she might do so now. This was not something he wanted to happen . . . at least, he didn't think it was.

June Keenen sat in the bright coffee house and sipped her brew in leisurely fashion. Her blue eyes scanned Sir Warren's set features. He was displeased. Well, she wasn't exactly thrilled about what had happened last night either, so he needn't make it any worse by pulling such a face! She patted her amber hair in place beneath her chip bonnet of yellow silk and smoothed her matching spencer as she attempted to penetrate Sir Warren's thoughts.

"Perhaps, Sir Warren, this meeting between us is no longer necessary, as I now have little, if any, influence with Don Rodrigo."

His eyes flew to her face and he released a short, derisive laugh. "My interests in your regard"—his eyes now traveled the length of her neck to the low plunge of her V neckline—"have little to do with your influence with Don Rodrigo," he answered, and then, before she could further question him, he put up his hand.

"However, your disassociation with him might be a problem."

"Why?" She was curious now.

"Never mind that. I must think."

"Would you perhaps tell me what all this is about?"

"There is a young noblewoman whom I intend to wed," he answered simply. "She has everything I need. Position, wealth, beauty—even spirit. All the ingredients necessary to wean me from my happy state of bachelorhood."

"What has this to do with me?" June Keenen did not feel pleased sitting with this handsome man and listening to him expound the virtues of another woman.

"The lady of whom I speak seems momentarily diverted by a Latin light," he returned on a dry note, though he watched her face for a reaction. He saw that she understood at once.

"Don Rodrigo?" came June Keenen's surprised reply. "Are you telling me that Don Rodrigo is courting some English noblewoman?"

He inclined his head. "In a manner of speaking. He certainly has intruded himself upon her notice, though in truth I don't believe his intentions are serious. He merely amuses himself."

She shrugged. "He will tire of her . . . or he will soon leave for his own country and your path will be cleared."

"I am"— Sir Warren hesitated—"a proud man." His tone was grave. "I don't want it said that she took me only because she was spurned by this Latin." He considered June Keenen warily. "Nor do I enjoy the notion of this Latin hellrake toying with the woman I mean to wed."

"I still don't see how I can help in this matter."

"Nor did I when you first informed me of your new situation with Don Rodrigo."

"Well, then, we have nothing more to discuss in that regard." Again the invitation was in her eyes. She would need a new man in her life to pay the bills and keep her in style. Sir Warren, she found attractive enough to fill this post.

"On the contrary, my dear. I said when you first advised me of your break with Don Rodrigo, I found myself at a temporary impasse. However, I believe we may yet salvage my plan."

"We?" Her ginger brow was up; her hand went to cup her chin. He took her hand away from her face and brought it to his lips. His voice when it came was low and charged.

"Do what I ask of you, June, and I will reward you . . . satisfactorily."

"Hmmm, but what will I have to do?"

"What you do so well. Act, my dear, simply put on an act."

Lady Jessica found the inn in Covent Garden to be all that she had hoped it would be. There were notable poets present, and when her eyes rested on Sir Walter Scott, she felt her day had been made complete. While she oohed and aahed, Pauly pulled a long face and interjected, "I don't see what should have you all agawk, but there you are; there is no saying what a female will take into her head to fetch and goggle over!"

"Pauly, do but look. That is Sir Walter Scott. You must admire *him* at least."

This he reluctantly conceded, for Scott's scribblings, he admitted, were at least written with a man in mind. The others he scoffed were naught but dandies and tulips putting on airs. "For my part, 'tis those two barmaids that have m' interest!"

She laughed. "And you not even in the petticoat line!"

"Yes, but Jess, I'm told they are American Indians— and look at that one's braid. Why, it's dragging and dusting the floor, and deuce take it if that isn't some kind of skin she is wearing."

Lady Jessica considered the dark lean girl in the unusual costume. "Yes, and no doubt some poor man's scalp is dangling from her waistband."

He considered this suggestion as he surveyed the length of light brown hair she paraded at her waist. "You might be right there, though I think it's done for effect."

"Well, it certainly has created one." She looked around at the bustling crew of rowdy gentlemen. "Everyone seems very much in spirits for early afternoon, don't you think, Pauly?"

It was this very fact that had dampened his own amusement some moments ago and made him think that he should remove his charge from this inn at once. As he watched one of the cits get overzealous with a passing wench he was sure Jess should not be brushing shoulders with, he quite made up his mind. "Well, girl, if you have had enough, I think we had better pike off, for it appears to be some chap's birthday and everyone in this hole seems determined to celebrate himself into unconsciousness." He stood up and took her arm.

Common sense told her he was very right and that her great-aunt Charlotte would have both their heads for even being seen near this particular inn, so she readily accepted his decree and got to her feet. As he led her outdoors, however, a prime individual with more height than breeding and a great deal more brawn than Pauly cited Lady Jessica as a prime looker and took it into his head to halt their progress.

" 'Ere now, flash, where would ye be going wit that prime mort?" asked the brawny giant.

Pauly's pale blue eyes traveled the distance from the tip of the man's head to his sharp-toed boot and resisted the impulse to gulp. With more forethought than care he shoved Jess out the door while he turned to block the path.

The giant took grisly exception to the meaning behind this act, for he was too drunk to think of the consequences of mistreating the quality. He was on his turf, with friends at his back. "Curse ye, lad, is it insult ye be offering me, then?"

Unfortunately the young viscount did not have the opportunity to use his diplomatic tongue and calm the brute down, for the door at his back was thrust open, sending him headlong into the stomach of his protagonist.

It was inevitable that the greatest part of the inn's celebrating and assembled company decided this was time for a great-go. There were some wiser few who took to corners, their fives up to protect themselves from attack, but for the most part, gentleman, bully, cit, and youth swung freely, merrily, and in great earnest as they attempted to bludgeon the fellow they had just shared a bumper of ale with.

Pauly spent most of this time dodging one blow after another from his giant. Luckily the man was not as agile as he was powerful. Pauly was trying all the while to make his way to and out the door, hoping that Jessie had been wise enough to call a hack and get herself away from such a scene.

Chapter 13

Don Rodrigo climbed into his stylish curricle and closed the door. He leaned out of his window and threw Simon Bolivar's wife a long kiss and laughed to his friend who clenched a fist at him. He motioned to his driver to move on and sat back against his leather squabs with a sigh. The meeting with the prime minister had gone nicely. Soon he would be able to return home.

This should have brought a sense of pleasure, but instead the thought produced a frown. Home, his rancho, San Jacinto, his gauchos and peons, his stout and garrulous Maria who ran things for him in his absence, and his father. Thoughts of home should have him smiling. His father, crippled from his last stroke, was content to sit back and let his managing cousin take over for him. Why not?

The youthful image of his father's English wife, Rodrigo's mother, deepened his darkling frown and drove him into the past. Maria had never approved of the soft and gentle creature his father had brought home from England, but he and his father had adored her. Her memory touched him now. She had never been happy. She was quiet but restless, and there had been a bitterness in her that Rodrigo had never understood and that Rodrigo's father had tried to drive away.

Then Facón came! A gaucho as wild and dangerous as the sound of his name. Indeed, he had been a knife and he had cut out his father's pure heart when he stole Rodrigo's mother. Without a backward glance she had gone with the copper-skinned hell-bent gaucho. He had been, like all his kind, half-Indian, half-Spanish, but she had left her husband and child to be with him.

A year after her flight she died in the mountains of a fever and Facón was killed by persons unknown shortly thereafter. A long time ago, all this, but Rodrigo remembered it too vividly. Why were his thoughts there now? Because of the lady Jessica. No! She was nothing like his mother. She was English; she was fair—but so vastly different, wasn't she? No, she was a woman and therefore much like all her kind.

And then, there she was, as though to refute this argument, standing by the curbing looking angry and just a bit confused, and it was no wonder, for through the door at her back came the young viscount. He came all right, but not upright. He was followed by something of a mountain who seemed intent on picking him up only to throw him down again. At their backs they were followed by several other men with much the same ideas for one another.

Don Rodrigo cursed beneath his breath and called his driver to a stop. In a flash he was outside his carriage, taking Jessica by the arm and pulling her in his wake.

"Stop it! What do you think you are doing? Pauly is in trouble!" she attempted to explain as she was unceremoniously dragged along.

"Your Pauly would be the first one to tell you that you must get away from here as soon as possible."

"But that dreadful man means to kill him!" she cried in real concern.

"Do you think you can stop him from doing so?" Don Rodrigo countered as he opened wide his carriage door and attempted to see her safely within.

"No, but you—"

"I think, my dear, that Pauly will see himself out of this squabble, and besides, it appears that the beadles mean to put a stop to all of it." His chin indicated a flash of uniforms coming their way, and without further ado he pushed her within the confines of his carriage and hastened to climb in after her, taking only a moment to tell his driver to get them away at once.

As he attempted to take up his seat and be comfortable, he could not help but notice that Lady Jessica was picking herself up from the carriage's narrow floor. This because he had been too quick to get her inside to bother being gentle. He chuckled and reached for her arm to help her settle in beside him. She plopped herself down, yanking her arm away from him as she glared, her violet eyes on fire. "How dare you!"

"Now, this is gratitude. Has it not occurred to you, Lady Jessica, that I have just rescued you from a scandalous affair?" Egad, but her eyes glowed wondrously when she was angry. Hell and fire, but her lips were made for kissing.

She bit her bottom lip, making him want to do the same. Indeed, she would have been in a great deal of trouble if she had been caught up in such a mess, but it seemed so cowardly to run off and leave Pauly to his fate. "It appears, sir," she said with her chin in the air, "that you are forever coming to my rescue whether I wish it or no!"

"True, which leaves me to wonder about the good sense you seem to think you possess."

"Oh! You are insufferable!" she returned, beside herself.

There, he could not control himself any longer. His dark eyes devoured her as his voice, low and husky, answered, "So I am." At which point he went about the business of proving it. His arms were around her waist, drawing her to him as his head bent to hers.

She made no attempt to fight him off. She discovered, much to her shame (for she could find no ready excuse for her behavior), that her hands went first to his hard, broad chest, then up to encircle his neck as he drew her closer.

He was elated by her response. He felt his body burn with fever as his eyes closed and he took her to him, reveling in her sweet fragrance. His mouth closed on hers, tender in its touch, burning to teach her more. His lips parted as his blood raced, and he had to school himself to be gentle as his tongue entered her mouth and deftly wielded her sensations.

"Sweet passion," he groaned against her ear before taking its lobe and nibbling, "There has never been one like to thee."

His words were magic, not quite understood, but there was enchantment in his tone. She hungered for more, hoping that his desire was driven by love of her. She sought to encourage him to this declaration by thrusting herself instinctively against his hard, lean body. She encouraged him very well.

"Ah, sweetings," he said as he found her full breast beneath the spencer of her gown. He was tempted to take her here and now and be done with it, but his better sense was still in control. "This is not the place."

Her momentary happiness was illogical, but as there was no time for anything but feeling, she was struck by an odd desire to giggle. In bantering style she riposted, her eyes alight with the tease. "Yet you manage . . . very well."

He threw back his head of glistening black hair and laughed outright; here was a strange child indeed. A virgin surely, yet a willing morsel well able to hold her own. "Even *I* might fumble the affair in these tight quarters."

She frowned. Now, whatever was he talking about? In her innocence she did not yet realize he was speaking about something altogether different from the foreplay she had allowed. However, there was no time to question him, for they had reached her uncle's town house.

The curricle came to an abrupt stop and already Don Rodrigo was adjusting his clothing as he hopped down from the carriage door and turned to reach out his hand for her. She gave it and felt a thrill of pure delight as he squeezed it reassuringly. She felt carefree, mindless, and happy at that moment and laughed out loud for no reason at all as he rushed her up the slated steps to her front door. It was opened by the admiral's formidably stiff valet, who immediately informed Miss that she was wanted in the parlor by her great-aunt. She ignored this and turned to Don Rodrigo. "Do you come in, sir?" Her smile was inviting, reckless.

He was tempted. He was loath to quit her company. He silently reprimanded himself. What would it accomplish? No doubt her great-aunt would not leave them alone, and even if she did, he could not very well seduce the girl in her own parlor. "No." He smiled apologetically. "I think I will return and see what has become of your young viscount."

"Oh, would you?" She beamed. He was doing this for her. Wasn't that proof of how he felt? "And you will send me word as soon as he is safely out of it?"

"You have my promise," he answered sincerely. He looked around at his waiting coach and then quickly dropped a kiss upon her wrist. "Until later, sweet passion."

A moment passed and he was gone. Did she float into the house? Was that her aunt calling her? She couldn't tell, didn't want to listen. All she wanted was the seclusion of her room so that she might relive every moment she had just spent with Don Rodrigo, hear every word he had said to her. She loved him. There was no denying it to herself now. She loved him hopelessly and completely. And he? He would soon love her. She would make him love her, for he was certainly worth the effort!

Sir Warren watched Don Rodrigo lead Lady Jessica into a country dance. She was looking exquisite in her gown of red silk. Her flaxen waves had been piled high with a tress here and there allowed to escape and tickle at her bare shoulder. Short thick wisps of gold curls framed her forehead and teased her dainty ears. Her breasts were full and provocatively alluring above the heart-shaped neckline of her gown, and her trim waist taunted a man to touch.

Sir Warren was frowning darkly, for it was apparent she had eyes for no one save this Latin! And the Latin? This, too, seemed more than odd, for the man had an air of seriousness in his address. Could it be that Don Rodrigo's intentions were honest in her regard? Then there was that puppy, the young viscount! When she wasn't casting the Latin meaningful glances, she was petting the puppy! Why the lad's eye was blackened, he could not guess, but no doubt he had won the injury protecting Lady Jess. Why else would she accord him so much loving concern?

Well, it would appear it was time for June Keenen to enact the game they had set upon. In the meantime he would see what he could do to win a smile or two from the lady Jessica. He walked in her direction, waiting patiently for the dance to end. It did and he bowed over her hand as Don Rodrigo looked on.

"Can it be that the lady Jessica has no time for an old friend?"

She smiled warmly, for she liked Sir Warren and felt a wave of guilt. Had she been ignoring him? Indeed, she was vaguely aware that she had paid little heed to anyone other than Don Rodrigo.

"Sir Warren, it is I who should be complaining, for I'd swear this is the first time this evening you have sought my company."

"Not true, my love, but I found it difficult getting past your press of suitors. They grow in number each moment you are out in society." He was taking her hand, linking it through his arm, leading her onto the floor for the cotillion, then being struck up.

She felt the velvet of his black cutaway, felt the tenseness of his muscle beneath, looked up to discover his profile, lean and quite attractive, and even then she turned for yet another look at Rodrigo. She was gratified to find Rodrigo watching her every move.

As Don Rodrigo watched Sir Warren take hold of Lady Jess's gloved hand and lead her off, he was consumed with a jealousy that threatened to overtake his temper. Damn the man! He wasn't fit to look at Lady Jess, let alone lead her out. Ah, nor are you, another voice answered. You would have seduced her this afternoon had you the chance. Yes, but she was so willing, yet a third voice returned defensively. Logic intruded with its answer. She is an innocent, fancies herself in love. Look there, even as Sir Warren leads her out she turns to find your eyes.

He inclined his head to her and threw her a kiss. He had the satisfaction of seeing her blush in response, and there was such a look of longing there that he nearly moved across the floor to take her away from his rival. This was absurd! He was going to have to put the child aside, forget her, and refrain from hurting her any further. Hurting her? Had he done so? Well, she will have learned a valuable lesson by the time he had set his sails for home.

"Rodrigo," called the young viscount coming up to slap the man's shoulder, "come on. They are getting up a game of cards in the next room. Have done with all this dancing about and join me."

"Cards, eh? Right. I find that an excellent notion!" Better to leave her be. Even so, he found it difficult to do so, and every nerve strained to find a way to keep him in the ballroom. No, his mind was made up. Leave her to Sir Warren, whose intentions at least were to make her a bride, not a mistress.

So it was that during the machinations of the cotillion Lady Jess looked for Don Rodrigo and, with a wild sensation of loss, watched his broad shoulders leave the ballroom in Pauly's wake. "What?" she answered Sir Warren absently, for she had not really heard him. "What were you saying?"

He was irritated by her lack of interest. This was the first time he had ever encountered a woman who was not captivated by his charm, and charm was an effort he was exerting in great depth for Jessica's benefit. He could see her looking after Don Rodrigo, and it was difficult to suppress his temper, but he managed, for the stakes were high. "I was saying that I hear June Keenen's performance at the Drury Theatre is reputed to be superb. I have been wanting to get over there for a night's entertainment."

Now, here was something that Lady Jess heard very well. Sir Warrren was quick to note her violet eyes snap to attention at the mention of June Keenen's name. So then, the lady Jessica was aware of the connection between Rodrigo and the actress.

"I have never had the privilege of witnessing one of her famous performances." She hesitated. "I hear that she is very . . . beautiful."

"Indeed, she is a diamond," he answered simply, and then in a low, meaningful voice, "Though for me, my lady Jess, there are no eyes that draw me but yours."

She smiled. "You are as always very gallant, Sir Warren. I thank you but in truth know better than to believe you." She meant to lighten the moment.

"What is this? How can you doubt me? Jess, my dear sweet child, don't you know you are being hailed in the clubs as the 'incomparable'?

"No, I know nothing of the sort." She very nearly snorted.

"Well, you are, but that is another matter altogether, for even if other men could be blind to your beauty, I could not, Jess. Haven't I made it clear to you how I feel?"

She blushed and was all too grateful that the music had stopped, for she could see her great-aunt Charlotte making her way toward them and hailed her relative. "Aunt Charlie," she called, avoiding Sir Warren's intense glance.

Lady Wilton was pleased enough to find her great-niece away from Don Rodrigo's influence. That was a man she wanted well away from Jessica. She would further the match with Sir Warren if only Jess would listen, but Jess simply was not reasonable these days. She was patting the mauve silk turban she wore on her short gray curls and mumbling about the manners of sporting gentlemen, all of whom she held to be no better than idiots, when Sir Warren bent over her gloved hand in greeting.

"Ah, Lady Wilton, enchanting as ever," he said smoothly.

"You do that so well, Warren lad, that an old woman might even believe you." She was smiling benignly at him.

This now was the moment, he decided, and smiled at Lady Jessica as he directed his conversation with her great-aunt. "I was just mentioning to Jess that I intend to get up a party to take in June Keenen's play over at the Drury and it occurred to me that while the admiral is out of town, you and your niece might like to join me. We could take dinner at Claridges afterward."

Lady Wilton jumped at the chance. An evening away from that Latin rogue was just what Jessie needed. "Why, Sir Warren, that is a marvelous notion."

"Excellent. Friday night, shall we say?"

Jessie was frowning. She didn't want to commit any night to any affair that would not include Don Rodrigo. At these soirées, balls, and fêtes he could be found, but at a select party for the theater, she was quite certain she would not find him. Especially if that party was to be put together by Sir Warren. However, there was nothing she could do when her aunt was already accepting for both of them. And then she was startled to see Don Rodrigo taking leave of his hostess. He didn't even look in her direction. What was this? What was wrong? Had it been only that very afternoon when he held her in his arms?

How could mind and heart sustain the highs and lows she was experiencing? Why was he leaving? Hadn't he kissed her in passion? Hadn't it meant anything to him? Wasn't he jealous that she was now being attended to by Sir Warren? Was Don Rodrigo going to June Keenen? Was that it? Oh, God, she suddenly felt miserable and sick. Was this love?

Chapter 14

Henry Holland did justice to his reputation when he built the Theatre Royal in Drury Lane. It proved to be one of London's two great theaters. In its boxes the fashionable *haute ton* were able to recline in sparkling elegance. In its corridors they were able to mingle discreetly. In its green room they were able to take wine and negus. In the theater's pit the less fortunate were able to look up and around with their eyes and mouths wide open.

One city merchant nudged his companion and indicated a box just to their left. In it sat a young beauty whose smile had totally captivated the man. His crony groaned in broad cockney, "Ay, now, mate, she be beautiful . . . so beautiful. . . ."

Indeed, the maid's buttercup curls styled à la grecque and ornamented with a black and silvery twirling feather were thick, long, and bouncy. Her eyes were of deep violet hue, her gown was off the shoulder, heart-shaped at the bodice, and its silvery shades of silk were adorned with embroidered black velvet fern leaves. Her smile was sweet, her face enchanting, and, as though she were aware of the two lads below, she looked their way.

The first chap who had sighted her nearly fainted. The other was quick-witted, took off his top hat, and made her a sweeping bow. She laughed but stilled any further pretensions by then looking away. At any rate, Sir Warren was then calling her attention to Lady Jersey's quip. Lady Jessica listened as attentively as she was able, for she found her attention span these days not what it should have been, certainly not what it had always been. Three days. Three days had passed without a word from Don Rodrigo!

What was wrong? She had not seen him at Almacks. She had not seen him at the Venetian breakfast Lord Amherst had held yesterday, and now at the theater he was nowhere to be found. It was Friday, and, true to Aunt Charlotte's word, they had allowed Sir Warren to escort them to Drury Lane. He had selected Lady Jersey to be one of their party, as well as both Lord Amherst (an elderly gentleman, and one of Aunt Charlie's favorites) and the viscount Paul Bellamy. However, Pauly was off somewhere in the pit, which he declared suited him just fine but was no place for Jess, so here she was, listening to fashionable gossip, and something inside of her wanted to explode!

"Ah, the orchestra is telling us that the screen is about to go up," said Sir Warren. There was a strange quality in his voice that caught Jessie's interest, and she glanced his way. He looked unusually animated, as though in anticipation of something more than the play that was about to be enacted on stage.

An arm slid around her back and pulled one of the long, twirling buttercup curls that hung there. She looked around and found Pauly taking his seat behind her and she smiled. On her left Sir Warren watched out of the corner of his eye. On her right her great-aunt Charlotte conversed amicably with Lord Amherst and the Jersey.

"Where were you, beast?" She smiled at him.

"Having a jolly good time of it below, that's where. Bored, are you? Well, never mind, look, they are snuffing the candles. They mean for us to have an eyeful of the Keenen when she enters. She likes to make a show of it.''

''Does she?'' Jessie attempted to shade her interest.

The orchestra lifted to a crescendo, the curtain began to rise, and a hush fell over the audience.

Jessie's violet eyes rounded and her heart took on an extra beat before it sank as she took in the full measure and scope of June Keenen. Her mind presented facts she did not want to hear. Look there on stage, it said; there is a woman! Indeed, June Keenen in her full costume stood a tall, graceful, and bewitching creature. She had a certain aura, a charisma that immediately captivated her audience. Jessie studied Don Rodrigo's mistress and felt she could never compare with such as that.

As the scenes of the innocuous but thoroughly entertaining musical comedy progressed, Jessie found herself captivated by the actress's finesse. Over and over again one thought kept repeating itself: *Here was Don Rodrigo's mistress!* This very naturally suggested a series of questions. Why had he bothered to flirt with her, why? Here was a woman he surely loved. She saw herself by comparison no more than a green girl, a silly, inexperienced child. What could Rodrigo see in her when he had June Keenen to satisfy his needs?

Well, here was an answer to the question of where he had been the last three nights. Waiting attendance on Miss Keenen, no doubt. Jessie's poor heart, young and unable in its present state of confusion to cope with such competition, attempted to shield itself. After all, Don Rodrigo *had* kissed her. That must have meant something to him!

During intermission Pauly remarked that he had never before had the pleasure of watching Miss Keenen perform.

''First-rate, you know,'' he told Lady Jessica, ''and the play ain't half bad either,'' he added generously.

Sir Warren, hearing this, suggested idly, ''I know what you might like, my lord.''

''Eh? What's that?'' returned Pauly, who was not

overly fond of Sir Warren and found himself even less so this evening. There was something about the man, something he could not name, that made his bristles stand on end.

"I have the pleasure of Miss Keenen's acquaintance and should be pleased to convey Lady Jess and you to her dressing room after her performance tonight." He turned to Ladies Wilton and Jersey and Lord Amherst. "Perhaps we might all pay the actress our respects afterward?"

Now Lord Amherst's bent head of white came up with interest, but his gloved knuckles were rapped soundly by Lady Wilton for his effort. "I think not," said Lady Jessie's aunt Charlotte knowingly. She was well aware that June Keenen was reputed to be Don Rodrigo's mistress. She was quite certain that Sir Warren had something up his sleeve, and silently she applauded his efforts. "You know very well, Amherst, that you have promised to see the Jersey and me to Claridges."

"She is right, you know." Amherst nodded sadly. "But won't you young'uns join us?"

Pauly pulled a face. "Sorry, promised to friends after the theater . . . but I tell you what, Sir Warren. If you and Jess mean to have a look in on the Keenen, I'll go with you."

"Good!" responded Sir Warren, clapping and then rubbing his gloved hands together jovially. "May I consider the matter settled, then, Lady Jess?"

Lady Jessica was silent. Her sound common sense advised her against such a meeting. Why subject herself to possible heartache? Her mind went to war with this timid suggestion. Heartache? Why should there be any discomfiture in meeting this famous actress? Why not see for herself the sort of woman Don Rodrigo admires? Common sense and logic did battle, and her poor heart simply went along with the outcome. Mind's curiosity won the moment and swept away all other considerations.

She inclined her lovely head, and so the matter was indeed settled.

White's buzzed that evening. Spirits were lively, gaming was entertaining, and the assembled company in the gold room were amusing one another with their silly antics. Don Rodrigo leaned back in his comfortable chair and watched with a tolerant eye. Why he should love these English was more than he could say, but he very often discovered that he did. His mother had given him every reason to mistrust them, but more often than not, he felt his English blood overpower his Latin.

His grin widened as he watched Lord Alvanley (a bit in his cups) rise unsteadily to his feet and announce that he would outlive his companion Copley, by damn, he would!

His voice carried in resonant tones, turned heads, and brought quizzing glasses up. Copley, a stout individual who had imbibed even more than his long-time friend, hiccuped and said they must call for the betting book.

Simon Bolivar eyed them with distaste and quietly advised his friend that he thought them, these English, a gathering of cold and silly men with nothing to do but concern themselves with trivia. "No, my friend," answered Rodrigo with a sad sigh, "they are much like us, tracking through life. . . ."

A lackey arrived on the scene, and within moments it was set down that Copley had wagered Alvanley that he would outlive him by five years. The bet was set at twenty guineas and was to be paid by a fund set aside in advance.

"Astounding," said Bolivar, "and mad. Yes, Rodrigo, they are all of them mad, and I grow impatient with the lot. I am grateful that Pitt has finally agreed to the promise of neutrality so that I am now free to take my Beatrice and return home."

"Yes, it is well that Pitt has agreed. I am only surprised that the promise came so easily," said Rodrigo thoughtfully.

Bolivar shrugged. "They will not throw in with Spain. It would do nothing for them against the Frenchman, Napoleon."

"Agreed. I don't think they will throw in with Spain, and still I know better than to trust them entirely."

"But why? What can they do? They must remain neutral. It is the sanest course."

"True, but then you have only just a moment ago said that you think them mad." chuckled Rodrigo, momentarily diverted.

"*Sí, amigo* . . . but not *that* mad!" laughed Bolivar, who immediately sobered. He and Rodrigo had achieved something of importance—perhaps not all that he had hoped for, but it was certainly better than nothing. Other matters now fretted him. His young bride was not herself these days, and the English doctors had not yet helped her. He wanted to get her home, where his family with their own physicians and their own ancient remedies would do her some good. "It is farewell, Rodrigo, and this I bid you with deep sadness." He was touching his friend's shoulder. "But always my home is yours, and I pray that both our homes will soon be free of Spanish rule."

"Must you go already, Simon?"

"*Sí*, my Beatrice languishes in this climate. I must see her home." He got to his feet. "*Adiós*, Rodrigo. Make it soon, your visit to Venezuela."

"*Vaya con dios*, Simon." Rodrigo was on his feet as well, clasping his friend's hand. "I don't know when that will be, but I, too, will be leaving England. My vessel awaits my word in Southampton. In fact, I don't know why I tarry."

Simon laughed. "I can't imagine. Perhaps it is the color of the English flower . . . the buttercup yellow?" he asked audaciously.

Don Rodrigo stiffened. He would not be questioned along this line. His private concerns were just that, and he rarely confided such things to anyone. "There are many English flowers that fascinate, but none to keep me from home'' was all he would answer.

Simon Bolivar shook his head and made his departure. Don Rodrigo watched him go with a sad sigh. He would miss him, and then for the hundredth time that day he thought of Jessie. Damn, but he had to get the chit out of his mind. It had been three days that he had kept himself away from any assembly that might include her. Odd, instead of getting her out of his head, he found his abstention only served to bring him into a constant state of restlessness.

He was an experienced man and knew that what was needed was time. Once he was away from England and in his own country, attending to his ranch, she would be put aside. This should have eased him, this sure knowledge, but strangely enough, it did nothing of the kind!

Chapter 15

June Keenen believed, like Shakespeare, that all the world was, indeed, a stage, and *she* meant to write the next scene. It would not win Don Rodrigo back, but it would certainly serve to satisfy her spite.

She heard the knock at her dressing room door and immediately dissolved into tears, putting her elegant head of curls upon her folded arms on the vanity table before her. An open letter written in what was a fair copy of Don Rodrigo's hand was spread out on that same table. Her stage was set.

Sir Warren opened the door a crack when she failed to answer (as was prearranged), "June?" he called merrily, and then, finding the actress in distress, he stepped boldly within. "My dear, whatever is wrong?"

Lady Jessica and the young viscount were left in dubious confusion within the framework of the open door, but Jess could see that the woman was crying, and she looked at Pauly. In a whisper she said, "Should we leave?"

"Od's life, there isn't anything I'd like to do more, but don't know if we can. . . . Might be in trouble, you know. Can't leave a lady in distress."

"To be sure, one must not lose to the dragon by default," said Lady Jessica, her sense of humor tickled by Pauly's sudden sense of honor.

"Oh, Warren, Warren, please forgive me," sobbed the woman, her attempt to hold back her tears quite neatly perfected.

He put a comforting arm about her. "Only tell me what is wrong, or I promise you, I shan't forgive you."

She patted his arms. "We are such old friends that I am very nearly tempted . . ." Apparently she was unaware of the two interested individuals standing in her doorway.

"Warren, I—I am so ashamed."

"Nonsense," he said, bolstering her. Apparently he had forgotten both Lady Jessica and the viscount's presence. He discovered the open notepaper and frowned as he looked its way in what was glorious subtlety, but not so inconspicuously that both Jess and Pauly did not notice the letter. "What is toward, June?" His voice was grave.

"I—I have made a fool of myself," she said, her eyes downcast.

"You mean that *he* has served you badly?" returned Warren angrily.

"He . . . he never loved me. He . . . he wants me to . . . lose . . . lose the child. He—See for yourself." She handed him the letter.

Sir Warren made a show of reading it. "The scoundrel!" He put a comforting arm about her shoulders.

The viscount felt this was the time to remind Sir Warren that not only was he present, but Lady Jessica as well, and that this was the sort of scene a young maid should not be exposed to. He cleared his throat. "Er . . . so sorry . . . Er . . . may we be of some service?"

Both Sir Warren and June Keenen looked around in utter surprise. Sir Warren stepped forward and blocked the entrance. "Jess, forgive me, but I am afraid this is not the time." He turned to Pauly. "My lord, would you mind seeing Lady Jessica home?" He eyed him meaningfully.

"Mind? Not at all . . . greatest pleasure in the world."

He could see that June Keenen had turned her face away and was attempting to shield herself from their curious eyes. The viscount immediately took Jessica's arm and directed her back into the corridor. Sir Warren smiled to himself and closed the dressing room door, but his next words were clearly audible all the same.

"Damn that devil, Don Rodrigo! Fiend seize him for a rakehell. Ah, June, how did you let yourself get captivated by such as he?"

In the hallway, the viscount felt Jess suddenly miss a step. She seemed to fold, and he held her up with a look of concern.

"Steady, ol' girl. Are you feeling quite the thing?" He knew that she was a sensitive soul, and he doubted that what had just taken place had gone over her head. She had understood all too well, and he could see now from her expression that she was deeply affected.

"Yes, yes, I . . . am only tired, a bit tired."

He patted her arm. "Of course you are. I'll hail a hack and get you home."

Once in the hackney coach, he settled down beside her and gave her face one quick survey. She wasn't talking, and that worried him. Usually Jess was wont to throw a hundred questions when something untoward took place, and here she was looking glum and blue-deviled. He decided to broach the subject and see what she had made of it all. "Sorry affair, that," he said in way of comment.

She looked at him, her emotions threatening to take over, but she managed a calm exterior. "Pauly, from what we heard . . . it would appear that June Keenen is with child, and that the father wishes her to . . . to . . ."

"Just so," he answered simply, and then took her hand and slid it through his arm before giving it a squeeze. "These things do happen, Jess, though *you* should not be hearing about them."

"But how can he? How can he wish to kill the child he fathered?" She was white with the shock. Don Rodrigo had turned out to be more than a rakehell. He was past redemption. He was the lowest form of life. He was without feelings, without honor.

"Well, he can't marry her, Jess. It wouldn't do. She *is* an actress . . . and, Jess, she ain't in her first blush."

"Meaning there have been other men in her life?" She considered this.

"Meaning just that."

"All the same. He should take the responsibility of his child."

The viscount gave this a moment's thought and nodded. "Ay, that he should. That's the way a gentleman usually handles it."

She closed her eyes. "Oh, Pauly, I had very nearly made such a dreadful mistake."

He frowned. Women were the strangest creatures. What was she talking about now? "Never say so!" he answered, hoping she would enlarge on this statement.

His hope was not realized. Instead, she dissolved into tears. He took her into his arms and stroked her head. "Jess? Jess, what is all this? Jess, she'll be all right. I'll see to it meself if you like."

"Would you, Pauly?" She gulped.

It was not something he wished to do, but he rather thought he might visit the Keenen in the morning and offer some financial help.

"Promise," he answered at once, and had the gratification of seeing his old Jess return. She took in a long gulp of air and bolstered herself. "I have been a fool, Pauly, but no more." She shook her head with determination, "Oh, no, my eyes have been opened."

"Good," he said with more conviction than he felt. He thought it prudent to refrain from questioning her when she was in such a disturbed state of mind. Instead, he took up her chin and lifted her face to his. She looked such a frightened child, such an innocent, and he was struck suddenly by the fact that she was quite, quite beautiful. Friendship between male and female has its bounds, but unless one is always very careful, in moments of crisis those lines might disintegrate. It was such a moment. His desire to assuage her, combined with his sudden awareness of her womanhood, bent his face over hers. His kiss was tender. It caressed, it spoke of a certain kind of devotion, and Jessie received it in this vein. When it was over she collapsed into his arms to quietly say his name.

Don Rodrigo had left White's and was taking a stroll. The fact that his steps took him unconsciously toward the admiral's town house was not something he had the time to analyze, for something else quite caught his attention. A hackney cab had entangled itself in a web of traffic, caused by several vehicles attempting to make a turn where there was not enough room. Idly his eyes discovered the occupants of the hackney coach and there became transfixed. He watched the handsome lad take a quite lovely maid into his arms and he watched as that familiar figure slid into the boy's arms.

Fire burned through his veins and drove him unthinkingly toward that carriage. Rage took each rational thought and tossed it to the gutter. His hard strides had him at the hack and flinging the door wide open before he knew what he was about, but breeding restrained his words as his voice came, steel-glinting and cold.

"You may not have noticed, as you were otherwise occupied, but there seems to be something of a mishap in the street. May I suggest, my lord, that you remove Lady Jessica from this scene, and as her house is not far off, we may yet escort her there more ably than this hack." His teeth, he noticed, were gritted, and he made the attempt to set his mouth at ease and give the couple a sweeping smile.

Don Rodrigo was the last man on earth she wished to see at that moment. Plague take his soul! After what she had just learned about him! She looked to Pauly, who was frowning. He, too, was quite displeased with Don

Rodrigo, but he was a male and thought perhaps there was more to this business than met the eye. After all, his emotions were not involved in the affair. He looked about, saw that Don Rodrigo was quite correct in his summation, and attempted to save them all from Jessie's temper, which he could feel rising out of control. "Right you are, sir," he answered lightly as he jumped out of the carriage and took out a coin from his inner waistcoat pocket. This he flipped up to the driver with his thanks before reaching his hand for Jess. "Come on, then, girl."

"Thank you, no. I prefer to ride out the distance," answered Lady Jessica in a haughty tone.

She had not even looked at Don Rodrigo but it was clear that her snub was meant for him. The viscount grimaced. "Don't be a ninny," he whispered, "Now, be good, Jess, for me."

She relented. "Oh, very well," she answered, and gave him her hand, allowing him to help her out of the carriage.

Don Rodrigo was all too aware of the fact that she was coldly ignoring him. Why? Because he had avoided her these last few days? Did that excuse her behavior in the coach with the puppy viscount? Did she always make a habit of teasing a man into lovemaking in the confines of a carriage? He was beyond reason as this thought drove his blood into flames. "I can understand your preference for the coach, my lady," he said to her on a dry, hard note, "when one thinks of its—*snug* comforts."

The viscount frowned. Had Don Rodrigo witnessed him kissing Jess? He blushed, and his mouth set in firm lines. "You overstep, Don Rodrigo," he answered on a grave note.

"Do I?" returned Rodrigo, dark brow up. "Perhaps, then, felicitations are in order?"

Jessica blew up. She turned, hands on well-shaped hips, her fury taking her face into almost blinding beauty.

"How dare you?" Her hand went up and out to still her friend. "No, Pauly, do not bother to answer this . . . this unfeeling cad of a man." She put up her chin. "I take leave to tell you, Don Rodrigo, that you are beneath my contempt and wish you will quit my company immediately!"

The viscount was aghast at her rudeness. "Jessica!" he objected in shocked accents.

Don Rodrigo's stature was rigid. He looked at the lady with something akin to murder in his eyes, and his sneer was pronounced. "It is my wish always to surrender to your will, Lady Jessica." With a curt nod at the viscount he had turned on his heel and left them.

She wanted to cry, to scream, to pull her hair. She could feel her heart thumping out of control. She could see Pauly was about to lecture her and put up a signal for him to think twice. "*No!* Just see me home. I don't want to hear a word, not a word. . . ."

"No," said Pauly with a shake of his head. "I don't suppose you do." In silence he took her home and in solemnity he bade her good night.

When Jessie had retired to her room it was to find herself pacing wildly, clenching and unclenching her fists as her hands came together and pressed themselves to her firm little chin. "Oh, faith! It is a devil of a man . . . a devil, and I—I despise him." This she found to be nearly more than she could bear and dropped to her bed in a fit of sobs. Astounding, how love, the best of all emotions, can arouse all the very worst. Had she not fallen in love with Don Rodrigo, she would not now be driven to such misery.

Chapter 16

One week had passed since the incident in June Keenen's dressing room. The young viscount Bellamy eyed the missive he had in his hand, and his youthful features were drawn in a frown.

Dearest Pauly,

Aunt Charlie says that a change of scene is all I need to swish away my blue devils. Perhaps she is right. At any rate, we leave for her New Forest Manor home this afternoon.

I feel a wretched coward and know the answer to *my* problem does not lie in running—but run I must.

Have you seen to that matter we came across the other night? Please visit me in the New Forest, Pauly, and we will ride the wild country. When I was a child all I wanted was to come of age and now . . . now all I want is to be a child once more.

As ever,
Jessie

He had received the letter yesterday, and he was still undetermined how to handle the matter of June Keenen.

Clearly Jess expected him to keep his promise and administer to the actress's problem. At the time he had felt inclined to involve himself, but now he was not sure it was the thing to do.

How did one, after all, take care of another man's mistress? Sticky, very sticky. On the one hand, there was June Keenen with child. On the other, there was Don Rodrigo. Clearly he had no place in it himself. There, too, was Don Rodrigo to consider. He liked the Latin. Indeed, he liked and respected him, as did most members of the *beau monde*.

The question uppermost in his mind was had Don Rodrigo really left June Keenen to her own devices? This was not only ungallant, ungentlemanly, dishonorable, and heartless; it was also a despicable act that Pauly could not believe Don Rodrigo capable of committing. It was out of character with the man Pauly knew.

A knock sounded at his study door, and his butler opened it to announce one of the viscount's youthful cronies. "Francis Crabtree."

Pauly looked up absently and nodded as he put aside Jessie's letter. "Oh, hello, Crabby."

"Have you forgotten," started the chubby individual with the red hair and the freckled face, "we were promised to Crawford for the afternoon . . . cockfight." He hesitated, for the viscount did not appear to be dressed for an evening's casual entertainment in one of London's more questionable quarters.

The viscount eyed his friend for a long moment, "Eh, so we are." He got to his feet with a plan forming in his mind. "Know what, Crabby? You go on. I'll meet you."

"Deuce take you, Paul. What do you mean go on? Came out of me way to collect you."

"Right, then, come with me. Must make a stop first."

"What's this? Stop where first?"

"I need to see Don Rodrigo. It's important."

His friend cut him off with a snort. "Then it's to

Southampton you'll have to go, and we'll be missing the cockfight!''

"Southampton?" riposted the viscount in some surprise.

"That's right. Met him at White's a couple of days ago. He was taking his leave of Alvanley and some others. Said his schooner—the . . . the . . . oh, some blasted Spanish name—had been awaiting his return long enough. Means to set sail for home."

"Damnation!" the viscount hissed. "That's it, then. I've no choice left. Crabby, you go off. I'll join you later. It can't be helped!"

Lady Jessica's long, thick flaxen waves of hair swayed in the summer breeze. Her simple gown of white muslin clung to her alluringly lovely figure. Her violet eyes, though, like the droop of her full cherry lips, indicated a lingering despondency. She had hoped a change of pace would make her forget the devil Latin. She had hoped that here in the New Forest that she had often visited as a girl she would find solace, something to wipe out the disillusionment of adulthood.

There was, however, no going back. Knowledge once attained can not easily be put aside. Innocence shed cannot be recalled. Don Rodrigo had toyed with her, and she had been fool enough to think him better than he was, and herself magical enough to make him forgo his libertine ways. More than that she had discovered, for he had been revealed as a cad, a man who would father a child and then leave both mother and unborn infant without a care.

Wild pony herds grazed within easy reach, and she watched their peaceful, graceful movements. A gathering of wild deer peeped out between the trees and leaped the fencing as they made their way to the other side of the road. It was time to return to the house, for it would soon be dark.

Aunt Charlie was entertaining some locals. They were all of them nice people with daughters her own age. She would have to sit down to dinner with them and make conversation. It would perhaps divert her. Perhaps. If she could concentrate on what they were saying, if she could banish Rodrigo's dark eyes from her head, and if she could forget that she was here to forget. . . .

Don Rodrigo sat in his stateroom aboard his yacht and worked his charts. It occupied his time, it was necessary, enjoyable employment, and it kept his mind off the violet eyes that might haunt him.

He knew better than to allow such a thing. He knew better than to sit idly by while thoughts of Jessica stirred him into frenzy. He would keep busy. There was much to do. Thank the saints for this craft. The sea, ships, sailing—these were things, like his ranch, that were very much in his blood. Early in his youth he had learned to navigate and sail. It had become a passion and then two years ago he had sat with an American, Palmer, and together they had designed his yacht.

She was a sleek craft. He had wanted her so. He had wanted her built for speed, and he hadn't bothered about the cost. When it had been completed, the ship came off the ways looking very much like one of the privateers. She measured eighty feet long at the waterline, sporting square sails on the foremast, fore-and-aft on the main.

He had indulged a whim and had her painted with horizontal stripes of bright colors on one side, while the other side was painted with a herringbone pattern. Within, her captain's quarters consisted of two rooms. His stateroom and his private saloon were both furnished elegantly as well as practically. An adjoining door between the rooms was usually hooked open. He looked now from his desk in the saloon and his eyes strayed to the four-poster, with its gold satin coverlet, and he thought of Jessica.

For a moment she came vividly to life. He could hear her delicious, infectious giggle. He could see her twinkling violet eyes, see her full cherry lips curving into an inviting smile. Oh, hell, how she could invite—damn it all! What was the good? Tomorrow morning he would leave for home and he would see Lady Jess never again.

Ah, but he would remember the childlike mischief in her voice, the devilry in her spirit. He would remember the way she would toss her head and hip when displeased. He would remember the unshed tears of compassion he would see spring into her eyes when she chanced to look upon a cruelty she could not change. How she could rage, how she could melt as she had that day in the coach when he had taken her into his arms.

Yes, damn it! She could melt to a kiss very nicely. She did just that for that puppy, Paul Bellamy, didn't she? Didn't you see her kissing him that night in the hackney coach? Didn't she tell you to quit her company? He remembered this as well, and his heart hardened. There would be no more Jessica, no more England. He was going home to work his ranch, to free his land of Spain, and then perhaps to marry a simple Argentine girl who would give him sons and be obedient to his will.

His passions he would still indulge. Love? Well, love was an emotion he would shun. Jessica. She was a passion he had not satisfied, he explained to himself. That was why he still hungered. She was the fruit he had not tasted, nothing more.

The young viscount's kid-gloved hand was raised to June Keenen's dressing room door when the sound of voices within made him hesitate. It was still early evening, and there were another two hours before she would go on stage, but even so, perhaps he should not now be disturbing her. And then it was with some surprise that he recognized the male voice conversing with Miss Keenen.

"You were a wonder, my dear. She will have naught to do with Rodrigo now."

"Hmmm," said June Keenen absently, "so long as you pay me the remainder of what you had promised."

He put it down on the dressing table and sighed with satisfaction.

"It was worth every sou. Her aunt has taken her to the country, where I mean to court her in style."

"Catch her on the rebound?" asked June. "Doesn't it matter to you?"

"What matters to me is her fortune, and that it will be mine after we are wed. In return for my lady's funding she will have a husband who will care for her, respect her, and travel with her in the first circles, for I mean to move politically all the way to the top."

"And I, dearest Warren, can help you in that regard. You would be astounded at the things men tell me in the boudoir." With this she tittered.

There was a sudden quiet, and the viscount turned away feeling just a bit sick. He had eavesdropped. How could you? he asked himself even as he had done it, and still could not stop himself.

He was twenty-two years old and fancied himself a man about town, yet every feeling was repulsed by what he had just overheard. To hear his Jessie talked about by such as they utterly distressed him.

He had to do something. It was clear now. Why hadn't he seen it before. Don Rodrigo and Jess. When she talked about that certain "someone" she hoped might be interested in her, she had meant Don Rodrigo! Why hadn't he understood? Now she thought Don Rodrigo was a cad, and Rodrigo was leaving for South America. This was terrible. Something had to be done. He rushed back to his lodgings, went straight away to his desk, and took up paper and quill to jot down:

Dearest Jess,

What a muddle it is! Don Rodrigo is presently on his yacht in Southhampton harbor. Don't let him leave. I will explain everything when I arrive tomorrow evening. Can't get away before then.

Yours,
Pauly

With this he stepped out into his hall and called for his butler, who appeared promptly, as he could see his master was greatly agitated. "Have this note taken by one of my grooms to Wilton Manor in Lyndhurst's New Forest. Tell the lad to ride hard if he must and to see to it that Lady Jessica gets the note personally."

This done, he took in a long breath of air, swallowed a glass of brandy, adjusted his clothing, and checked the mantel clock. It was just past seven. He had time still to catch up with his intimates at the Blue Bell and witness the cockfight. Right then. Leaving instructions to pack for his trip on the morrow, the young viscount put the business temporarily aside and set out to enjoy himself. It never occurred to him what his laconic missive would do to Jess. How could it? Hadn't he said he would explain all when he arrived?

Chapter 17

The New Forest always seemed to Lady Jessica like a place captured in time. She could imagine the Normans ferocious in their feudal reign, hunting through the forests. The wild ponies roamed still as they had hundreds of years before. Even as this thought occurred to her, a herd of deer lunged through the park's lush greenery, flew over the forest fence, and vanished in the dark of the trees.

It was so lovely here. A full moon lit the gravel path she was now on, the gardens lay behind her, the house ahead. It was a warm house, full with its history. The third lord of the manor had restored it, renewed and redecorated until it sported all its early glory. There was an aura about the mellowed gray walls with their dark oak beaming. She felt the house's invitation, "come and enjoy me," and, indeed, being here had softened some of her tears. There was always something about the woods and the country that calmed her when she was low.

The hour was late, and she could imagine her great-aunt pacing the library floor. Indeed, even at this distance she could see the diminutive form of her aunt Charlie standing at the glass garden door of the library. Jess suppressed a sigh. She needed to be left to her own devices, to shake her mood in her own way. However, she knew her great-aunt loved her and was worried. She put on a smile and finished the remaining distance to the library door, which her aunt threw open for her.

"Really, Aunt Charlie, what did you think would happen to me on our own grounds?"

"I thought the night air would swallow you up, and then what would I tell the admiral?" rallied her aunt.

"You would tell him that I am a perfect hoyden, playing with elves and imps at nightgames," teased Jessie, her eyes glinting naughtily.

"Well, that is precisely what I do not want to tell him. Jessica, you simply must not go on like this. I think it time we removed ourselves to Brighton, where your uncle will eventually meet with Prinny. Why, it is the place to be, where all the gaiety abounds, where nearly everyone will be by the end of the week."

"Perhaps," returned Jessie quietly. "Perhaps in a few days, but now all I want is to romp on my horse and wear britches and take a swim when no one is about."

"Jessica!" reproved her aunt with a deepening frown. "This must stop. I know you will never be a biddable girl, but you cannot go on in this hoydenish manner."

"Oh?" returned Jessica on a dangerous note. "Can't I?"

They were at this moment interrupted by the appearance of a weary butler who felt it was time he was allowed to retire. He announced Lord Bellamy's groom in resonant but stiff accents so that Lady Wilton took pity on him and whispered that as soon as the lad had been seen to, he would be free to retire to his quarters. He thanked her and stood aside while the dust-covered boy entered the room. The lad was no more than fourteen years, lean and wide-eyed as he removed his wool cap and stood at attention.

Jessica in some concern stepped forward, "The viscount, he is well?"

"Ay, that 'e is, m'loidy. Oi've been riding these last

three hours to bring ye this." He handed her a rumpled envelope, which he had produced from an inner pocket.

Jessica took up the envelope and broke the wax seal, unfolded the notepaper, and read the curt message in some surprise. She then turned the paper over as though looking for more.

"What is it, Jessica?" demanded her great-aunt in some impatience.

Jessica had not confided the details of her experience backstage that night. She had merely said that June Keenen had not been feeling well and they had not visited her for any length of time. Her aunt had questioned her about her blue devils, but she had said only that she was tired of routing about London. She now looked at her aunt and knew that something would have to be said.

"Pauly was supposed to see to a mutual friend. He writes to tell me he will be here tomorrow, as the matter is now under hand." She turned so she wouldn't have to face her aunt with a lie. "That, er, that is why he didn't accompany us down here. I dare say we shall all leave for Brighton together. You will like that, Auntie."

"Yes, indeed. In fact, I have been watching you two," said her aunt speculatively. "You and Pauly, that is, and I wouldn't be surprised if there was a match brewing between you." She was sending out lures and watched for a reaction.

Jessie was about to scoff, but instinct held her silent. Instead, she dropped a perfunctory kiss upon her aunt's cheek and bade her good night.

Once in her own room, she dismissed her maid, saying she would see to her own gown, plopped upon her pink satin quilt, lit an additional branch of candles at her nightstand, and produced the letter again. "Dearest Jess," she read out loud. "What a muddle it is! Don Rodrigo is presently on his yacht in Southampton harbor. Don't let him leave. I will explain everything when I arrive tomorrow evening. Can't get away before then. Yours, Pauly."

She frowned. "What does this mean?" she asked of no one in particular.

Dawning sent a fear through her entire body. Don Rodrigo was on his yacht. Don Rodrigo was leaving. He would be gone. She would never see him again. Oh, God! How could she bear it? Southampton harbor was no more than twenty minutes' ride on horseback. Pauly wanted her to keep him from leaving, but how? She didn't even know the name of his yacht!

As she undressed, questions frenzied her mind. She took a brush to her flaxen hair and stroked as she attempted to calm herself. She could ride over to the harbor and inquire about his boat. After all, it would have a Spanish name, no doubt, and a Spanish crew. The quay would be familiar with it, for it must have been there during all these months.

How could she keep him from leaving? What if he had already embarked upon his voyage. Oh, no, no. She couldn't think of that. She wasn't ready to think. Fiend, seize it! What was she saying to herself? Don Rodrigo was a cad. If he left, it would mean heartache for poor June Keenen, not for her. Not for her. If he had already left, it would be even easier to forget him. Wouldn't it? This question brought his handsome face to mind and his dark eyes—oh, his dark eyes, how they penetrated all logic and etched emotion in her heart.

She would have to ride out early. No one must see her. She would leave a note for her aunt, something noncommittal, telling her not to worry. Tomorrow she would deal with Don Rodrigo. Od's life! How? How? Just how would she do that?

The heavens offered a wondrous morning. A sailor's dream with wind enough to fill a sail and a sea softly promising to be kind. Don Rodrigo snapped out orders as he worked with his men and put all thoughts of Jessica away. It was early still, scarcely six A.M., and there was much to do if they were to disembark on schedule.

A milkmaid passing at that moment stopped to tuck the hem of her skirt into her waistband when the form of a tall, athletic man in an open-necked shirt caught her eye and her breath. She stood, open mouthed, and took in the details. His black silk waves of hair blew around his handsome face, and that face—coo, she breathed, chiseled and with a mouth made to make a girl melt. A shiver went through her, for at that moment he was climbing down from the rigging and he looked her way. His dark eyes lit in amusement and he jumped to his deck to make her a bow.

This set her to giggle, and she turned quickly to call to a friend as she hurried off, pleased enough that he had noticed her. Don Rodrigo smiled to himself and turned his attention to his ship. His nine-man crew was in merry spirits, for they were all eager to set sail for home. Belowdecks his cook worked, giving orders to the young steward at his disposal. Don Rodrigo's first mate was dockside, seeing to the delivery of some last-minute purchases.

A frown etched itself across his brow. In London he had seen to his employees, giving all of them references and one month's additional remuneration. His horse-flesh he had sold to worthy friends, and the lease on his lodgings would soon be terminated. There were no loose ends. Right, then what was wrong? Why did he feel incomplete? Why did he have this emptiness inside of him? He was vexed with himself. He felt as though his emotions were out of his direct control, and, fiend take his soul, he had to stop thinking of her!

Quietly Jessie slipped out of the house. She had piled her long, thick hair on top of her well-shaped head and plopped a servant's wool cap over it. She wore boy's britches and an old buckskin riding jacket that fit too tightly to conceal her womanly figure. The morning's sun gleamed on her face as she hurried out of the house and made her way to the stables. There she hushed the sleepy groom with a finger to her cherry lips and told him not to fret, that she had left a note for her aunt and would return by luncheon.

Quickly he helped her saddle the bay gelding she had been using all week, and some moments later she was mounted and trotting down the long, winding drive to the main road. She patted her horse's neck and put him into a collected canter as they hit the road. He was not yet fit, for he had been only lightly exercised before she had come to the manor. However, he was muscled enough for the short trip to Southampton harbor.

The road was empty, for it wanted some twenty minutes to six, and even the local farmers were still in their barns feeding their livestock. She reached the pike and took the fingerpost to the village docks, where she met some light traffic and one or two curious eyes. An inquiry directed at a passing seaman set her off farther into the quay's mainstream. It was nearly six now, and she was beginning to worry. What if Rodrigo had already set sail?

Another passing seaman was hailed. "Sir?" She waited for him to stop by her horse's flank and look up at her. "Could you tell me if there is a Spanish yacht docked in our harbor?"

"Spanish, is it?" he asked, and attempted to consider the question while he scratched his gray-stubbled chin. "Aye, could it be the *Amistad* ye be wanting?"

"Is it manned by a crew from South America?"

"Aye, but there were another one some weeks ago. It went on to Dover, though."

"Thank you. Do you think you could point it out to me?" She pursued.

"Aye, take the quay till ye see the Old Bell Tavern. Last I looked, she was sitting there."

She took out a coin and flipped it to him with a smile. "Your breakfast on me, sailor."

He tipped his hat at her, wondering, for her voice was that of a gentry mort, and what she could be doing at the docks, decked out like a lad, was more than he could fathom. He settled it in his mind that it was an affair of the heart, and with a shake of his head went about his business.

Just as Lady Jessica was urging her horse forward, Don Rodrigo spied his youthful first mate somewhat overburdened with packages.

He laughed and called out to the lad in Spanish, teasing him as the boy balanced his load and made his way on board. "What is this? Have you bought out all of England?" He noted one particular box wrapped in pretty fashion and took it up. "Oh-ho! Now, what is this, Antonio? For a sweetheart, no doubt? Could it be you still remember Carmella?" He touched his chin in mock thoughtfulness. "As I recall, you had done with her when we set sail? Hmmm, I seem to remember you saying something about the unfaithfulness of women, about the duplicity of a dark, rolling eye. Very poetic on the subject, you were."

"My captain," said Antonio with a wide grin behind the largest of his package. His tone held great respect. "Go to the devil."

This set all the crew within hearing into ribald laughter and brought down Don Rodrigo's hand onto Antonio's curly dark hair.

"So I shall, but not, I hope, before we see Buenos Aires once more." He led the way toward the companionway, saying lightly, "Dispose of your . . . er . . . purchases and meet me in my saloon. I want to have one last look at the charts I drew up before we set sail."

Something inside Lady Jessica's stomach quivered as her violet eyes found the *Amistad*. She could see the crew, brightly clad, merry, and preparing to disembark. "My word," she breathed to herself, "already he is leaving. I am only just in time."

Hurriedly she called to a passing urchin who ambled to her. He was no more than twelve with a shock of unruly hair beneath his dark wool cap. His sailor's jacket was two sizes too large for him, and he looked at Jessica with some surprise as she placed a coin in his dirty hand and asked that he hold her horse. "Coo . . ." he breathed, for a second glance told him it was not a boy who had just hired his services, but a woman in britches.

Unnoticed, Jessica made her way on board, for the nine men working the rigging had no opportunity to pay heed to a small lad crossing the deck of their vessel. It was no doubt, thought one or two of these men, someone delivering something to their captain. Jessica correctly assumed Don Rodrigo would be in his cabin belowdecks and made her way in what she hoped was its general direction. She gave no thought to the propriety of her situation. She only knew she had to get there; she had to see him. She had to do as Pauly had asked and prevent Don Rodrigo from leaving. After all, there was June Keenen and his child to think about.

Don Rodrigo rolled up the chart he had just surveyed with his first mate, clapped him on the back, and with silent resignation gave the order to set sail.

"Do you not come up . . . to say *adiós* to this English soil you love so much?" bantered Antonio. He sensed that all was not well with his captain.

"Not this time, my friend. I leave it to you to make my farewells as quickly as may be. Full sails . . . full sails, lad." said Don Rodrigo quietly.

A frown marred Antonio's cherubic countenance. He had been taken on by Don Rodrigo four years ago when he and his family had been starving in the streets of Buenos Aires. He loved the man, and it disturbed him to see, for he could, that his captain was laboring under some unhappiness. God knows, he thought silently, the man has already suffered enough. He bowed his head and left the saloon.

Jessica heard a door opening and dodged behind one directly at her flank. This proved to be the door to a closet, and she stood, holding her breath, until she heard the sound of footsteps on the companionstairs she had just descended. She opened the door and peeped around before breathing a sigh of relief and making her way to the captain's saloon so designated by the elegance of the heavily molded and richly stained oak door. Before she opened this door she forced herself to knock, and when she heard Don Rodrigo's deep voice she was amazed at the sensation it aroused within her breast.

As invited, she opened the door, went within, her head lowered so that he could not at first see her face. Carefully, quietly she turned and closed the door at her back and then took a step toward the figure at the porthole.

Don Rodrigo had looked around with only mild interest at first. However, finding a figure in a rough English riding costume, his attention was arrested and then excited as a certain glimmer of recognition touched him. And then he was looking into violet eyes. His hand brushed his forehead in sudden consternation. Was he going mad?

There he was! Oh, God, how her heart was beating. His black eyes burned, and there was a haunted look in them that drew her to him. For a moment, just for a moment, she felt she was his. There was no June Keenen. There was no Pauly asking that she detain his departure. There was no Sir Warren asking for her hand in marriage. There was only this wild dark-eyed man who set her to trembling and froze her in time.

He was across the room in two purposeful strides. Was he indeed out of his mind? Could this be Jessica? Did he want her so badly that he was seeing her eyes, her face, through the blur of unhappiness he was experiencing. Without a word he had whipped off her wool cap so that the buttercup shades of long, thick hair that had already escaped their ribbon beneath the cap came tumbling down her back.

He groaned, and, still without speaking, he was taking her into his powerful embrace. His mouth closed on hers and his willpower was given to the winds. Here was the woman of his desires asking—yes, damn it, in coming here she was asking to be taken. Why should he deny her? Why deny himself.

Jessie bent to his touch, molded to his body, gave herself to his kiss. Something called her from afar, and she heard the voice in the back of her brain only to close its door. It was so good to see him, to have him touch her, to feel his hard, masculine body against her. His mouth parted her lips and gave her a kiss that set her on fire, that drew out her soul and made it his own.

She had never been handled in just this fashion by a man before. She could feel him start to remove her buckskin riding jacket, but it thrilled her rather than frightened her, for he held it close to her body, using it to bring her nearer to his own. He played with it as he lowered it to her bottom so that she was aware that he was undressing her and in taunting slow motion. All the while he nibbled at her lips, whispered magic into her ears in a voice that sent shivers down her spine.

He taught her in those moments what he wanted from her, and guided by emotion and a startling wantonness she responded and found a lust in her heart she had never realized she was capable of feeling. Were those rockets blasting in a dark velvet sky? Such fine bright stars, they filled the room; they twinkled hypnotically behind his handsome head. His glistening black waves fell around his rugged face, his dark eyes mesmerized, and his voice enchanted. She felt herself falling and then suddenly she was scooped cradlelike in his arms. He was slipping his hand into her white linen shirt, finding and releasing her breasts with one easy movement. He was bending his head even as he walked with her, burying it into the fullness of her breasts, moaning as his lips discovered the sweetness of her pert nipples.

He was taking her through a doorway toward his enormous four-poster. She saw all this through a haze of light as she clung to him. She marveled at his strength, at his grace and ease of movement, and she was obedient to his every need. She could not object; she could not think. She only responded to the ache in her limbs, thrilled to the excitement of his fingers, to the bewitchment of his aura. She saw only his eyes, felt only their united desire as he gently removed the remaining confines of clothing.

What was this he was feeling? As his hands glided over the softness of her body he reveled in the innocence of her response, fevered at the excitement her touch engendered. He gloried in the sweetness of her scent, the silk of her wondrous thick hair falling over her naked breast. All senses were riveted on her, on pleasing her, warming her to his needs, and his kisses grew more passionate as he discovered the embers burning in her core. She burned for him, he knew it, and it took him soaring.

As they met they were suspended in time. There was naught for her to do but to surrender to his deft handling. She arched her naked body, pressing against him as he managed his britches and kicked off his boots. There was a moment of sudden, very nearly spell-shattering fear when his skillful hands found the honeyed crevice between her thighs and she stiffened. He immediately assuaged her fear.

"Ah, babe, worry not, *muchacha* . . . sweet life. . . ." he whispered, and his voice instilled her with a hunger for more. She wanted more of him, more of what he was making her feel. He knew it as he kissed her earlobes, moved his lips down her throat, cupped her breast, and teased her nipple with his tongue.

There was something in the huskiness of his voice that thrilled her in a way she could not comprehend, so that now, when his finger found and explored, teasing, manipulating the sweetness between her legs, she opened them wider, groaning with pleasure as his fingers penetrated.

"Ah, *querida*, you don't know," he moaned as the hardness of his manhood pulsated and demanded more

161

of her. He wanted to hold off, make sure she was ready, but it was difficult, so difficult to restrain himself. He wanted to plunge himself deep . . . deep . . .

It fevered her brain to hear his endearments spoken in his native tongue, to hear the Latin in him now released, always in the past so carefully withheld. It was she who drove him to this ardor. She knew it and exalted in the knowledge. Softly she said his name. "Rodrigo." Almost shyly, yet with a lacing of incongruous boldness she whispered, "I—I want to please you."

Magic! Her voice, timid yet very nearly audacious, spurred him into fathomless hunger. He had to have her. He had to take her now. "Jessie, open for me, then; that's it, *querida*." He was raising her legs, bending her knees, positioning her for his entrance, taking her slender hips into his firm hands, stationing his rod at the lips of her opening. "Don't you worry, Jess. I mean to be pleased, and, eventually, you will be too." He was gently prodding now, and as he felt the tightness of her womb take hold, he groaned with delight. "Sweet *muchacha*, you are so small, so good. You feel so good."

She felt his entrance and again stiffened against him. "No," she said doubtfully. "No."

He wasn't listening. Indeed, how could he? He plunged in, taking hold of her body to him, kissing away the cry that sprang to her lips. She was virgin-tight, and it felt as though he were ripping her wide open. The sudden pain was quick and it was over, but it had served to rouse her into terror. She moved away from his embrace, pushing at him. "Stop, oh, Rodrigo, stop."

He had never had a virgin before. It was something that strangely excited him, being her first. He treated her caressingly, taking her for the child she was. "Not now, little one. It will be better, I promise." He had her hips again and was moving into a steady beat, urging her to receive. "Sweet *vida mía*."

The aura of his tenderness soothed her, and she discovered in herself an easy willingness to relax and let him do what he would. And then once more she was pleasuring to his touch, responding to the enchantment of his voice, soft, loving, full with Spanish endearments. She found herself giving to him, tentatively at first, and then, as she felt his fever mount and knew she was his source of pleasure, she lost the last of her inhibitions.

His fingers moved erotically as he took up her firm rump and raised it to his thrusts. She realized as he raised her legs what he wanted her to do and she bent up her knees for him, succumbing to the rising wildness of his dance. He frenzied then and took her lips with ardent need as he built himself to his peak.

She moved to his passion; she ran her hands over his back, to his shoulders; she marveled over his hard, muscular body as she gave herself over to the rhythm of his lovemaking, and then she felt herself rise in a way she had never dreamed possible. He took her to her climax in decadent, wanton, and beautifully paced propulsion. He heard the intake of breath as she reached her peak. He felt her ebb and relax, and it furthered his own fire to ecstasy before he, too, took on his moment.

Even as he held her, enervated from their passion, satisfied in its release, he knew he had not had enough of her. This feeling was different. It brought a frown to his brows as he took her close into his embrace and rolled over, keeping her across his chest, kissing her forehead as she closed her eyes. What was this? He should feel satiated, but he did not. His heart twisted suddenly in his chest. This would not do!

He had, some years and many experiences ago, bidden farewell to love, its hopes and its joys. He knew better. He had keenly observed womankind and had drawn for himself a boundary. He had within him a willpower to walk away, and he had always done so before—before Jessica. His need to be free of ties that bring heartache and then finally break a man (as they had his father) was a stronger need than the fleeting desire for one woman!

He looked down at her face as she slept. *Madre de dios!* Was there ever such a face? Angelic in repose, beautiful, sweet virgin. Ah, that was it. She was his virgin. He had never taken an innocent before. He had seduced, yes, but she had come to him; she had wanted him. Again, that stirring in his loins. He was trapped between his own brand of logic and the flicker of his heartbeat. Heat came once more to banish thought as he bent his head to kiss her pursed lips. She smiled and murmured something unintelligible and it brought a light to his dark eyes. How she moved him. And then he was kissing her mouth more urgently.

Her eyelashes moved and her violet eyes opened wide as she came to life. She felt his hands move from her waist and back and make their way across her body, over her breasts. "What . . . what, sir, do you think you are doing?" she whispered sleepily.

He hushed her as he pulled her on top of him, as he kissed her throat, the crevice between her breasts, parted her thighs with his upraised knee and then held her tenderly as he said, "Ah, Jessie, just look what you have done. . . ."

Part Two

*"There's a divinity that shapes our ends,
Rough-hew them how we will."*

—Hamlet

Chapter 1

Don Rodrigo's young first mate looked up at the darkening sky with some misgiving and wondered for the hundredth time in two hours what his captain could be doing for so long. They had left England's shore behind them some three hours ago and Don Rodrigo had not bothered to come up on deck. It was not like Rodrigo, though Antonio felt a wave of pride that his captain trusted him to handle the disembarkation on his own.

He sighed and scanned the ocean ahead. Waves of deep blue, finely capped in white foam, rolled, dipped, and lapped at the yacht's sides. She seemed a friendly sea and yet there was that sky at their backs, every moment closing in, that made Antonio wonder if he should send the steward to disturb his captain.

Don Rodrigo awoke with a start. Was something not right? And then with slow-dawning realization he knew. "My God," he breathed out loud, and moved bolt upright. The slap of ocean waves was all too audible. The pitch of his vessel told him they were on the high seas. He ran his hand through his black hair and looked furtively at the small bundle in his bed, at the length of thick sunflower hair streaming over the quilt, at the pert nose, the long lashes, and the cherry lips. "Well met, Rodrigo!" he said to himself in some disgust. "Now you have done it!"

He got to his feet, picked up his britches, and hopped into them as he moved to the porthole. The sight that confronted him confirmed all suspicion. *They were on the high seas!* He pressed his fingers to his forehead. Hell and fire! He was in for it. What did he do with Jessie now? Turn back, of course, but even then he would be met, no doubt, by her uncle and called to order. No less than marriage would be demanded. Marriage? Damnation!

He paced back to the bed, and a heavy frown shadowed his fierce dark eyes. She had been a virgin, and he had been trapped. Had she known they were pulling out? Damnation! *He had known.* Why hadn't he stopped his crew? Why hadn't he thought to call out to Antonio to put off their leave-taking? How had they disembarked without his feeling it? Why? How? Because he had been like a man drugged, drugged with passion. All he had known was the glory of Jessie in his arms. Nothing else had existed. Well, it would have to be handled. Perhaps he might yet be able to sneak her back into England. There was the customs in Southampton. Perhaps he could beach her nearer to her home.

He went to the bed, pulled on his stockings and his high-top boots before turning around and taking her bare white shoulder in his firm hand. Even now the feel of her sent a shiver of pleasure through him that was inexplicable. He should feel satiated, but he didn't. He wanted more of her.

He managed to shake this notion off as he gently stirred her.

"Jess?" His voice came in harsher tones than he had intended. It was his present predicament overriding all other considerations. "Wake up, girl."

She rolled easily onto her back, her eyelashes fluttered, and then she was resting her lush violet eyes in a soft expression on his face. Her first discernible thought was that he was wildly handsome with his black hair glistening across his forehead, with his mouth set so sternly, with his dark eyes. She sat up then, pulling the covers around her. Something was wrong. She could see it in his eyes, "What is it?" she asked at once, brushing the sleepiness away.

It was hard to resist the angel quality of her concern. It was nearly impossible to resist the pixy shyness that hung around her. Involuntarily he took up her chin and said, this time more gently, "Get dressed, little girl, and as soon as may be, I will see you safely home and hopefully out of this mess we are now in."

"What?" Then suddenly she felt the roll and pitch of the ship. "Faith! Oh, never say . . ." With this utterance she was out of the bed with her coverlet all around her and dashing toward the porthole. There, she, too, discovered their predicament and closed her eyes. "Rodrigo, how did this happen? How did you allow your crew . . ."

He was irritated by her question. Ah-ha, he thought. So the chit (like all her kind) meant to trap him into an admission of fault. Once blame was laid he would be expected to make amends, marriage being the prize sought. The fact that he had asked himself this very question was, of course, beside the point! "And what of you, my fine lady Jess? You knew I was disembarking when you made your way on board my ship and came to me in my cabin!"

His words were careless, spurred by his irritation with their present circumstances. He didn't realize how they would sting a young heart, and Jessie's pride was not about to show him. She felt as though he had slapped her, but she didn't buckle beneath the blow. She pulled herself up, her eyebrow raised, her violet eyes cold, but she didn't have to find a retort. He hurried on in fine ranting style. "That's right! Put up your chin. Stand there like a stock and say nothing. Why should you answer? You had nothing to lose and everything to gain. What happened, *muchacha*? Didn't Sir Warren come up to scratch? Did you fancy a Latin ranchero in his stead?"

Her hand came up and would have whipped across his face had he not caught her wrist. "So, my kitten has claws?" he whispered, only vaguely aware that he might be hurting her.

A tear formed somewhere in her heart, and she fought it down. Hurt? No, she told herself, she must not be hurt, only angry. "I take leave to tell you, sir, that you are a demon rake as bad as you have been painted." She stood glaring at him and pulled her wrist out of his hold. "You will get me home with all possible speed." That was all she would say to this man. That was all he would hear from her on the subject.

He was furious with her coolness, but he made her a sweeping bow. "With pleasure, ma'am. May I suggest that you get dressed . . . or is it that you have a local minister on standby?"

There, her own fiery temper was unleashed. "To do what? Marry us?" She shook her head with contempt for the notion. "Not if my life depended upon it." And then, her eyes glaring, she added with grand haughtiness, "Do you think, honestly think, *I* would marry *you?*"

He grinned in spite of himself. "I have, er, excellent reason to think so, ma'am."

"Nonsense." She cloaked herself in disdain. "Don't flatter yourself that far, Don Rodrigo. I came to you because Pauly asked me to see you . . . on business, and if I fell into your arms, it was because . . . I found that my attraction for your physical charms overrode my good sense. Naught else was involved. Marry you, indeed!" she scoffed, doing it up brown. Her violet eyes were dark pools of vivid color hiding the feelings that were tearing her insides in two. "Why would I marry you when I have promised myself to Sir Warren? You see, you were not only crude in your choice of words, but you were inaccurate, as well. Sir Warren did, in fact, ask me to marry him, and I was very pleased to accept!"

Inexplicably this sliced through his senses in alarming

fashion. However, he had himself and his thoughts in order. "My . . . felicitations, Jessie sweet, but then, I have already kissed the bride." As soon as the words were out, he felt the cad. This was inexcusable, but he had no time to rebuke himself, for this time, Jessie found her mark.

Her foot came out and gave him a quick, solid kick to the shin. She didn't manage to do the damage she would have liked to have done, for her feet, like her body, were quite bare beneath the coverlet's folds.

"Fiend!" she exploded in hot wrath. "How dare you!" She very nearly dissolved in tears, for she had no defense. She had come to his yacht. She had gone into his arms and into his bed. What could she say?

He was ashamed of himself and unconsciously admiring her pluck. He laughed out loud as her foot landed its blow, and he grabbed both her arms behind her back and brought her up against him. She struggled against him and he smiled in sporting fashion as she hurled abuse at his head. "So I am, tigress, so I am, but what is to be done now?" In answer to this he dropped a kiss upon her cherry lips. It was odd how sweet he found her kiss even when she did not respond to him. "Come, *querida*, do not fight me now, for we must make haste. I don't want your name ruined, and mean to stand by you in this."

"Go to the devil!" she snapped. "And don't dare tell me that is where you are destined, for I know it." She flung out of his hold, but his hand caught her waist and brought her back.

He was grinning. "Now, what sort of way is that to talk to me? Don't you want me to return you to English soil? Perhaps you want to go to Buenos Aires with me. Is that it, my sweet?"

"I'd be hanged first!" she retorted sharply.

"Or married to your popinjay, Warren?" His mercurial temper was on the rise.

"He will make me an excellent husband," she answered him, her violet eyes glinting.

"Will he, by God! And will you tell him where you had your first lesson in bed?" Damn, how could he be saying such hellish things to her. He saw the color drain from her face. He saw the violet eyes lose some of their sparkle and retreat in pain, and he was furious with himself.

"It will not matter," she said on a dull note. "I said that Sir Warren wants to marry me. I didn't say that he is in love with me."

"Ah, Jess, you mistake there." His voice was suddenly tender, softer than before. "But it doesn't signify. I will stand by you in this, and if he does not wish to fulfill the marriage settlement, I will, of course, take the consequences of my act."

"You will bear the conse—" She nearly spluttered with rage. "You . . . you . . ."

He laughed harshly. "Anything you wish, my dear, but for now, words are a waste of time." He bent, scooped up a white linen shirt, and stepped out of the room.

She stood her ground for a long moment. She was stunned by the force of the blow. There was an emptiness of heart, a despair, that she had never before known in her life. How had everything changed? Just a short while ago all had been blossoming around and within, and now? Now all things were dying. She had been wicked and wanton, and, of course, she was paying the price. That was the answer, the only answer. Everyone had to pay the piper in the end, and her dues had just come up sooner than expected!

Chapter 2

Summer gales are cruel things. When all is peaceful and serene, when all is quiet and the sky is soft, it is then that they strike, gathering sudden willful winds and hauling them before the unsuspecting seaman. Antonio called out an uneasy command to the nine-man crew, for he had never seen a gale just like this. There was something about its color, something about its style, that struck terror in his youthful heart. Where, for pity's sake, was his captain? he asked himself again.

From the southeast the gale flexed in proud array, rotating toward them, giving the men on the *Amistad* a full view of what they might expect to meet. Counterclockwise, it spiraled, a mass of dark, threatening weather, devouring everything in its path. Don Rodrigo pulled his shirt over his head as he came topside and tucked the shirt into his britches in hasty fashion as he looked for his first mate. And then he saw what held his men spellbound.

"God's death!" he breathed out loud. In Spanish he called his men to order. "What? Are we babes in the wood? Do you stand and gawk, or do you work to save?" he bellowed. He had a leader's momentary satisfaction, for he saw his men respond to his voice, jump to do what was called for, and as they climbed the rigging to take in sail, he called to Antonio, "How long have the winds hauled from the south?"

"Not long." He couldn't help the curious glance he cast his captain and the bait in the remark. "Certainly not as long as you have been below."

What was this? Rodrigo would not be questioned by anyone. Was the lad presuming to admonish? His thick dark brow went upward, and his expression was unapproachable. "That was *not* an answer to my question, lad."

Antonio blushed, abashed, and sorry to have displeased. He worshipped Don Rodrigo, who was very much the boy's ideal, and he answered him at once, his curiosity temporarily put to the dust. "Five . . . maybe eight minutes . . . no more." He looked at the rising waves. "Shall I have the men prepare to scud the wind?"

Rodrigo shook his head grimly. "No, to do so would send us hurtling into the center of the storm." He moved toward the quarter-deck and called out an order to one of the crew regarding the clewing up of the sail before turning to explain further. "We shall have to point the bow against the wind, take the might of the storm, and hopefully shoulder ourselves away from the storm's heart."

"But how?" Antonio returned doubtfully.

Excited by the prospect they faced, Don Rodrigo laughed out loud and clapped the youth on the shoulder. "You will see, lad, you will see, for I mean to use the storm's power to get us out of its path!" With this he took to climbing a mast and handing a seaman a length of rope before aiding him in clewing up. There was a great deal to be done if they were to ride out this storm, and it would take every man on board to see them through.

In his stateroom cabin below, Jessie made an attempt to pull herself together. Her heart had taken the blow and stood up against the pain. He did not love her. Over and over again this thought thrust at her relentlessly.

She had hoped, oh, how she had hoped, just like any silly green girl could hope. Sweet words during his love-making . . . but they had not been more than sweet words. He had not said he loved her. He had not made her any promises. She had given herself willingly, wantonly, and that was her own shame to bear!

Yes, but hadn't there been a look in his eyes? Hadn't she felt something communicated between them? Wasn't there a spirit that touched both their souls and mingled them as one? Or was it all just the chemistry of physical fever? She sighed. Did it matter? Wasn't the end result the same? Soon she would be parted from him, and never again would she want a man the way she wanted Don Rodrigo. He had touched her, taken her, caressed her, in a way she could never allow any other. Marriage to Sir Warren was probably her destiny, but oh, oh, she wanted only Rodrigo.

Fiend seize her heart! Why should it throb for a devil, and devil he was with those fierce dark eyes. She closed her own and took up a hairbrush she found on his high dark oak dressing table. She smoothed her long, tangled flaxen locks with quick, impatient strokes before pulling on her britches. Quickly she splashed some water from the washbasin onto her face and dried herself with a neatly folded cloth. Stockings and then boots were pulled on, her riding jacket of buckskin was slipped into, and she was peeping into the corridor.

She could hear the crashing of the waves, and as she reached the companionstairs she could see the sky growing increasingly dark. Ye gods! Could it be evening already? Her aunt Charlotte would have the whole of the New Forest out searching for her. Pauly will have arrived by now. He would have told her aunt that she had gone to see Rodrigo. They would find her horse at the docks. Oh, faith, there would be all hell to pay!

She closed her eyes a moment over the vision this thought presented, and she recouped her courage. There was nothing to do. She would have to manage the situation step by step. Resolutely she started up the stairs, when the ship lurched and she found herself reeling backward both by the force of the tilting vessel and by the sturdy form of a falling sailor.

Antonio lurched with the sudden dip of the vessel and would have caught himself had he not been taken aback by the sight of an exquisite fair maid in boy's clothing. This so startled him that he quite forgot precaution, and before he could remedy the situation he was landing with a nice thump upon the pretty. In hurried Spanish he begged the maid's forgiveness as he took her hand and tried to right them both.

The ship did not cooperate with their efforts, and once more its rough swaying found Jessie entangled with the tall, dark youth. This time she found him pinned to the wall, and as she put her hand against his chest to steady herself, she smiled ruefully and said softly, "Faith! It is I who must apologize, sir, for I find I am not yet quite seaworthy."

English! This beauty in boy's attire was English, which of course he must have assumed from her gold hair and her fair complexion, but how did she get on board? This was his first silent question and took up the moment as he attempted to discover an answer to his very reasonable question. "Dios!" he managed to breathe as he bent over her hand. "You—you are English?"

No time for the reply. Once again the ship was throttled by the rising waves, and Jessie went into the boy's arms. It took them a moment or two before they were able to stand, and in this time she scarcely realized that she was clinging to him for support.

It was at this moment that Don Rodrigo, having been thoroughly soaked by the ocean's spray, wondered where Antonio had gone off to. He had sent the lad in search of his rain slicker, which he kept always on a wallhook just at the bottom of the stairs. With a curse below his breath he took the first two steps below and stopped short to find his lady Jess very neatly in Antonio's arms.

In addition to this fact was another: The two seemed to be smiling quite amicably at each other.

His voice came in stern accents. "I am certain, Antonio, that while you must, as all men do, find Lady Jessica quite fascinating, you shall have to quit her company for the time being, as you are needed on deck." He eyed Jessica with something near contempt. "And, my lady, I must ask you to return to your quarters until I send for you. "

Antonio was blushing furiously as he scooped up his captain's slicker, had it snatched from his hand before he passed his captain, and returned to the topdeck. Don Rodrigo's dark eyes glared, for Lady Jessica had made no attempt to comply with his command. She meant to show him she would not cower before his boorishness.

"Well?" he said in frigid lines. "What are you waiting for? Another of my men to come along and entertain you?"

Angry beyond reason, past expression, she turned on her heel and very nearly stomped off (as best as the rolling ship would allow) to his stateroom. There she opened and closed the door with some resonance before she took to pacing.

Don Rodrigo watched her go off in her high fury and, in spite of himself, his sensuous lips curved in a half-smile. She was a spirited lovely, and he had no right to treat her thus. More than that did not at that moment occur to him, for there was the storm above to contend with. All other matters would have to be put aside.

Lady Charlotte wrung her hands and paced the Oriental carpet of her tearoom with great energy. The door was opened and her butler announced the young viscount Paul Bellamy, whereupon she ceased her pacing and turned expectantly to him.

Pauly entered the room, his clothing damp from the light mist that he had encountered, his face white with worry as he stepped forward and took up her ladyship's cold, thin hands. "Aunt Charlie, I—I have . . . awkward news."

"Awkward?" she screeched. "Do not play on words with me, boy! Tell me outright. Where is Jessie?"

"I found her horse and brought it back with me," he started, leading her to the brocade sofa.

She allowed him to seat her but irritably answered him on this score. "Hang her horse! Where is my Jessie-girl?"

The young viscount closed his eyes. Oddly enough, he was not overly distressed. He knew Jessie too well. She had gone into town dressed in britches. That much he got from the boy she had left her horse with. She had of her own will (and as per his request in his letter to her) gone on board Don Rodrigo's yacht. Therefore, no premeditation there. Don Rodrigo did not plan to abduct her, if indeed that was what he had done. What then? She had not come off the ship; that much was certain. Instinct told the viscount that Jessie was where she wanted to be, yet the ship had put to sea and he knew she would never leave her aunt to worry over her. What, then, was the answer?

"I have reason to believe," he said slowly, "that somehow Jessie must have found herself in a position where she was unable to leave Don Rodrigo's ship."

"What?" ejaculated Lady Wilton, jumping to her feet. Her purple turban tilted and went askew over her forehead. "Never say the scoundrel has abducted her?"

There was a dangerous moment when Pauly, affected by the strain of the day, the fears of the question, and the sight of the little, aged woman with the crooked turban, very nearly burst into indecent mirth. He managed to control himself. "That is something we can only speculate on." He frowned over the problem. "I suggest that there may be a simple explanation."

"Such as?" demanded Lady Wilton.

"Well, you know what Jess is? No doubt she talked

Don Rodrigo into giving her a tour of the Channel?" he said on an unconvincing note.

"Bah!" returned Lady Wilton. "What a piece of nonsense. Our Jess may be full of pluck and mischief, but she would never put me to worry over her. Disappear all day without sending me word? Never!"

"True," agreed Pauly on a frown, for this is what had him puzzled as well.

"You must ride to London at once. Go to the Horse Guards. They will know where the admiral is."

"The admiral?" returned Pauly, his eyes opening wide. "Don't you think we should give her till morning?"

"No. Something tells me there is no time to spare. Pauly, you must tell him that Don Rodrigo Cesares has abducted his niece. You must, for that is precisely what that Latin rogue has done!"

Chapter 3

Don Rodrigo's vessel was built to take the harshest gales, but its might was being tested, as was its crew. Rodrigo bellowed out to a nearby sailor as he charged up the mast to save a seaman desperately clinging to a line. The wind was filled with driving rain and the ship was very nearly on its side as it plowed the cruel Atlantic.

Thunder deafening in its force broke through the heavy masses of dark clouds, furiously roaring out from the heavens, making all around tremble. Lightning blazed through the sky in sharp staccato. The mastheads and yardarms were laden with composants, beads of electricity as low down as the lower yards. The sails were furled, and even so, the hurricane winds managed to find their edges and shred their hems out of their gaskets. More than once Rodrigo and Antonio had to lie flat to hang on, and so it went for hours.

There was a moment when Jessie, huddled on Rodrigo's canopied bed, thought the storm would bury the ship, and just at that moment a sudden lull came upon them. She sat very still, wondering, almost ready to move, when the stateroom door opened and she could hear Don Rodrigo in the outer room, doing what, she could not tell, and then he was entering the bedroom cabin.

He hardly glanced at her as he shed his wet garments and reached into his wardrobe cabinet for fresh clothing.

She averted her face as he dropped his wet britches and stretched into a pair of buff ones. He pulled on dry stockings and another set of top boots that came up to his knees. A waistcoat followed, and then the rain slicker was pulled over his head.

This surprised her and she managed on a low note, "Is—is it over?"

He looked her way and a frown descended over his dark eyes. Not only was it not over; they were some distance off course. Here was a problem, for here was an English wench whose family would expect him to . . . marry her. God's death! He walked over to the bed, for she looked vulnerable all trussed up in the quilt with her huge violet eyes opened wide. "No, my lady Jess, it is not over, and there is no going back. We are too far off course for it to matter, so when we get through this gale, we will be bound for Buenos Aires."

She jumped to her knees on the bed. "No, I can't. . . ."

He misunderstood and his sneer moved his lips and mingled with the light in his dark eyes. "Never fear, I will do the honorable and give you my name."

Her chin and her pride came up. "I don't want your name," she said at once. "I want to return to England."

He frowned. "That is impossible at this time." He was tired. They had been fighting the storm in the rain and cold for nearly five hours. There were many hours more that they would have to do the same. He sighed. "It will be better to write your family once you are safely and respectably wed in my country."

"No," she answered, "not if you were the last man on earth would I marry you."

She had the knack to work up his ire as no other woman had ever done. She infuriated him with her look of cold contempt and it was in some exasperation that he threw up his hands. "I don't have the time or the patience to waste in argument with you, woman. You shall do what is expected, as *I* must and shall." He started to turn on his heel, feeling that his words had been enough to silence her. He was, of course, quite wrong.

"Rodrigo!" She called him to order in sharp tones. "I certainly intend to do what is expected, and as I am expected to marry Sir Warren, that is precisely what I mean to do!" There! She glared at him, her own temper fueled by his disdain. How dare he think he could order her about. How dare he behave as though all this were her fault and that he was the only one who could set things to right. She had her pride and she would show him that she had alternatives.

He was moved to rage and walked toward her purposefully. In a moment he had her shoulders roughly in his grasp. She could feel the strength of his grip beneath the buckskin of her riding coat. His eyes, faith, how they blazed into hers.

"And your Sir Warren," he said with derision, "will he want you when he learns that he will not be your first, that a Latin rogue was before him? Will he want you when he learns that you fevered for another man, or, like a female, do you mean to deceive?"

"I don't have to lie to Sir Warren, nor does he to me" was her reply and then softly, "It will not matter to him."

He pushed her away from him and with a sneer said, "Ah, but then I find it matters to *me*! I will not have it said that I took the prize only to have another man pay the price!" So saying, and before she could think to answer this, he quickly left her alone once more.

She sat back against the pillows, staring after him. No, she could not, would not, marry him on such terms. He did not love her. She felt the tear in her eye swell and silently spill over. Enough! Look at him . . . at all he has said and done since the first moment you met. Yes, you could have him as husband, but he would be with you out of his warped sense of honor and obligation. That would be humiliating.

She gulped back a flood of tears and defiantly decided she would rather die a spinster than hold to him in such a manner. In spite of her pride, she bent her head to her upraised knee. Faith, it hurt, but it was the child in her that was hurting, not the woman. The woman was squaring her shoulders and preparing for the next battle.

In the quiet of the prime minister's richly appointed study, affairs of state were being decided. A hush had fallen over the room with Pitt's announcement. Admiral Stafford, the Earl of Redcliff (Lady Jessica's guardian uncle), stood pulling at his lower lip. "I must tell you here and now that I am against such a move. After all, you gave the Latins your word."

Pitt gravely shook his head. "Did I, Thomas? I think not. What I assured them had nothing to do with what they asked."

The admiral considered the prime minister doubtfully. There was no denying that Pitt was all for Great Britain, but he was not the man he used to be. He was a man obsessed with his determination to make a success of the Third Coalition. With deliberation the admiral said softly, "I was under the impression that you offered them our promise of neutrality." He stood, his large hands at his back.

The prime minister moved irritably, but before he could answer, Sir Warren was on his feet, taking the attention with the charm of his smile. "Why, Admiral, we are, I believe, realistic adults, and aware in that capacity that all is fair in . . . love and war?"

A long sigh as the Earl of Redcliff considered his past career and his present predicament. He could not in good conscience play Don Rodrigo and Simon Bolivar false, and that is precisely what he would be doing if he took a fleet to invade their country. It wearied him, and he turned to the street window for a long moment.

"Thomas"— it was the prime minister—"always the idealist, my friend." He put his hand on the large shoulder of the aging seaman. "You know, don't you, that Great Britain's economy is in serious danger. Liverpool's raw cotton imports are down beyond belief and grain—damn it, man, we are in trouble. Open your eyes. We need timber to build our ships. The situation calls for desperate measures." He drew himself up in all his portly height. "I will do whatever it takes to set this country of ours on its feet, and, Thomas, it is my belief that you will too."

"Treachery is for diplomats," returned the admiral, unconvinced.

"You would be committing no such act," put in Sir Warren. "You would be faithfully adhering to your country, your government's wishes."

"So the administration favors military expeditions to South America?" asked the admiral bluntly. He stood waiting for the inevitable reply. He never thought he would ever find himself in a position where he would decline any office his government required of him. He had the choice and, by damn, this time he would make it. He would take no ship to invade a friend's country when word to the contrary had been given to that same friend.

Pitt waved Sir Warren off and answered slowly, carefully. "Argentina is a hope for a new market into which our merchants and British traders may be diverted. Therein lies your answer."

"I see, and do Beresford and Popham agree to such a scheme? Do they know that Great Britain gave its word to these Latins?"

"It is my intention to call upon Popham and the viscount Beresford's naval skills in this instance."

"Then I can have no qualms in declining."

There was a sharp rap on the door before the butler opened it wide and in some agitation of nerves announced the viscount Paul Bellamy. Pauly scarcely waited for the retainer to finish announcing him when he thrust himself into the room, excused himself and his intrusion with more haste than sincerity, and advised the men at large, "But you see, sir, I am here on a matter of the utmost urgency, indeed. We have not a moment to lose."

The admiral's thick brows were up, and as his nerves were already on end, he found himself out of patience with the youth. "Zounds, boy, will you stop babbling and bleating at us and spit out what has you in such a fidget?"

"Your niece, sir . . ." Pauly managed to utter in hushed accents. The swift ride to London had done little to calm his fears, and now that he was finally facing the admiral, there seemed no very polite or intelligent way of putting the matter to him.

"My niece?" riposted the admiral on a note of surprise. "What the deuce do ye mean, halfling, for if ever—"

"Please, my lord," interrupted the young viscount, "there is no time to waste. I have just ridden from the New Forest."

"Ay," agreed the admiral disparagingly, "ye have the look of it. Now, if you don't mind, will you please tell me why?"

"I am trying to do just that," answered Pauly, putting his hand through his windblown locks. His hat he had lost somewhere between London and the New Forest.

Sir Warren had in the interim poured a snifter of brandy, which he now placed into the young viscount's hands. "Buck up, lad, and try if you will to tell us calmly what is wrong."

Pauly (who had a dislike of Sir Warren) eyed him a moment but took up the glass gratefully. "Obliged . . ." he managed before gulping the fire liquid down and starting once more. "Sir, we have reason to believe that your niece has been abducted." There, it was out!

"The devil you say!" returned the admiral, thoroughly astounded by this disclosure.

"Abducted?" stuck in Sir Warren, frowning darkly. "By whom? How?"

"How can this be? Her great-aunt sent me word that they go on tolerably well."

"So they did, but nevertheless, Jess has been abducted!" returned Pauly portentiously.

"Damn it, man! You can't go about claiming such things without giving over the facts!" returned the admiral.

"All I know . . . is that . . ." Here he hesitated, not wishing to advise the admiral in front of the prime minister and Sir Warren that Jess had gone to Rodrigo's ship of her own volition. Carefully he chose his words. "She was seen on board the *Amistad,* which is Don Rodrigo's yacht, and that vessel sailed early this morning, and as Jess has not returned home, we can only assume . . . Indeed, the flunky who had charge of her horse was certain that Jess was still on board when the ship disembarked!"

"Upon my word!" breathed the admiral, stunned.

Sir Warren's eyes narrowed into slits. He felt a wave of hatred stretch through him as he thought of his intended bride perhaps even now in the arms of the Latin rogue. It was not that he was moved by love. It was that she was his chosen piece of property, a coveted treasure he did not mean to share with any other man. He stepped forward, and his tone was ice. "If this turns out to be so, then Don Rodrigo is as good as dead!"

Chapter 4

Lady Jessie stood on deck leaning against the bulwarks, ignoring the spray of the waves as the wind played in soft harmony with the sea. All was peaceful now between heaven and ocean. Hardly was there a trace of the fury that had raged only a few days before. A few days? Five, to be exact. She had been at sea for five days!

The first two they had spent wildly, for the gale had taken them into its fury, tossing and teasing them alternately in unreasonable fashion. It had been two days of on-and-off spurts of temper as the hurricane would swirl around them, keeping them off course. In those two days she had managed to stay out of Don Rodrigo's way. Indeed, she had scarcely seen him. Every single man had been needed during the storm, and they had taken shifts to eat and sleep, doing little of either. During that time Jessie had found her niche, helping Cook with the serving of the meals, the sewing of sails, the preparing of dry clothing for the men. All through this each man came to question her presence, to wonder silently about the answer, and to accept her as a part of their team. That she, in some manner, belonged to their captain they took for granted, but her bright smile, her undeniable beauty, her boyish antics in the clothes she had adopted, put them at ease.

She stood now, her long thick waves of flaxen gold caught by the wind. With her buckskin jacket tugged tightly around her, Antonio's white sailor's belled pantaloons tied up around her small waist by a red satin sash, she cut quite a picture.

She was lost in thought. The ocean dipped, peaked, sweetly, calmly, allowing her to use it as a backdrop for her thoughts. What was she to do? Her reputation was gone. What had Shakespeare's Othello said? "Reputation, reputation, reputation! O! I have lost my reputation. I have lost the immortal part of myself, and what remains is bestial." Ironically, she had come upon those words only last night when she had been lazily scanning the pages of this tragedy. Well, she grimaced, like the moor, she had "lov'd not wisely, but too well."

The question returned, what to do? Don Rodrigo hardly acknowledged her presence. He had given over his bedroom quarters to her and had taken to sleeping in his stateroom. Now all questions seemed to loom above her head, for it finally dawned on her that there was no easy going back. She could not force Rodrigo to sail back to England with her, and even if he did, ye gods, what trouble and scandal she would cause her family. No, it was better that she make no further fuss about traveling on to Argentina. What then? Marriage with Don Rodrigo was unthinkable under their present strained relationship. Why, he did not even want her as a woman any longer.

Last night there had been a moment when she thought he might make some attempt to have her. She had lain in his canopied bed, staring into the dark, feeling the gentle roll and pitch of the vessel, listening for him. He had been restless in the adjoining room. She had seen the lamplight go off and then through the cracks in their connecting door she had seen that he had relit it. She heard him pace, pull out a chair, and probably sit at his desk, but he had not come to her.

"Ah, *señorita*, you are looking so sad." It was Antonio who had from the start fallen a victim to her smile and declared himself her slave. It was a puppy's worship, nothing more, and Jessie, touched by it, extended an easy friendship to him.

"Do I? I am not, you know, so don't fret, Antonio. I am fine," she answered, touching his arm.

His hand covered hers for just the space of a moment. "Yes, but always you laugh, you giggle. But just now you were far away and your heart was in your eyes and it—it was crying." His voice was soft.

She pursed her lips and put her hands on her hips, looking at him archly. "Now, Antonio, I didn't know you had the soul of a poet. Listen to you! La, but I declare I should grab a quill and jot that down." She opened her violet eyes wide. "Look again, my bucko, do you see any tears?"

Doubtfully he answered, "No, not now, but . . ."

"But nothing, sir. Come, have you had your breakfast yet, for I swear I could eat a dozen eggs, I am so famished."

He laughed out loud and bent his arm. "Cook will be much pleased to hear it. He says you ate naught at dinner and shakes his head saying, bah, *los ingleses*, when he thinks of the wonderful food you spurned."

They laughed together and made their way to the companion stairs. Neither was aware that Don Rodrigo, standing at the bow, had managed to turn just enough to watch their interchange. He couldn't hear any of what was said, but he had not missed the affection that passed between his first mate and . . . and the woman he now intended to wed.

He frowned in supreme irritation. Damn, but at every turn she surprised him. After all, here she was, away from home and in a difficult situation. He had not been exactly gallant the last few days, and yet she managed to get on with his crew (without the benefit of introduction) and she managed to stay in lively spirits. She maintained a smile and kept Antonio at her beck and call and, hell and fire, she managed to reach his soul without saying a word!

It was impossible. He would not be fooled! She had come on board to push him over the edge. She had succeeded. Right then, she had him where she wanted him; why, then, did she say she would not marry him? He had dissected the problem carefully. She had been a virgin, captivated by him, so upon hearing that he was leaving England she rushed from her great-aunt's home to see him one last time. Very well, that meeting had led to the inevitable, for she was as passionate as she was beautiful, and their mutual attraction had taken them to the bedroom. He sneered to himself. She had no doubt expected this and thought to force marriage on him. Yet she said she was betrothed to Sir Warren.

Ah, bah! He growled out loud. There was no understanding this girl! Look at her. She seemed unconcerned about her future. She seemed unconcerned about . . . never mind. Perhaps she meant to tease him with her refusal to wed him. Perhaps she realized that she had no choice and meant only to put up a front? Of course. That was it. Well, he would let the chit know that he was not a schoolboy whom she could play her games upon!

Admiral Stafford, Earl of Redcliff, stood on the quarter-deck of his flagship, *Britain*, and looked out at the small, busy ship-building village of Bucklers Hard. Some days had passed since the young viscount, Paul Bellamy, had interrupted his meeting with Prime Minister Pitt and given over the shattering news of Jessie's abduction.

He had rushed to the New Forest, to his Aunt Charlotte, to confirm this news and found it to be true. The Latin rogue, Don Rodrigo, had indeed sailed off with young Lady Jess. It was incomprehensible. So it was that he had sent word to Pitt accepting his commission to sail to Buenos Aires. Damn, but no Latin would run off with his niece and live to boast about it.

He looked around his warship. It was impressive. It sported 37 guns and 1100 men, all fit and able to take on all of South America. Ah, Jess. Sweet, pretty Jess, with her entire life ahead of her. How had such a thing happened? Why would Don Rodrigo abduct her in this underhanded way? Plague take the devil's soul. The odd thing was that the admiral had liked the Latin. He had liked and respected the man. How could he have been so wrong?

Sir Warren had gone into a white rage. He had declared himself Lady Jessica's champion and announced his intention of accompanying the admiral on his expedition. At this recollection the admiral's eyes narrowed. Of course, if they were successful, it would be a great boost to Warren's political career.

Then there was the lad, Pauly. Jessie's friend. He had made it obvious that he did not trust Sir Warren to see Jess safely out of this ugly business. Bluntly he had offered, "There is the chance, my lord"—Pauly had taken the admiral aside—"that Jess won't have Sir Warren. . . ."

The admiral remembered the look in the young viscount's pale blue eyes and puzzled at it. "Is there something you are not telling me?"

"Well, the thing is . . ." Pauly had started, then, thinking better of it, decided against confiding in Jessie's uncle all his suspicions. "The thing is, I mean to make this trip with you. After all, it was my fault Jess went to see Don Rodrigo on board his ship, and if she won't take Sir Warren's offer, she'll take mine!"

The admiral closed his eyes now. His poor Jess. Was she still his vibrant, sweet treasure, or had the Latin rogue broken her spirit? Damn Don Rodrigo to Hades! He would see his heart cut out for this piece of work. How could he bear it if he looked into Jessie's eyes and found her broken? No! She could weather anything, his Jess. She was strong enough to cope. She had to be. . . .

*　　*　　*

Beautiful in repose. Gentle in her sadness. Lonely in her uncertainty. Jessie sat on Don Rodrigo's canopied bed, her slender legs folded under her hips, her alluring form concealed in the length of Rodrigo's dark print dressing gown. Her long buttercup shining hair fell all around her waist as she pulled a hairbrush through its lengths.

The flame from the whale-oil lamp was reflected in the deep recesses of her dark violet eyes. Broken? No, her spirit was not broken, but it had certainly received a beating. They had been at sea nearly two weeks. She had managed to befriend most of the sailors on board, and had been of considerable help to the cook daily, as they took inventory of their stores. More often than not, however, she took her meals alone in her cabin (by order, of the captain) and found herself alone, like this night, immediately after dinner.

Now and then she could hear him in the next room, where he had set up a sleeping cot. From the glimmer of light she could see through the crack between floor and door, she knew that he was up still and probably working at his desk. On one occasion she had worked up the courage to interrupt him during one of these late-night sessions. He had been curt and very nearly rude, dismissing her in fine style. She had not attempted to approach him for company since.

The one question that seemed to pop into her mind the last few nights was *Didn't he want her?* It had been two weeks since their lovemaking, and that had been a magic thing she still could not totally understand. A major part of her mind revolted against herself. She still wondered how she had allowed herself to lose control, and she did a nice job of raking herself over the coals. Then there were the questions, inevitable in her inexperience. Hadn't she been adequate as a woman? Hadn't she pleased him? Was she so very resistible that here, out at sea, after two weeks he still made no attempt to have her again?

It didn't matter, did it? She had quite made up her mind to say him nay if he tried, yet she wanted him to try. She wanted the satisfaction of turning him away. She wanted, oh, how she wanted, but he just didn't seem interested. He was always busy at something. There was a knock at her door and in some wonder she responded, "Y-yes?" Her brow was up, her emotions were in hand, and her determination to save her pride maintained her façade of coolness.

He had already opened the door. This was the first time he had ever extended himself on her behalf, and as he took in the sight of her on his bed, he felt a shiver run through him. This was absurd! With more politeness than friendliness he said, "Cook has sent some refreshment. I thought, since you were still up, you might like to take dessert with me." *Certes!* Those violet eyes were dangerous. He would have to remember not to look too deeply into them.

Faith! she thought as she looked at him in his open-necked shirt. He was so magnetic, but so arrogant! What was he trying to do, ease a guilty conscience? Night after night he had left her alone, and here he was offering kindness. How very magnanimous of him. "Now, why would I want to do that?" she answered in freezing accents.

His temper flared. He calmed it with logic. After all, he had been purposely avoiding her. He had ruled that she eat dinner alone and then remain in her cabin afterward. He tried charm. "Cook will be devastated. It is my firm belief that the chocolate confection he whipped up was in your honor."

She cocked a brow. "Oh? Why do you think that?"

"Because I heard you tell him this morning that you love chocolate above all other sweets."

The smile came to her lips, but she remembered her grievances and banished it almost immediately. "Then I will have my dessert in my cabin . . . where I had my dinner."

Again his temper tickled his blood, but no, if marry her he must, then have her he would. "Then I will bring the tray to you here and we can explore its delicacies on my bed." His dark eyes twinkled devilishly.

Startled, she scurried to her feet. "Never mind. You needn't go to such trouble. I will join you in your cabin."

His eyes roamed over her. She was enticing in the silk of his robe. He could see her pert nipples peeping at him through the material. He allowed his gaze to linger so that she would have no doubt of his intentions as he raised his dark eyes to her face.

So. He had decided to have her, eh? The question came to her mind with a snap. Well, well. This would prove interesting, because now, now, she had no illusions to coat the moment. A smile curved her lips, but had he known her better, he would have seen the steel in her violet eyes.

He felt her body as she brushed past him. He found the scent of her sweetly intoxicating, and he knew himself dangerously stirred. This would not do. He had to be in control. He would conquer the sensations she aroused in him. He sustained this intention by drawing on his ability to make light and easy conversation. All the while, he made himself busy at the table tray, where a marvelous chocolate cake took center stage.

Glibly he teased her about Cook as he made elegant work of cutting her a handsome wedge and delivering it before her with a flourishing bow. She was seated at the linen-covered round table. There was the candlelight casting its shades over her beautiful face, and the room was filled with the aura of romance, of expectation. This occurred to her, and she lowered her lashes over the thought, afraid to meet his inquiring eye.

"So . . ." he continued as he put a plate of the same down for himself and took up a chair opposite her, "it would appear that even my old cook has succumbed to your many charms, for this confection must have taken some doing with the limited means he has on board."

She smiled. "He is so funny and has managed to keep me busy taking inventory with him these past few days. He says we must sight land soon and make a stop to replenish our supplies."

"And when you are not with Cook, there is always Antonio," he said on a dry note. "Indeed, you have a knack, *querida*, for how Antonio finds the time is more than I can fathom."

She frowned. "I should think that Antonio would be allowed a moment or two, sir, to amuse himself." She was on the defensive and did not think what her words might portend.

"And is that what he does in his spare time, amuse himself with you?" The question scorched his lips.

She put up her chin. "Some people find me good company." The meaning behind his query had not yet hit her.

"I do not doubt it, madam!" he answered her harshly, fully aware that she was evading him in her innocence. He didn't know what to make of her yet. There were moments when the devil lit in her eyes and she teased him across the ship's deck. There were times when he could swear she invited him with the provocativeness of her moves to reach for her. There were other times, more so lately, when she never seemed to look his way at all, yet he would always find her laughing pleasantly with Antonio. She stirred his jealousy as no other woman had ever stirred it before. It was a feeling he did not enjoy, would not admit to, and willed himself not to feel!

"Then what is all this heat?" she found herself asking. "Why should it annoy you if I dispel the loneliness of this voyage by befriending Antonio?" She didn't wait for an answer, but sighed. "In some ways, he is much like Pauly."

He frowned over this, for her statement and her sigh of longing did little to assuage his ruffled temper. He didn't know what he was looking to hear from her, but thus far, he had not found it. "And so, perhaps he is, but as I recall, there was an evening when I could not help but notice that you and your young viscount were most—intimate." He was speaking about the night he had seen her in Pauly's arms in the carriage. "I will not allow such behavior with my first mate."

There, he had done it! He had struck home with these words as no others would have done. She felt the blow, but bolstered herself in spite of its force. She was up like a queen, drawing strength from herself, putting on a look of utter disdain as she pushed away the plate of cake. Her violet eyes flashed with her temper, with the contempt she wanted him to see. How dare he? He thought she had dallied with Sir Warren and Pauly alike? How could the thought have touched his brain? What sort of man was he? She bristled, but her tone was perfect as she retaliated. "Oh?" Her finely shaped brow rose. "Well then, sir, do tell me—and quickly, if you please, for you must know my hot blood will not wait. With whom will you allow me to be . . . intimate?"

He was at her in the devastation of that moment. He felt fire touch and burn his heart. His grip was around her slender arm and his dark onyx eyes were bright and hard with his rage. He had pulled her to him and his head was bent to-hers, his voice a low growl. "Hot-blooded, are you, wench? Damn your traitorous heart! But you *were* virgin and *I* was the one who spilled that blood, so I will be the one to give you a name, but mark me, woman, no other shall ever touch you!"

"Really?" she countered. She would not be frightened by him, though her knees trembled and her heart quaked. "How, then, shall I make up for your neglect?" What was she doing? As soon as the words were out, she realized how he would take them. What was she inviting?

"Neglect is it, jade?" Somehow his tone had altered but his hands were rough as he pulled her closer still, as his arms encircled her and his mouth closed on hers.

She felt his lips singe her own before they parted to

allow him more. Oh, faith, what was she doing, melting to him in this way? She put up a hand and made some feeble attempt to stop him.

He was wild and he was in heat. He wasn't even aware that her hand pushed at his chest. Her kiss thrilled him, spurred him on, as did the feel of her pliable, alluring body against him. He had to have her. That was all that mattered. Only that thought was in his head. Now she had to be his. His handling was deft yet laced with a certain riotous force. His skill was natural as he tore away the silk robe from her body and exposed her breasts to his dark eyes. "Ah, Jess, and so your hot blood matches my own."

She was pulling away. "Stop it! Rodrigo, stop . . . I don't want you to . . ."

He laughed, and it was a harsh sound of disbelief. "Don't you, *gatito*? Don't you?" Again he had her in hand, pressed her naked form to him as his hands teased her breasts, played with her nipples, and his lips made sweet love to her mouth.

She had to stop him. How would she stop him? He felt so good. His kiss was so right. No. She couldn't allow herself to be this weak now. If she allowed him, he would have the upper hand and she would be nothing but his slave. She found the strength somehow and pulled hard and free. *"No!"* she screamed at him, and fled the room.

He stood a moment, staring with disbelief after her, for she had closed and locked their adjoining door. He could break it down and demand his rights. His rights? He wasn't her husband. She wasn't his wife. He had no rights. Damn it to hell! He was on fire and it was a fire of her making!

On the other side of the door, Jessie leaned. Her robe was on the floor of the cabin she had just left, and she stood shivering in the dim light, but it was not from cold that she trembled. She couldn't believe what had just happened. She put a hand to her forehead and moved across the room to her bed, picked up the quilt, and wrapped it around her, standing still, marveling that he hadn't broken down the door and charged in after her.

Her fault. He had attempted to ravish her, but it was her fault. Something inside of her had taunted him to it. She had teased him to the point and now, in the quiet of the room, she knew that she had wanted him. Yes, fool that she was, she had wanted him to take her in his arms, to kiss her, to touch her. No, oh, no, this would never do. She had stopped him, though. That was something. Wasn't it? Well, wasn't it? An interesting question but at that moment she just didn't have the answer.

Chapter 5

Northwest of Buenos Aires, the San Jacinto Estancia, the Cesares's rancho, lay in regal measure and thrived just as Don Rodrigo's great-grandfather had envisioned. Cattle in stupendous numbers ranged and grazed idly on its rich green plains. Gauchos worked the herd, broke horses, tanned leather, and played in high glee on a land that was as wild as their natures.

Don José Cesares contemplated a group of these half-Indian, half-Spanish cowboys as they sucked yerba maté through silver tubes thrust deep into brightly colored gourds. Wild, hungry renegades, these gauchos, and always he found himself admiring their indomitable spirit. He watched a servant's children as they ran barefooted out of their play area and were quickly called to order by their mother. His was a prosperous ranch, yet he knew something was missing. He sighed. Just now it was Rodrigo that was missing!

His son. Bold, free-spirited, and in recent years touched with a cynicism Don José could not like. It was not a surprising thing, considering the circumstances of the boy's youth. Women had not been kind in Rodrigo's eyes. First there had been his mother, but Don José pushed all thought of her away. It was no longer painful, after all; it had been fifteen years since her going, fifteen years. He frowned and blocked her memory as he looked down at his useless legs. Ten years since his stroke had left him in his wheelchair, but why was he thinking of that now?

"José?" It was a sharp sound. It was his cousin, Julia, and he turned his head, to find her ambling down the red brick walk toward him. "José, what are you doing here? I have been looking all over the grounds. You know Emmanuel is coming. You must sign the papers."

"Emmanuel! He is a pig," returned José gruffly. "Why do you foist the fellow at me?"

"He is your solicitor and he handles the estate for you while your son gallivants through his precious England!" Her double chin was accentuated as she stiffened over her words.

"My son works for his country!" snapped her brother with a reddening of his face.

"Your son should be here, attending to his lands. He should marry, have children." She put her hands on her wide hips as she scolded.

"Ah, so that is it! You want him for your Maria and he will not comply . . . and no, I am glad of it, for your Maria is not woman enough for him!" He didn't mean to be so harsh, but Julia had a knack of bringing out the worst in him and rousing it to a peak. He could remember still how she gloated when his wife had left all those years ago.

"How can you?" she gasped. "Maria is an angel. She would make him an excellent wife, bear him many sons. . . ."

He sighed, tired now. "Enough, Julia, enough. Wheel me indoors, will you? I will await your precious Emmanuel there."

There wasn't a cloud in the sky. Blues of all shades mingled into a heaven that softened sore eyes and assuaged weary minds into restfulness. A bright sun glimmered high overhead as the *Amistad* sailed through gentle waters.

Antonio looked at Jessie's profile and felt himself stirred. She was so very beautiful with her long, loose flaxen hair blowing away from her creamy face. She looked out at sea, playing the game with him, giggling now and then in a musical lilt that went delightfully through him. Here was the danger. He was more than just a bit infatuated with her and it would not do. Mercy! It would cause him a great deal of trouble if Don Rodrigo were to notice, for she was the captain's woman, wasn't she? Herein lay the problem. His infatuation with her was spurred by the fact that he could see she was neglected. He wanted to comfort her, see to her needs, assuage her loneliness. It was obvious that the captain did not mean to attend to the lovely. It was a strange thing, but he was not in the captain's confidence. Indeed, he had never known Don Rodrigo to confide in anyone.

"There! Look there!" cried Jessica merrily as she pointed out to sea. "Don't deny that is a sail, Antonio. That makes three ships I have spotted in two days. You are not doing very well."

"That is because I am blinded," he answered softly.

She turned and eyed him quizzically. She was fully aware that he was a bit taken with her and meant to steer his feelings into friendship. "Antonio," she answered him, her tone that of someone older than he, more experienced than he, "you are an accomplished flirt, my friend. I am sure the girls in Buenos Aires are all pining for you by now."

"They are nothing," he returned impatiently, "my lady Jessica. How can I tell you—"

She cut him off. "No, Antonio. You *may not* tell me." Her eyes were soft, and she patted his cheek with her open hand to sugar-coat the words.

Don Rodrigo's dark eyes snapped, as did his temper. He could stand no more! Sharply his steps brought him to Jessica. Scaldingly he drew his first mate to order.

"Antonio! I am certain there are things you may find to occupy your time that would better *serve me!*"

Antonio turned a deep shade of red, lowered his head, and in some embarrassment hurried off. He was in the wrong of it. He coveted his captain's woman. He had neglected his duties, though it was one of those days when the men were able to take it a bit easier. Some were gathered below, in fact, playing at backgammon. Still, there was paperwork he had put off, all because he wanted time with Lady Jessica. This was unpardonable, but even so, how could Don Rodrigo demean him so? He had never done so before. Yet his life he had long ago pledged to his captain, and he saw himself totally in the wrong of it.

Lady Jess met her captain with different feelings, mixed emotions, but she met him with every intention of giving measure for measure.

"You are a boor!" she snapped. "There was no reason to speak to Antonio like that."

"How I speak to members of my crew is my own business!" he answered on a low hiss. "How I choose to speak to you will be for *you* to determine."

She frowned uncertainly. "What do you mean, Captain Cesares?"

"We may conduct our affairs here, or below, your choice, but speak to you, madam, is what I intend to do now!"

They had not been alone since that night. Four days had passed. She felt herself go hot at the memory, and she lowered her violet eyes.

"I don't think we have anything to discuss, sir," she answered quietly, reluctant to converse with him on deck before the crew and unwilling to go below with him.

"I, on the other hand, feel that we have a great many things to discuss. We will be in Buenos Aires in a few days' time, and I want certain matters settled before then." He waved his hand for her to precede him.

"I don't wish to go to your cabin with you," she

responded, and managed to raise her violet eyes to his face.

His dark eyes discovered the deep hue of hers, and their gazes locked for a moment before he answered her. "Nonetheless, madam, you will do so."

Faith! The man had gall! He didn't even promise to behave. He didn't promise her anything. She squared her shoulders. "I don't think so, sir." She could be just as stubborn.

He released an oath and a moment later she was scooped up in his arms and his lips were near her ear. "You may make a scene, my dear. That is up to you. It will not matter, for they are my men and will do naught to interfere with my . . . pleasures."

"Fiend!" she breathed, her cheeks flushed, her violet eyes flaring.

"Yes, you would do well to remember that," he answered her, taking on the companion stairs, seemingly unhampered by her weight.

She held tightly to him, for he had the air of a man who would gladly throw her the distance to get her where he wanted. She glared, she seethed, and she gritted her teeth. Once again he was taking over. Oddly enough, the answer that suggested itself to her mind created a delightful shiver of anticipation in her body. No, she shouted at herself. No. She couldn't, wouldn't, allow herself to soften in his regard. He was a boor, a cad, a deceitful dark-eyed devil, and he had broken her heart. He should not have taken her knowing that he did not love her. He should not have done that. After all, he was the experienced one. He should have had control! But no, he had decided to add her to his list and she, fool and blind, she had allowed it to happen. She was still as much enraged with herself as she was with him.

There was no time for further thought on the matter as she found herself roughly deposited on the sofa he had been using for a bed in the last three weeks. As she scrambled to her feet he took two long strides and locked his hall door, and then he was turning to eye her up and down.

It was here that they took measure of each other. She could see, much to her mental discomfort, that he was looking more than dashingly romantic in his open-necked white shirt. It displayed his broad chest and wide shoulders to advantage, as did his tight buff-colored britches. She raised her eyes and discovered his glistening waves of long black hair had fallen across his forehead in a most engaging fashion. Quickly she looked away, not wanting to meet his dark eyes.

In that same flashing moment he found a fair-haired minx, an alluring vixen in boy's clothing. Her long flaxen hair fell loosely to her small waist. Her lips were full, rosy, and pursed with her determination. Her violet eyes were rich with their color, glinting with her wrath, and it amused him, coaxed him into a softer mood as his gaze traveled down her slender neck to the curves of her body. Her breasts were full, high, and heaving with her agitation. Her nipples, hard now, were pertly pressing against the white linen of her open-necked shirt, and he found himself aroused and yet strangely angry with her. Hell, but it was damned indecent of her to walk around like that! "Look at you!" he spat before she was able to utter a word. "It's a wonder Antonio hasn't raped you by now, the way you flaunt your body at him!"

She went rigid, turned a deep shade of red, and felt her body go hot with sudden embarrassment as she realized he was looking at her breasts through the material of her blouse. Was the shirt that transparent? She had worried about it when she chose not to wear her coat because of the warmth of the day. "I do no such thing," she managed to answer him. "And so he has no such thought."

"And what do you know of his thoughts, of any man's thoughts?" he sneered. "Damnation, woman! Look at you!" He took her shoulders and swung her around to the dark-wood-framed long mirror.

She could see herself with the sun's rays streaming through the porthole, and indeed, he was right: the contours of her body were all too visible. But suddenly his voice changed as he stood behind her, and before she knew what he was about, his arms were around her and his hand was moving up from her waist and taking firm hold of her breast. "That's what you tease a man to—" He was turning her around, bending her to him as he gently played with her nipple and his lips met hers, parted them, and took her mouth in a kiss that sent them both into a bevy of emotion.

No! Her mind recoiled from his touch. *No!* Her logic shouted down the fire that threatened. "No," she heard herself say as she forced herself to pull out of his hold, but her voice sounded as unconvincing as her rationale did to her heart. She wanted him; oh, how she wanted him.

He stared hard at her, attempting to regain power over himself. Here was a woman, and at the moment he needed a woman, but more than that, he was suddenly aware that he needed *her*, this rumbling vixen, this Lady Jessica! It was a startling realization, and he was not pleased with it. "No, my Jess? Indeed, if you do not wish a man to so use you, then do not invite him. . . ."

"I—I did not invite you to take a liberty with me," she answered, her lashes lowering and shading the doubt in her violet eyes.

He tugged at the sleeve of her shirt. "When you sport your body for all to see, *you invite*," he said firmly. "Especially on board a ship whose crew have not had the opportunity to . . . er . . . enjoy other women."

"It was too hot for my coat," she answered simply, still not meeting his eyes.

He took her chin. "Too hot for the vest I left you in your room?"

She blushed, for, defiantly, earlier that morning, she had taken the vest and flung it away as soon as he had left it with her. She had been angry with him for attempting to rule what she should or should not wear, but she could see now that he had a point. Indeed, she had noticed one or two of the crewmen casting her an over-long gaze. For answer she said quietly, "I—I will wear it now, sir."

He was surprised at her easy capitulation. Had he found a way to tame the vixen? Did she so hate him that she would do as she was told to avoid his touch? He felt oddly irritated by the notion.

"And my lady Disdain so easily surrenders?" He could not help the taunt.

She was in no mood to stand there and fight with him, not with her heart beating so wildly and her body yearning for his hands to explore it. "No, I merely acknowledge . . . good sense." She managed to take a step away from him.

He reached out for her arm. "Jess?" His voice was a caress, for he wanted her so badly, he could taste her lips still. He needed her in his arms.

"*Land ho!*" was bellowed out in Spanish, and the bell was clanged in furious accord. "*Land ho!*"

He was caught by the new urgency. It would be the South American coast that had been sighted. They needed supplies, for it would be another four days' journey to Argentina and they were low on food and out of fresh vegetables and fruit. Without another word he had turned on his heel and left the room.

Land? The excitement of putting her feet on something that would not sway banished all despondency as she rushed to get the waistcoat and follow him on deck.

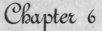

Some hours had passed since the first sighting of land, and Lady Jessica was surprised to find Don Rodrigo solicitously, almost possessively, standing beside her during the busy affair of docking. Quietly, with a hint of excitement, he gave her some history about the port, El Salvador.

"There are some who consider this the oldest city in Brazil." His dark eyes softened at her wide-eyed expression as she looked around, trying to take in everything in one sweep. "Look there. That is a merchant vessel taking sugar and tobacco to Portugal and France. In return, El Salvador manages to acquire a nice array of finery. I mean to take you to a dress shop or two."

She stiffened at once. She didn't want him buying her a thing. What was she, a kept woman? How humiliating. "That," she said tartly, "will not be necessary."

He laughed, understanding at once. "Oh, but it is, *gatito*. I can not, after all, present you to my family in your present raiment."

She blushed and reluctantly cast an eye over the boyish attire she still wore. It was quite true. She couldn't go about in britches and boots. She relented a smidgen. "Very well, but you will present me with all bills, which I will be pleased to turn over to my uncle upon my return to England. He will, of course, reimburse you for everything.''

Don Rodrigo's resolve to be gentle was cast aside. His brows drew together. ''And *that* is a very nice opinion you have of me! Damnation, woman! Do you think, after taking you across the Atlantic, I mean to return you to your uncle ruined and hand him a wallop of bills as well?'' He shook his head. ''No, my kitten. You made your bed—'' a smile curved his lips in spite of his ruffled temper—''and now 'tis time you dealt with it.''

''I intend to, but not as your wife!'' was all she could think to answer him.

He considered her for a long moment. ''No?'' He shook his head. ''As it happens, I don't want a wife, but a sense of honor leaves me with no choice, and, my girl, if I have none, you have less!''

She had turned away from him. She had been frustrated, irritated, and very near to tears. To be married out of a sense of honor? To have a man take her as wife out of pity was beyond anything she had ever thought she would have to endure. All pride stuck in her throat, and then what page must she turn to later in her room, but Byron's words:

Away! Away! my early dream,
Remembrance never must awake:
Oh! where is Lethe's fabled stream?
My foolish heart, be still, or break.

What she wouldn't do for a drink of Hades's river now so she could forget Rodrigo's dark eyes and devastating smile.

His words *I don't want a wife . . . a sense of honor* . . . came back to her now as she sat in the dressmaker's shop and watched him flirt outrageously with the proprietor, Madame Rinaldi. Lady Jessica's violet eyes considered the plump, attractive, and sophisticated woman as she batted her lashes at Rodrigo and spoke in soft accents.

There was something in the manner of their conversation—Italian, she thought as she caught a word here and there—but it was the way their eyes met that made Jessie think Madame Rinaldi and Rodrigo were old friends.

Jessie frowned and turned away from the laughing pair. How could she bear it? His open dalliance with the woman was cruel. Marry him, indeed! What, so that he could keep her home with a brood of children while he careened over the countryside. Ha! Ruined, she might be, but it was preferable to being saddled with such a rake for a husband!

The woman in Jess couldn't help but notice as she moved restlessly about the shop that the gowns were certainly designed in the first stare of fashion. It was clearly evident that the rich silks, brocades, satins, frothy muslins, and organzas had come straight out of Paris (aided no doubt by a Spanish privateer) to this busy seaport.

Madame Rinaldi cast only a curious eye at the petite figure in boy's clothing, for she was fully occupied in her attempt to intrigue with her old flame. Jessie could see them from a corner of her eye and made a brave attempt to ignore the sensations their play aroused in her breast. Then suddenly his quiet, firm voice was near, so very near, and she thought she felt his lips brush her ear as he spoke.

"Here, *gatito*, put this on."

Affection? Was that affection in his voice? Nonsense, she answered herself at once. That was certainly an emotion he did not feel for her. Did he? No. Hadn't he proved it over and over again in these last three weeks. Why, he had scarcely looked her way.

She turned halfway and stopped as she found herself very nearly in his arms. Her violet eyes scanned his face before she could stop herself, and her glance discovered that his dark eyes held an expression to match his tone. It was absurd how her knees suddenly melted. A self-defense trigger went off in her mind and she went rigid against the feelings he inspired.

"Thank you," she answered him coldly. "But I think not."

His dark sharply defined brow went up. "You think not?" he returned, but there was an amused light twinkling in his eyes. "Ah, perhaps you need assistance?" His hands were already on her coat, pulling at it.

"Stop that!" she shot at him, and stepped backward. "What do you think you are doing?" This because he proceeded to pull away her coat and seemed intent on going for her shirt.

"You behave like a brat, my lady Jess, so I have no alternative but to treat you as such," he answered her glibly.

She yanked the gown off his bent arm, and her eyes blazed a fury at him. "You are insufferable!"

"So I am, my pet, and the sooner you understand that, the better it will be for you." Then without waiting for a retort from her (which was caught somewhere in her throat) he turned to Madame Rinaldi. "You will lend my lady whatever assistance she requires," he said softly.

Jessie fumed past him curtly, advising Madame that she could dress herself. The Rinaldi woman looked to Don Rodrigo, who was smiling strangely, and he allowed Lady Jess her face-saver, taking Madame's hand and saying quietly, "She will no doubt need her buttons done up. Perhaps a seamstress might go in to her."

Madame looked at him quizzically. "Most wise, my love, and understanding as well?"

He released a short laugh. "Surprised? Am I such a beast that you didn't think me capable of finer feelings?"

She arched her chin, considering. "No, but I did think your finer feelings beyond a woman's reach." She looked toward the doorway where Jessie had just passed. "That one seems to have touched them."

He didn't answer her, for at that moment from the recesses of the dressing room they heard, "*Blast!* Oooh! Double blast!"

Rodrigo chuckled and said softly, that strange light in his eyes still, "Go quickly. Send one of the girls to help her."

Maria heard her mother. "Maria is an angel. She would make him an excellent wife, bear him many sons. . . ." Well, that was precisely what she did not want to do, at least, not yet. Her hand moved from her waist and her dark eyes narrowed as she thought of Don Rodrigo. He was certainly attractive, and she had often dreamed about him, about what it would be like to have him make love to her. Yes, and she had every intention of marrying him and being mistress of this great ranch and all its wealth . . . but not yet.

She touched a long strand of thick black hair, and her dark eyes searched out the big corral until she found Varjona. She felt a quickening of her heartbeat. She was nearly eighteen and her blossoming womanhood kept her awake at night yearning for Varjona. It couldn't be. He was a gaucho, every virile inch a gaucho, and she wanted him. She moved now in his direction, swinging her yellow skirts as she swayed his way. He looked up and saw her, and his smile widened into a grin as his eyes roamed leisurely over her body. She sucked in her breath and inclined her head in a greeting.

"*Belleza,*" he acknowledged quietly, and took the two strides that put him at the weathered fencing standing between them; his dark eyes invited her to linger.

She watched the men working the wild horse in the center of the corral. "You have a job in this one," she said softly.

"Ah, but she is a filly worth the effort," he returned, his eyes twinkling.

She put up her chin. "Indeed," she answered curtly, putting him in his place and turning to walk away in haughty style. At her back she heard his laughter ring out. By all the saints, she knew that one day she and Varjona would find each other's arms, but for now she must be careful. There was Don Rodrigo and his rancho to be had first!

Chapter 7

Lady Jessica's view of the world had been limited to rural England and the bustle of London. South America was a place she had heard about, read about, but could not at first believe. She was reduced to a child full with exclamations of glee and her "ooohs," "aaahs," and, "oh, looks" were accompanied with wide-eyed violet stares that Don Rodrigo found inwardly hard to resist.

He discovered himself contemplating her during the long carriage ride, and he found himself drawn to her in a way he could not understand. Amused by her avid enjoyment of all things new, he quietly took command, giving her bits and pieces, teaching her about the land, its people, its history, and her response was eager and warm.

"What a man your great-grandfather must have been!" she exclaimed upon hearing that it was he who had sailed for Argentina and created the Cesares Rancho. "I mean, to set out from all things familiar, to leave his estates in Spain . . ."

Rodrigo smiled ruefully. "He was a second son and meant to establish his own estates, you see."

"Still, what courage it must have taken. Rodrigo, look, this is still a wild country." Her hand went to the open window expressively. "Imagine what it must have been *then*!"

He considered this for a moment. It was true—the lands, plains, and forests they had already passed through on their journey from Buenos Aires to his home were roughhewn and wild. Rich and full, certainly, but sparsely populated and barren of the civilized pleasures both Spain and England had in abundance. There wasn't time to give this thought, because Jess was now in her rough-and-tumble manner very nearly out the open window of their carriage and squealing his name in high glee. "Rodrigo, oh, Rodrigo, is that your ranch?"

He laughed out loud and reached for her trim waist, pulling her back into the carriage and down beside him in a firm, authorative fashion. "You are acting like a perfect hoyden," he admonished affectionately. "Sit down, or do you want my family to think I have brought back a mere babe from England to be my wife?"

She sobered. Perhaps she had not heard the tenderness of his tone. Perhaps she recollected the circumstances of her situation. All at once she was Lady Jessica, regal, on guard, and on the defensive. "I don't wish them to think me a child, nor do I wish them to think I am your bride. I am neither, Don Rodrigo."

"What, then? My mistress?" he returned scathingly. "Ah, yes, that will do nicely. Here, Father, I have made an English noblewoman my mistress, but don't fear; I mean to ship her back to London straight away! His sneer was marked. "Famous!"

She blushed and sought an answer to this. "Sometimes the truth is uncomfortable."

"And is it the truth?" he countered, but did not allow her to answer. "No, it is not! You have not been my mistress during this passage, and I don't mean to cart you off to London . . . having used you! I have my reputation to consider as well, little girl, and you would do well to remember that!"

She tackled the problem logically. "We could say that

. . . that we had planned to be married and . . . and decided during the voyage that we would not suit."

"Lovely!" he snapped. "And you expect my father to believe that your guardian sent you off with me unchaperoned and unwed? No, I think not."

"What, then, do you propose to tell your family?" she asked testily, "After all, I *am* here with you unchaperoned!" Why had she never considered this end of it? Somehow the notion of meeting his people had never seemed real until this moment.

"I am going to tell them that I was denied your hand in marriage, that I couldn't bear the thought of sailing without you and did the unpardonable—abducted you against your will," he answered on a grave note.

"How very gallant of you!" she snapped. "But if you think I mean to allow you to take the blame . . ."

He cut her off sharply. "My lady Jessica. I, being hot at hand, will be forgiven my lapse in conduct, as I am doing the honorable and marrying you. On the other hand, you must not be found in the wrong, and as I will not have my future wife gossiped about, you will not contradict what I choose to tell my people!"

She didn't have an immediate reply to this and chose instead to turn her attention once more to her open window. An orchard of considerable size and blossoming beauty greeted her and she sighed, all at once remembering England. However, the sigh was immediately dispelled by the sound of Don Rodrigo calling out a warm greeting to one of the gardeners. The laborer was atop a ladder that leaned into one of the large trees, and Jessie was touched by the genuine pleasure she saw on the man's face. He was really pleased to see Don Rodrigo.

Everywhere straw hats bobbed as men and women alike worked in the orchard field and then a post and rail fence divided one scene from the other and she was looking out onto pasture after pasture of grazing cattle. It was all so incredible. Then the long drive made a sharp bend and she could see the hacienda on the crest of the hill. Its name, clear in gold letters against the black iron railing at its front gate: SAN JACINTO ESTANCIA.

Magnificent and vast and, for a moment, almost frightening. What was this strange new world she was entering? And then they were passing through the gate, passing the carriage house, the stables, the fenced dirt enclosures, until she caught sight, her first sight, of working gauchos!

Maria's thick, dark hair had been plaited and wound round at the top of her well-shaped head. A touch of color had been carefully applied to her highly defined cheeks. She turned from side to side so that she could look herself over in the long dark-oak-framed mirror, but she pulled a face and pouted at her mother.

"This"—she lifted the skirts of her ivory silk—"is for a schoolgirl, Mama. How am I to captivate Rodrigo with my body all tucked away like a child's?"

Her mother clucked at her and gently touched the girl's chin with affection. "What nonsense is this? Look at you. Maria, you are a woman fully grown, and this gown suits you."

"No, Mama, the bodice is too high, the waistline too old-fashioned, the skirt too full. They do not wear such in the drawing rooms of England. Don Rodrigo has been petted and cosseted by English maids in flimsy muslins that reveal their charms. Why should he look at me when I am naught but his dowdy cousin?"

"Ah, you are nervous; that is all. This gown is just the thing. Trust me. Don Rodrigo will not want his future wife to expose herself like an Englishwoman!"

"You forget, his mama was English," Maria answered thoughtfully.

"And we know what he thinks of *her*!" answered her mother.

Maria sighed. That was true enough. From all she had ever heard Rodrigo say of his mother (and that wasn't very much), he did indeed despise the woman. "Well, at least you have allowed me to put my hair up," she conceded.

"Yes, we don't want Rodrigo pulling at it like he used to do," said her mother with a quizzical smile. "We would rather he were moved to run his hands through it."

Mother and daughter laughed in unison. Their goal was the same, and both were sure what the results of their efforts would be. The moment the servants had rushed to the house with news that Don Rodrigo's carriage had been spotted on the open road, they had put their heads together and set the house into a bevy of preparations. They would show Rodrigo that what he needed was a wife to care for the smooth running of his establishment—and what better wife than the girl, Maria, who had been brought up within its confines?

"Come, Maria," Julia called softly. "We will give Rodrigo the time he needs to greet his father and then *you* will make your entrance. He will open his eyes."

In the courtyard, in his wheelchair, with his wide-brimmed hat to shield him from the harsh rays of the sun, Don José awaited the arrival of his son. Ah, Rodrigo. His soul cried for the sight of him. His ears longed to hear the voice. His blood ached to have its own near once again. He could feel his heart beating wildly and he made some mild attempt to calm himself. His dark eyes glittered with anticipation, and the smile that curved his thin lips was reflected in the depths of his old dark eyes. Ah, Rodrigo. Home. It was good, so good. And then the carriage was coming into view.

As the hacienda loomed before him, Rodrigo grew impatient. Here was his home. Here was his father. His father. Damn, but he wanted to see that man again. How he loved him. Why wasn't the carriage moving any faster? Come on, come on!

Jessie had retreated to the protection of the inner coach. She was no longer hanging out its window. Not even the lure of the intriguing gauchos held her entranced any longer. Here they were. They had arrived. In a few moments they would be meeting his people. She would have to face his family. Faith! How could she do that? So it was that she had now sat back against the squabs and Rodrigo was the one hanging out the window.

There! He could see his father sitting in the wheelchair with the ridiculous old hat he loved to wear. He waved his hand and laughed out loud. Damn, but he looked good. He had been worrying lest he return home and find him altered, but no, there he was, looking as spry as ever! "*Mi padre!*" he yelled, and then he had the carriage door wide open and was nimbly jumping to earth before the carriage had pulled to a halt. "Papa!" He was already at his father's side.

"Rodrigo!" Don José said softly. Here was his cub. His wild, hot-at-hand lad, and he was proud, so proud.

Theirs was the touch of love that needs no words. In silence they held each other; in silence they released each other almost roughly, to stand apart and gaze. Rodrigo was on his knees still as he took his father's bent, ungloved fingers and put them to his lips. "Papa, I have brought someone with me whom you must meet." He was on his feet, avoiding his father's look of surprise as he walked to the coach and opened its door.

Inside, Jessie was watching the pair from her corner. Was this Don Rodrigo?

Here was another man, surely. She had not suspected Don Rodrigo capable of such feeling. How could she face Rodrigo's father? What would the man think of her? She blushed and felt herself hot with humiliation.

Rodrigo saw the color in her cheeks and frowned. "Come, Jess," he said softly.

There was nothing for it. She had to buck up and face the music. She bolstered herself and gave her gloved hand to Rodrigo. At least she was dressed in the very first stare of fashion, with her blue silk traveling habit and the blue confection on her head of gold curls.

Don José saw one dainty blue silk foot step out of the coach and his gray brow went up. So, what was this? It dawned on him. Could it be that Rodrigo found a wife in England? Immediately he thought of his own disastrous marriage and almost as immediately shrugged that off. A different woman, another time, extenuating circumstances. Even so, he watched Jessie intently as his son walked her the short distance to meet him. Quietly, seriously, Rodrigo said, "Lady Jessica Stafford, my future bride. My father, Don José Cesares."

Lady Jessica's curtsy was low and quite beautifully executed as she gave Don José her hand and brought up her violet eyes to meet and explore his aged ones. "I am honored," she said softly.

He smiled. "And I am not only honored, my child, but delighted as well." And then as Rodrigo took her arm and brought her up, Don José added, "My saints! She is a diamond, Rodrigo, a veritable first-water diamond!"

"Precisely, *mi padre*. All of England acknowledged her as the '*incomparable*,' so what could I do but steal her away right from under their noses?" He spoke in a lively, bantering manner and was pleased enough to see his father sparkle. However, he felt Jess stiffen beside him and touched her elbow, whispering, "Don't ruin it, my lass."

Don José was mannered enough to continue in English. "That in their teeth, eh, my son?" He nodded his head with approval and cast Jessie a penetrating look, for there was something in the air he could not quite understand. "And you, sweet child, were you willing to be off with this brute of mine, or did you find yourself whisked off willy-nilly?"

She released a short, musical giggle, for her sense of humor prompted her. "Well, now, you seem to know your son quite thoroughly, Don José, and therefore I am persuaded you have the answer to that." There, she had sidestepped the question, for she found that she did not want to lie to the man.

"What is this?" Don Rodrigo's hand went dramatically to his heart. "Torn to pieces by my father and future wife? Such treachery in my own home?"

Don José caught his son's hand and gave it a squeeze. "We are neglecting our lady Jessica, my son. Please to see that a bath is prepared for her in her rooms."

Don Rodrigo bent slightly over his father's hand, smiled, and took a step toward the house, only to pull up short at the sight of Maria and Julia in the arched entranceway. Maria he had always been fond of, for she had been careful to dote on him during his youth. Julia, too, had always held his affection, and it was with genuine pleasure that he went forward to take them both up.

Even as Don Rodrigo took his cousin into his embrace, Maria's dark eyes looked past his shoulder to give Lady Jessica a scathing greeting. What was this? His bride, she had heard him say. Impossible. Don Rodrigo and the rancho were hers!

At that moment, her mother, Julia, was thinking much the same but with more irritation than the pure hatred her daughter was already feeling for Lady Jessica. She was also too clever to display her agitation and went forward to greet Lady Jessica after she had patted and cosseted Rodrigo.

"So, what have we here?" she asked in Spanish. "An English flower?" And then to exhibit her superiority over the Englishwoman she spoke in English. "Ah, but you don't speak Spanish; come, child. I will take you to your rooms and order you a bath. You must be exhausted after your long drive." She rapped Don Rodrigo's shoulder as she pulled Lady Jessica along. "Eh, what is the matter with you, keeping your poor bride standing, my dearest dolt?" Then, to Maria, "Take your cousin about, Maria, and show him the work that was done on his stables, *sí*."

Maria laughed, linked her arm through her cousin's, and managed the moment well. All of these procedures were not lost on Don José, who sat back with a raised brow and watched most thoughtfully and with some concern. Rodrigo, however, was caught up by the fact that Maria had bloomed into womanhood and was in that space of time enchanted with her newly adopted manners.

Jessie? Ah, Jessie. She knew herself a stranger in a new land, thrown into a circle of people, all of whom had reason to resent her.

Chapter 8

Lady Jessica stood, her long, flaxen hair in loose array to her waist, her supple body encased in a soft pink wrapper, her violet eyes staring at the stone patio outside her lead-paned glass doors. Bright yellow and rich red flowers bloomed in profusion from deep-red-painted flower boxes atop the high stone wall that surrounded her private retreat. Black wrought iron chairs were prettily appointed around a table made of the same. A dwarf citrus plant gave off its captivating scent as the breeze came to her in gentle waves, but all Jessie wanted to do was cry.

She should have felt refreshed, revitalized, in control after her bath, and instead, all she felt was out of place and alone, so very alone. She did not even have Antonio now to wile away the time with his youthful conversation. Antonio had remained with the ship in Buenos Aires harbor. Pauly. What would Pauly be thinking? Odd that he should come to mind now after all these weeks. What of her Uncle? Good faith! Or should she be saying *"Madre de dios!"*

Don Rodrigo. Herein lay her problem. Every inch of her wanted him to love her. All she could think was how perfect he was for her, how he fulfilled her dreams, how he dissipated her restlessness when he was near. "I have no other but a woman's reason; I think him so because I think him so," she said out loud, quoting Shakespeare.

"And *I* think you so, because you *are* so!" said a gruff male voice in broken English.

Jessie spun around and discovered Varjona. He wore his low-crowned suede hat rakishly tilted over his brow. His black eyes gleamed in attractive contrast with his copper skin. He wore a brightly printed scarf and an open-necked yellow shirt. Around his trim waist was a wide silver belt. His trousers were a baggy linen material of buff and he sat his horse in a proud, tall manner. So, thought Jessie, here, close up, was a gaucho! How he had managed to ride so near her enclosed stone patio she did not know, but she could not help the open look of appraisal she cast over him and blushed to hear him laugh.

"Ah, me, I speak the English, but you, Lady Jessica, your tongue seems tied, *sí?*"

She smiled. "It would appear that I am bested, for not only do you speak the English, also, you know my name, while I do not know yours." It was a statement, not a question, but he took it to mean that she was interested.

He straightened, his ego inflated, and beamed proudly. "I am Varjona. My mother was Indian, my father Spanish. I learned the English from Rodrigo." He frowned. "There was a time when we were friends, but that was many years ago."

"Do you mean you are no longer friends?" she asked curiously.

"I work for his father as my father did. We are no longer boys playing boys' games."

"Perhaps that is because we are men and I no longer admire your style!" came a harsh male voice at Jessie's back.

She spun around and found Don Rodrigo coming in upon them and felt the color flood her cheeks. Varjona was on the other side of the wall, yet she felt as though she had somehow sinned. Such was Rodrigo's blazing expression.

Varjona sneered and tipped his hat. "And the hero returns home," he said in Spanish.

"To find his old playmate ever ready to stab him in the back if he could," answered Don Rodrigo in the same tongue, but this time his tone had changed subtly.

"You mistake. When I strike, and I will, your eyes will be on me," Varjona answered.

Don Rodrigo's sneer was a practiced art and outdid the gaucho's nicely. He accompanied it with a slight inclination of his head, saying with deep sarcasm, "I am honored, though I give you warning—if I can see it coming, I surely will catch the blow and return it twicefold."

The gaucho made a low, growling sound before he turned his dark roan criollo horse and took off in a ground-eating lope. All this while Jessie had been watching the two men, her small sweet lips parted in surprise. Rodrigo turned to her, and his anger was still visible in his voice and in his dark eyes. "What do you think you were doing, standing out here in"—his hand swept the air—"*in that* and allowing yourself to flirt with a stranger?"

Her chin went up and she moved off the patio to go into her room.

"I was not flirting, and besides, everyone in this country is a stranger to me . . . until I determine otherwise."

His hand shot out and found her arm. In a moment she was pulled up against him and his head was bent low, his lips hovering close to her own. "I don't want you near him . . . or near any other gaucho on this ranch. Do you hear me?"

"I hear you, Rodrigo," she answered softly. "And if you want me to obey, I shall, if you promise me something."

224

"Oh-ho!" he exclaimed in some exasperation. "The lady Disdain wishes to bargain, does she?"

She frowned. Why should he refer to her in such a way? However, she answered him all the same in a calm and collected manner. "Yes, indeed, I wish to bargain with you."

"What, then?" He was curious in spite of his rising temper.

"My freedom. I want my freedom. Book me passage on a ship bound for England. That is all I ask of you."

"A bargain, my lady, usually offers something of an exchange. Your freedom for what?" He was toying with her now because he was angry, and he was angry because . . . because . . . suddenly the question loomed— why was he angry?

"I will attend to you until I leave. I will do all that you ask if only you will let me go home." It was very near a plea, but it was calculated to shame him into complying.

He considered her and thought he knew her too well to be taken in. "So, I may take you to my bed, as my mistress, until your ship departs for England?"

She hesitated. Was he serious? Would he shame her like that in front of his family? She called his bluff. "If that is your wish, sir. I rather thought you might ask me to cooperate only in other areas."

"I am not interested in . . . *other areas*." He dragged out the words. "I want you in my bed, madam, and that is where you shall be. And you will be there as my wife!" It was quietly said, but there was no mistaking the authority behind the words. Then because his pride was pinched he said, "Why do you go on in this way, Jess? You will be mistress of this great rancho, respected and cared for by all my people." He frowned darkly. "If it is England you want, England you miss, I may permit you a visit—"

She cut him off with a loud, deep, intake of air. "*You may* . . . you *may* allow me? What? Am I your prisoner? Am I subject to your whims?" She made a fist at her side. "No, I say, and no again! I will choke as your bride. Do you hear me? I will not marry you. Rodrigo, let me go . . . or I shall run. I swear it."

This sent a shiver of fear through him. It would not do for her to try to run off on her own. This was a wild country. She would not survive. He took her shoulders. "Thank you for the warning, love, for I shall take every precaution to see that you do no such thing! Jess, I mean to do the honorable by you, and then, if you still wish to leave, you may do so. There, I have compromised. Does that please you?"

She directed a penetrating look at him. "Please me? There is little that you could do to please me." She pulled out of his hold and moved away from him.

He took a step after her, caught her hand, and forcefully brought her to him as his other hand went to her waist. "Nevertheless—" He was not allowed to finish that sentence, as the door opened at his back and a gentle voice said in shocked accents, "Oh, please do excuse me. I did not realize . . ." It was Maria, looking all innocence.

A pronounced feeling of wariness tingled through Jess as her violet eyes encountered the cold, dark eyes of Rodrigo's cousin. Maria would be no friend. To herself she sighed and moved away, but she could not help noticing that Maria's small hand touched Rodrigo's arm in a familiar manner.

"I will return to your lady Jessica later," she said in soft Spanish, her dark lashes lowered. "Please forgive the intrusion."

"Nonsense." Rodrigo's smile was genuine as he put his arm around her delicate shoulders. "You will talk to her ladyship now if it pleases you." He turned to Jessie. "As I am certain it will her. Isn't that so, Jess?"

Politely, hopefully, Jessie reached out. "Yes, of course. Do stay awhile, Maria. After all these weeks at sea with nothing but a male crew"—she broke off in embarrassment as she saw Maria's eyes widen—"well, I would enjoy getting to know you better."

Rodrigo saw the color flood Jessie's well-defined cheeks. He was aware that she suffered a moment's humiliation, but he believed that Maria was too innocent to understand the implications. He made the women his bow and so left them.

Maria waited for the door to close at his back before she turned to amble about the room, not looking at Jess, who watched the pretty girl with a troubled expression. Maria finally turned around and faced Jessie full.

"So, you have trapped my cousin, it would seem, *sí?*" She did not wait for an answer, but hurried on. "Me, I do not blame you. We must do what we must do."

Jess's brow went up and her pride came hurrying to the fore. Fists went into position, but only in spirit as she brought her hands calmly to her midriff and clasped them. "*Trapped* your cousin? Perhaps you don't fully realize the meaning of such an English word. Perhaps you might wish to use another."

Maria released a short laugh, but it was without mirth. "Ah, you are careful. *Sí*, and I, *no soy un burro*! I am not a fool."

"I am sorry," answered Jess, moving to sit down and putting a finger and thumb to her chin to consider her opponent. "Did I give you the impression that I thought you one?"

"Ah, bah! Listen to me, and listen to me well. Don Rodrigo is mine! This rancho is mine." She shook her head. "You will never have either."

"Really? Have you informed Don Rodrigo about this?" Jess drew on her inner strength and maintained a cool exterior.

"He will see for himself in the end," Maria answered with an air of self-assurance. "When he left us I was not yet out. I was still something of a child. Now he will be made to notice me, to notice that I am more suited to be

227

his wife, the mother of his children, than some English flower who will wilt in his sun."

Jess smiled, got to her feet, and went to the door. She opened it wide. "I am so very glad we had this chat, Maria. I look forward to seeing you later when we may pursue our—mutual interests."

In a huff, and with a hand on her hip, Maria made her exit. The English girl had unnerved her. How had she remained so calm? Why hadn't she been frightened? Bah! These English! They were cold-blooded beings without passion!

The viscount Paul Bellamy gazed at the ships in the distance. They were English, they were warships, and in a few hours they would be coming astern for the scheduled meeting. The viscount Beresford and Sir Home Popham, each captaining a ship, each having made a name for himself in the British Navy, would collaborate with Admiral Stafford. *They meant to capture Buenos Aires!*

This was not really what the admiral wanted to do. He was retired. He had his scruples, and these dictated that such an attack was both unethical and unwise. However, his niece had been taken by a blasted Argentinian and she must be retrieved and honor maintained.

Pauly sighed. He really didn't think declaring war on a nation was the answer, and something inside of him said that all was not what it appeared. He couldn't really believe that Don Rodrigo had abducted Jess against her will. There had to be more to it. After all, he had left London without a backward look at Lady Jess, hadn't he? Yet she was gone. What if she had snuck on board (that certainly would be like Jess to do)? Right, so there she was when the ship disembarked. Perhaps she hadn't realized it at first. Then the captain, Rodrigo, being the kind of man he was, perhaps he meant only to teach her a lesson. Right. So why hadn't he then returned her to her home? Pauly sighed again. There had to be an answer.

He looked at Sir Warren, who was doing his damnedest these days to look larger than life. Here was a political morsel for his ambition. He could make a name for himself if they were successful with their attack on Buenos Aires. Famous! There Sir Warren would be, distinguishing himself on the scene and returning the hero with Lady Jess his prize. Egad! No wonder the man was in high glee. How London would eat that up. How he would shine in Parliament. Pauly shook his head and returned his attention to the sea. Ah, Jess, poor dear Jess, where are you now, and what in blazes am I doing here? Lending sanity to the proceedings? Indeed, Paul Bellamy, he told himself, you are growing up by quick degree.

Chapter 9

A warm sun gleamed brightly in a variegated sky of rich blues. It was early morning and only the servants were up and quietly going about their chores and activities in the complex of the hacienda. Lady Jess gave herself one last scanning in the long mirror, decided the riding habit of dark brown silk that Don Rodrigo had purchased for her would have to do before she opened her door to the wide corridor.

She stood for a moment, uncertain. She knew the way to the main portion of the spacious, rambling house, but what she wanted was a discreet route of escape to the stables. She didn't want to bump into Maria, her mother, or Don Rodrigo and be badgered with questions. She didn't want to see any of them. All she wanted was to go home.

Home. Yes, at this moment her hurting pride needed to run and be assuaged by familiar surroundings and people who would love her. Last evening at dinner all fears were confirmed, all hopes banished, but she wouldn't think of that now. Now she was headed for the stables. Now she was going to ride and feel the breeze whip some spirit back into her melancholy heart.

The corridor's length was quickly put behind her; a calculated guess turned her at its end to yet another corridor and then out the lead-paned glass doors to the hacienda's court. There she hurried across its cobbled width, skipped lightly over a low fence, skirted a fenced dirt ring, and came to the red-tiled high-roofed L-shaped adobe structure that housed the family's riding mounts. There a young livery boy in dirty white linen and bare feet came running forward, chattering in Spanish.

She managed with a few well-chosen words and much mime to convey the message that she wished to ride, and he vanished, only to reappear with a flashy-looking dapple gray. The boy chattered ceaselessly as he cross-tied the horse and went about the business of tacking him up. Jess didn't understand a word, but she rather gathered from the boy's tones that he thought this gray a rather special piece of prime blood.

The gray snorted as Jess ran a hand over his sleek coat, and he appeared alert, rather eager for sport. Jess's fine brow went up, for he wasn't muscled up, and she wondered how often he had been exercised. She noted the lad had brought out a cumbersome and heavily ornate lady's side saddle and she objected gently, indicating that she wished to ride astride. The boy verbalized his amazement at so strange a request, for none of the ladies that rode at the rancho had ever done so astride. Ah, well—he shrugged—here was Don Rodrigo's English bride, and she must be honored in all things.

A man's saddle with a high horn was put on the horse, and Jess inspected it with interest, as she had heard a great deal about these saddles but had never had first-hand experience with one. She noted that the bit was a fairly strong piece with shank enough to stop the highgoer should the need arise. Right, then. They went outside. She mounted and gently asked the horse to move away from the stables.

His head was up and his body was taut under her. He was a willful creature, proud, full of fire, and determined to display these facts. Jess laughed out loud as the horse pranced beneath her. Here was a horse indeed. "Easy now, Gray . . ." she cooed softly, for he was ignoring her hands, fighting the aids she attempted politely to use with him.

Again the gelding snorted and managed to lower his head and throw out a buck of some proportions. Jessie, now serious, got a determined look in her violet eyes as she spoke to him. "Want me off, do you? No, my friend, no, I think not." She shortened her reins and worked him in a trot, but he would only dance beneath her, refusing to calm down, refusing to listen to the gentleness of her request.

She frowned as she worked him, noting the lather he was already in. "What you need, Gray, is a run. You'll still need schooling in this ring, but not now. Now I think you and I have to run." She had been working him in both directions of the ring to the growing audience of gauchos that had gathered to watch the English maid tame the Spanish blood. She looked now for the lowest portion of fence and saw that it was well over three feet, but there was an open field directly afterward. Could he jump? Would he jump? She eyed the rails at the far end of the ring. Two were set up on crates and made questionable jumps, but enough to test him over. She took him to these, paced him, and he took them in fine and willing form from nothing more than a jog.

A low hush went through the crowd of brightly clad gauchos, for here was a female who could ride! Jess forgot that she was being watched. She forgot that she was in a foreign land and that her life was in the hands of strangers. All she knew at that moment was the feel of the marvelous creature beneath her legs. All she knew was the exhilaration of putting her skills on the line as she collected his canter and brought him to the fence.

There was a moment when she questioned herself. Why jump this? You could have easily asked for the gate to be opened. Why are you doing this? He is a strange horse with little or no schooling. She dug deep into her saddle; she got her heels down, down; she shortened her reins; and she drove him. The gray knew what they had to do, and he was eager. She felt his eagerness to clear the fence, but she still did not take any chances. She dug deep into her saddle, pushing him forward, going into her release only when she felt his fores leave the ground. Then she was up with him, exhilarated with the feat, with the sensation of the flight, with the thrill of the landing. This was familiar to her, being on a horse's back, feeling one with the animal, forgetting all worldly concerns. There was only the sky, the turf, and the field ahead. That was all she had to think about, that and the wonder of the animal taking her away from her problems! The gelding was pleased with himself, with his accomplishment. Hadn't he left the confines of the fences behind? This, this was what God had intended him to do, to run free, and, oddly enough, there was a comfort emanating from the sounds of the girl astride him. There was a certain calming effect in the feel of her hand patting his neck.

Jess laughed and allowed him full rein, never bothering to check as they bounded forward. "Go, sweet Gray, go . . ." she cooed softly, whispering endearments as she watched his ears flick to the sound of her voice. Forgotten was the hacienda and its people at her back.

There was with the fineness of her jump much commotion left behind. Gauchoes gestured in considerable admiration and were vocal enough to draw the attention of Don Rodrigo as he walked with his cousin just outside the hacienda. His expression of mild curiosity changed as he followed the line of their interest and watched Lady Jessica take the gray over the fence.

Oddly enough, he felt a pang of fear that was immediately followed by a rush of indignant anger. He stepped forward instinctively, thinking she would collect the gray on the other side of the ring, but no, off she went.

"Damnation!" he cursed out loud. "You little fool!"

He followed this with a clipped, almost violent-sounding order to get his horse saddled immediately as he strode hard and fast toward the stables.

Unaware that she had left some ruckus behind, Lady Jess rode out the length of the field, took a bend into the slope of grassland, and vanished over the crest. Here was life again, and after last night's ordeal, she needed just this sort of therapy. Rodrigo. How cruel he had appeared during the evening, staring at her with his hard, dark eyes, expecting what she could not, would not, give. His aunt, sitting in superior disapproval. Maria's dark eyes touching her with unconcealed irritation. How she had upset all their lives. Only Rodrigo's father had been communicative and kind, and that wasn't quite enough.

Gently Don José had patted her hand during an awkward silence. Quietly he had said, "Give it time, my dear. They will accept."

He was, of course, speaking of Julia and her daughter. They will accept? She doubted that. Why should they? She was an intruder, and besides, she didn't want to be here, forcing herself on them. Her home was England, and her future had naught to do with Rodrigo. The unspoken thought brought the frown once more to her fine brows. The mountains loomed ahead and there was a fallen tree down. Horse and rider glided through the air in perfect grace. Accept? No, they wouldn't do that, and it wouldn't be necessary, because one way or another she was leaving!

"Rodrigo?" Maria's eyes opened wide in her attempt to engage his attention. "What has happened? Someone said that the wild gray took off with Lady Jessica."

He was irritated by the statement, and as he mounted the large bay that had been tacked up for him, he shot her an impatient answer. "Took off with Jess? No, my cousin, it was quite the other way around." So saying, he, too, put on quite an exhibition as he took his large bay over the same fence his lady had just executed, crossing the field after her in speedy pursuit.

To his men this was drama of the best cut. Nothing could have caught their interest, attention, and affection more than the romance of such a scene. Here, hadn't they witnessed a wild, young lovely (English, yes, but a beauteous free spirit) take her horse whilst riding like a man, over open country? Hadn't they seen her man in (justified) rage take off after her? Wasn't this romance? Wasn't this life? Weren't these creatures regal? King enough, queen enough, to rule? Here was truth! Such were the gauchos' statements as they cheered after Rodrigo and turned to one another to place their bets. Bets? Of course. Some thought Rodrigo would not catch her up, and allowing that he might do so, they thought she would not come back willingly, tamely. Others thought he would bring her back willy-nilly. Some thought yet another wilder scene would ensue.

It was Don José who broke this up as he wheeled himself into their midst and demanded they return to their chores. They agreed, but not a one meant to leave the vicinity as they attempted to appear busy at their work. José was not fooled, but with mild tolerance he understood. He was himself seeing a new side to his son and was rather curious about the outcome of this latest tangle with the English maid.

He sighed out loud, for this brought last evening's events to mind. How coldly his son had behaved toward his intended bride. How remote, aloof, and untouchable Lady Jessica had been. Only when he had gone to her, made a special effort to engage her in conversation, had he seen the child in her putting up the shields. So, he had thought, that is it. She is only trying to protect herself. Why? Why does she think we would try to hurt her?

He had touched her hand and softly he had asked, "What is it, little Jessica? Have Julia and her daughter been unkind?" He hadn't waited for an answer, but hurried to explain. "You must understand; they have been waiting for Rodrigo to return." Then, apologetically, "I rather think Julia thought he and Maria would make a match of it."

Jessica smiled ruefully. "They should, Don José. It would be the natural thing." She looked away. What was she doing here? It was as though he read her mind. "No, not natural, convenient, and what is convenient is not always what is in the end quite the thing one wants."

She smiled at that, "*Sí*, Don José, and what is the thing one wants is not always quite convenient." She released a light, short laughter that was infectious and caught the attention of the others at the table. Rodrigo glanced at the pair whispering at their corner and attempted to bring them into the round of conversation.

"So, Father," he said in English, establishing that all discussion would proceed in that language, "how goes the gray criollo? He was quite wild when last I saw him. Has anyone attempted to school him for me while I have been away?"

"Ha! That one!" Don José made a derisive noise with an expression to match. "Only Varjona has bothered with him and then with the greatest of impatience. Var is not one to school a horse."

Without thinking, Maria cut him off. "What do you mean, Uncle? Varjona can outride any man we have on the rancho."

Her uncle chuckled and reached out for her cheek. Her mother sat in stony silence. "Can he, my dear? No doubt you have witnessed this fact yourself."

Maria's lashes dropped and her color turned a deep shade of red.

"One cannot help but notice the obvious," she said softly.

Rodrigo grinned. "And Var has ever been obvious." It was a tease, and he was surprised to see his cousin start up and, with her hands clenched, stop herself from responding to the bait. So, what was this? Did Maria have feelings for Varjona? This disturbed him. Var was a womanizer. With his flashy good looks he had always made easy conquests. In fact, he and Varjona had often enjoyed a night on the town together, and besides, he was a gaucho. It would not do. He decided to say something in spite of a certain instinct that warned him to stay out of it. "Maria?" he whispered.

She gave him her dark eyes. "*Sí*, Rodrigo?" Her tone was soft.

"You aren't finding yourself too attracted to Varjona, are you?" He took her hand and gave it a squeeze. "I know it an easy thing for a woman to find herself taken with his charms, but he is a devil."

She beamed. "So he is, and this is the first time you have ever called me a woman."

His smile was wide. "How very remiss of me." He flicked her nose. "Forgive me. I shall take care to think of you as such in the future."

"Do, Rodrigo," she answered in quiet Spanish. She used her dark lashes with coy abandon, and though Jess had not been able to hear or understand most of their conversation, this last piece of open flirtation was not lost on her.

Jess stiffened. Don José immediately noted the fact and touched her clenched fist under the table, saying gently, "He sees only his cousin, my dear; you have naught to fear in that direction."

It was kindly intended, and Jess was sorry as soon as her curt words were out. "Rodrigo's romantic inclinations are of no moment to me."

Don José's brow went up with some surprise. "Then he has indeed achieved a wondrous match in you, for that is certainly a very liberal attitude, Lady Jessica."

She bit her lip. "Don José, forgive me, but you see . . ." She was beginning to feel ill, physically ill. How much more of this could she endure? Something inside of her churned. Her head ached unmercifully, and the bread she had stuffed in her mouth a moment ago had definitely lodged in her throat.

She was spared the necessity of finishing her sentence. As though Rodrigo knew what was toward, as though he read her mind and the confession she was about to make, he called a jest to his father and drew his attention. It was a light remark, but enough to catch his father's answering smile, and conversation was neatly shifted.

Don José recalled all this, frowning when he thought of Jess later excusing herself for her own quarters. How lonely she had appeared. How sad those large violet eyes of hers had been. Why? Hers was not the look of a maid who had sailed across the ocean to marry the man she loved. Hers was the look of a child lost—quite, quite lost.

Around Don José his gauchos laughed as they worked. Some sat along the fence, repairing *correones*, cleaning the rough-worn matras. Others worked horses that needed breaking to bridle. Still others had left already for their work on the grassland with the cattle. Gauchos. A wild, happy breed. They lived life to its fullest extent. He closed his eyes. It had been inevitable that Facón would win Rodrigo's mother, take her away. She had been so taken with the unruliness of their breed and Facón had early caught her eye. Never mind! Not now. He wouldn't think of that. Besides, Rodrigo was a different man from what he had been at the same age. Don José thought of himself, the way he had been all those years ago. A quiet, gentle lad, forever poring over books, researching antiquities. Not Rodrigo. He had his mother's lust for life. And this English child, what of her lusts? Would they suit, Rodrigo and Lady Jess?

Chapter 10

Don Rodrigo was not thinking. In fact, he had not been thinking clearly for some weeks. Always he was moved before he could reason it out. Always her violet eyes would flash defiantly and he knew he had to tame her to his will. Was this such another moment? What was he doing here, running his bay madly over the grassland in her wake? Why had he flown into the boughs? Why put on such a spectacle for all his hacienda to see?

She had not taken off over the fence and into the mountains to defy him. No, of course she hadn't. She was the same English wildflower yearning for the breeze of the meadows. Then why had he reacted so irrationally? Because, because, damnation, he answered himself, she was on an unschooled animal in a land that was unfamiliar to her. That was why. Wasn't it? Of course. So right, then, calm down. No need to catch up to her and rake her over the coals. Indeed, she was alone in this new world and deserved a bit more understanding than that. Right. Our hero was in a better frame of mind as he managed to put the open field at his back and turn up the slope for the wooded mountain trail.

Jessie, too, was in a better frame of mind. Her hair was by now a mass of flaxen gold loosely trailing at her back. Her cheeks were flushed and her dark violet eyes were alight with the exhilaration of her exercise. She had slowed the gray to a jog and was humming an English tune when the sound of another horse's snort brought her head around. There, on an intersecting mountain trail, sitting tall and quite dashingly handsome in his gaucho gear, was Varjona!

Varjona tipped his wide-brimmed low-crowned leather hat to her. His smile was broad and his eyes were appreciative as he took in the unruliness of her appearance. Again he spoke to her in English. "The lady Jessica manages Don Rodrigo's gray better than she does Don Rodrigo?"

"Perhaps I make no effort to, er, manage Don Rodrigo?" she returned, willing enough to allow his rallying her. She could see he meant to tease, and mildly wondered why.

He ignored the remark and continued. "Do all English ladies ride astride?" He was genuinely interested, for he had never before seen any of the Spanish gentlewomen do so.

She laughed. "*I* do. As for all English ladies—it would depend on circumstances and their individual inclinations." She gave him a once-over, noting that he, too, like all the other gauchos she had seen, rode with bare feet. He clutched his metal stirrup between his first and second toes and his spurs were tied around his ankles. "Do all gauchos always ride bootless?"

He drew himself up proudly. "It is manly. A gaucho is capable of many manly things."

She gave him a coy look, amused by this. "Oh, of that I am certain."

They laughed together on this note and were not aware until they heard the sound of crackling twigs under a horse's hooves that they were not quite alone. When they turned, it was to find Don Rodrigo bringing his horse to a standstill, and his mouth was set in a hard, rigid line.

240

"How kind of you to entertain my lady, Var. As always, you play the friend." Rodrigo's voice was richly steeped in sarcasm. His black eyes snapped with the fire that was burning in his limbs. "I am, however, quite sure there are other things you should be doing."

This was all said in Spanish, yet Jessie rather thought she understood every word. Certainly there was no mistaking the anger or the air of rivalry between the two men. In spite of the fact that she had naught to feel guilty about, she did feel guilty and cringed inwardly as she awaited Rodrigo's wrath to turn on her.

Varjona frowned. What? Did Rodrigo think he would meet by clandestine arrangement with the Lady Jessica? Had Rodrigo's opinion of him dropped so low? It sent a surge of resentment through him, but he was not going to defend himself or his actions to Rodrigo. Not now, not ever! Thus, he turned a sneer on his one-time friend. "But Don Rodrigo, I can think of nothing more important than entertaining a beautiful angel." That he was in the mountains rounding up some stray calves he just would not explain. Such was his pride.

Don Rodrigo schooled his temper and his voice into a low hiss. "Don't draw me out, Var. It won't serve. I will repeat. Are there not things you *should* be doing?"

Varjona released a short, harsh laugh. "Should be doing? Ah, yes, but then, Rodrigo, when have you ever known me to do what I should?" So saying, he was once again tipping his hat, reeling his horse around on its haunches, and taking off for the deepest portion of the wooded slope.

A slow smile curved Rodrigo's sensuous lips for a moment before he turned his attention to Jess. Quickly the frown descended and he was dismounting, taking hard strides to her side, reaching up and taking hold of her waist. His grazing horse was forgotten as his attention, his emotions, found an outlet in Jessica.

Jess faced him and discovered that his dark, fire-lit eyes had the power to reduce her once again to a schoolgirl. Her body went limp as his strong, gloved hands took hold of her trim waist. She was very nearly hypnotized by the surge of feeling he was capable of arousing in her breast. Absurd, she told herself. This was so very ridiculous.

"What—what are you doing?" she demanded, attempting to get hold of herself and the situation.

What was he doing? He just didn't know. All earlier, better resolutions were tossed to the wind. All he knew was that he had come here and found her laughing with Varjona. Enough! She was his woman, no other's. This he would have her know, once and for all! Damnation! Why hadn't he seen this point of view earlier? She was repeating the question; he could hear the words touched with fear.

"Rodrigo, what is it? What are you doing?"

"Damn it! How dare you ride off on my gray!" was his answer, and though the words were firm, they were not harsh. "But then, since you seem to take what is mine, I find I should like to have the same privilege." This last was whispered on a low note just as he took her to himself, just as his head lowered and his mouth covered hers.

The feel of her in his arms was almost more than he could bear. Hell and fire! He wanted her, had been wanting her all these weeks, and, devil take it, he was going to have her, here and now. His kiss flowered into sweet passion, parting her lips, taking the reluctant response he felt from her and moving it into tender submission. He wanted her to surrender herself to his demands; more than that he had not thought out. He wanted her to be obedient to his whims. Blister it! Why not? She was a woman, why not *his* woman?

Jess discovered that his lips on hers ignited a raw passion within her that she couldn't believe she was capable of feeling. Her legs wobbled and she fell against him, allowing his arms to steady her, allowing his hands to manage her, and they did, oh, so well. His touch was like magic as his fingers undid the buttons of her spencer jacket. Stop, she told herself. She had to stop. Why? Because . . . because, but oddly enough, at that moment she could not think of one reason.

Easily, deftly, he had his own leather riding coat off and on the ground. Just as easily he had her entwined in his arms as he lowered her gently, purposefully, to the woodland ground cover of pine needles and rich ferns. His lips made a path from her mouth to her ears, back to her lips to linger, nibble, and proceed to her neck as his hands undid her linen blouse and released her full, youthful breasts.

She heard his husky voice in her ears and it was enchantment. She heard his words of endearment through the buzzing, soaring ardor burning in her head. Was this happening? Here, this way, could this be happening?

"*Cariña* . . ." he whispered as his gloves came off, as his hand cupped her breast, as his lips found the rosebud nipple and lingered there, teased there, before taking the route to her neck once more and finding her mouth parted, waiting for his kiss, his tongue. Readily she gave to him now, pressing her body against his hard, muscular chest. Almost shyly, hesitantly, she allowed her tongue to meet with his and share the tumultuous sensation of joining.

His hunger whipped at him, tore away all reason as he stripped her of her clothing, freed his manhood from his britches. He had wanted to take his time, stroke her into further passion, but this couldn't wait. He had to have her, and as she arched her body to meet, beg, for his, he knew she felt the same way. "Ah, Jess," he breathed, "my *azucena*, my white lily, give it to me now." He had placed his pulsating rod, and with the riot of his needs, he thrust hard and deep.

She groaned with pleasure as he entered. Her eyes were closed, and she floated away to a velvet world of colors and sweet scents. She held to him, moved for him, rotated in perfect harmony with him. She heard herself say his name; she heard herself ask him for more, ask him not to stop. She heard his moans and she opened her eyes a moment to gaze at his beloved face, steeped now in uncontrolled passion. Sweetly she touched his face with her lips before he was once again covering her mouth with his own.

Lightning? Was that lightning flashing across the sky? Was that thunder roaring in her ears or merely the sound of her heart beating for Rodrigo? He had her hips now in his firm hold as he urged her to move in rhythm to his dance. As he plunged, giving and taking in one beat, cherishing her all the while, she was very nearly sure she was in heaven. There was only Rodrigo and the beauty of their joining. There was only the moment. He had to love her, didn't he? He couldn't touch her in this way unless he loved her, could he? Suddenly she felt herself build to a peak and she held to him as she climaxed, crying his name, relaxing into his embrace.

He thrilled over the knowledge that he had already satisifed her. His mouth covered her own as his motion became frenzied and he lost himself to her. His lovemaking was near violent as he reached his own climax, and then he was groaning pleasurably as his breathing eased and he lay still, covering her body with his own.

Jessie lay beneath him now, and she was in doubt. How could she meet his eye? He had used her. Not once had he ever said he loved her. Not once had he ever given indication that he did. Oh, he wanted her as a man wants a woman, but love? No, he had never offered the word. Right then, what *did* he think of her? Would he think her a wanton woman? How would he treat her now?

She moved, pulling away and he objected, frowning at her, "Ah, no, not yet, my lady." There was an affection in his tone as he took her chin and turned her face to him.

She found that she couldn't look at him and that her cheeks burned.

"You mean you aren't done with me yet?" Oh, why did it sound so cold? Why had she answered him so blandly? Because you don't want your heart bared before him, that's why.

He was irritated by her response, but he bent and kissed her naked shoulder. "No, *cariña*, I am not done with you yet . . ." was how he chose to answer.

She bristled still further. "Of course, there is much to learn if I am to get it all right before our wedding night!" Oh, faith, she sounded like a shrew! Why, why was she behaving so?

"We spent our wedding night some weeks ago . . . on board my vessel," he answered softly, and then covered her mouth once more with his own.

It was precisely the correct thing to say, and it charmed her out of her agitation and sent her reeling once more beneath his touch. Later? She would worry about later, about the future, at another time. Now she was in his arms, and it felt almost as though he loved her. That was what stayed her there on their mountain bed and called forth her eager passion again.

Chapter 11

Jessie lay back against her pillows and closed her eyes. The night had turned nasty. Outside, something of a windstorm was gusting out its temper. In the distance she could hear the whinnies of some of the stallions in their individual grassy paddocks. In another portion of the hacienda Don José and his son were no doubt enjoying the game of chess Don José had asked for.

Her candlelight flickered and she opened her eyes to find that poem glaring at her again. Odd that she should pull out this book from the stack Maria had brought to her. Odder still that she should flip the pages only to come across words so very indicative of her own feelings.

HEARTS OF THUNDER
Author Anonymous

There—once again her knees are weak,
For she made the mistake of taking a peek.

At his face and then into his eyes—
Sampling his smile, discovering his wiles.

His passion catching her soul,
Taking her love as his toll.

Twinkling dark eyes taking her into fantasy.
Displacing the pain of harsh reality.

Sweet love—there it goes, its thunder!
As she holds him in gentle wonder,

> *Always in her heart.*

Jessie read it out loud and felt once again the constriction in her throat, the cringing of her heart, at the doubts it brought back to her. Had this afternoon really happened? Had she actually allowed him to take her up there in the mountains like some trollop? By God, she had. She really had. How? After all they had suffered at each other's hands, how had such a thing happened? Why had she let him touch her, kiss her, take her?

He didn't love her. Not a word of love had he spoken. Oh, no. On the ride home, when she was convulsed in shyness and needing the protection of his arms, she rode the gray, Rodrigo on the bay some strides before her. He was in spirits, announcing to her that he would arrange for the wedding to take place immediately, that he would ride into Buenos Aires that very afternoon and have dressmakers out to the hacienda in the morning, that all the valley would be invited to their wedding.

She had frowned through it all and just couldn't put up the argument that immediately sprang to her lips. Hadn't she just allowed him to make love to her? Yes, right then, so how could she declare her intentions of returning to England? It was absurd. And then he was saying, "And by the way, pet, I won't have you riding out alone. The next time you want to take the gray, you will also take a groom." His brow was up with the command.

Her own delicate brow rose and the fire in her violet eyes came back to life. "Oh?"

He frowned. "It is not done. I mean, a woman taking to open country unaccompanied."

"Really?" It was all she was willing to return, but her ire had been touched.

"Jessie," he answered her firmly, "you will honor my wishes."

"Your wishes? I rather thought you were issuing orders," she shot at him.

There it was, the clash of wills, and it lacked the declaration of strong love to smooth it over and diminish the battle. He pulled himself into his full, towering height. "As my wife, you will honor the name."

"I could not honor your name better than I have honored my own," she snapped at him. "And I was used to riding whenever and wherever I pleased!"

"Well, you will not do so here!"

"True enough," she responded in dangerously sweet tones. "For I shall not be here long enough."

They had reached the stableyard, and the gauchos within hearing managed to stop what they were doing to better view these two wild creatures having at each other. The argument was conducted in English, which they did not understand, but there was no mistaking the tones.

"Jess, my girl." His voice was low now but full with his threat. "You will be here for as long as I desire, and during that time, you will conduct yourself as *I* see fit."

"No, my lord tyrant, and no again. I will remain where I deem, and will behave only as *I* see fit." So saying, she was off her horse, throwing its reins up to him and swirling around on her heel. She knew he would not call after her in front of his men, but she fully expected him to storm in on her later.

She was right on the first count. He did not call after her. She was wrong on the second. Instead of his presence, he had a note taken in to her. She could almost hear his curt voice as she read it.

I am off for Buenos Aires as we discussed. I shall return later this evening. By then I am certain you will have examined your attitude and thought better of it. Rodrigo.

Oh! Was there ever such a man? Man? He was a fiend! One moment tender and passionate, and the next coldly indifferent, dictating orders to her. Well, who in heaven did he think he was? She was a Stafford! She seethed over the missive. She ranted to herself, to her four walls, stomping and running her hand through her long hair like a girl gone crazed.

There it was. Because she had allowed him to conquer her body in the mountains he now thought she belonged to him. He thought she would take his commands, follow his lead unquestioningly, stand by and allow him to order her life about. Ha! He would soon discover she was not so easily handled.

Then suddenly she knew what she would do. She would get Varjona to help her. He would deliver her to Buenos Aires (for she dared not go the distance alone), and he would arrange passage for her on the very next ship leaving for England. Passage. Money? What to do about money. She looked down at her ring. It was classical, Georgian in design, a cluster of rose-cut diamonds, and it was priceless, because it had been her mother's ring. She closed her eyes. Perhaps she could arrange to buy it back at a price through Varjona at some later date. Never mind. It had to be done.

The candlelight flickered now in her bedroom as a gust of wind swirled through her slightly opened window and she looked around. Well, she had gone to see Varjona just before dinner. She sighed as she recalled that meeting and its results.

Jessie had pulled the ivory silk shawl tightly around her delicate shoulders as she picked her way toward the stables. The night had already brought a cool wind and it whipped at her dressed golden hair. She couldn't help but notice the curious glances cast her way as she got closer to the barn where she had been told she would find the gaucho, Varjona.

He was there, sitting on a wooden barrel, cleaning his tack. His head of dark curling hair was uncovered; over his open-necked shirt he wore a colorful blanketlike vest, and he was chewing on a long, thick strand of straw.

"Varjona?" Jessie called softly. "I wonder if I might speak with you"—she looked around—"privately."

He eyed her for a long, thoughtful moment. He had no wish to quarrel further with Rodrigo. He couldn't help but notice that Rodrigo's mood upon his return from Buenos Aires earlier that afternoon had been decidedly better than it had been that same morning. Well, then, far be it for him to cause another rift. Why should he? It wouldn't further his cause with Maria, and it was Maria he wanted, wasn't it? Hence, he was not totally receptive.

"*Sí*, Lady Jessica?" Polite but formal was his answer.

She was surprised, but not turned off her purpose. "Come, then, sir. Walk with me."

He frowned. What did she want? However, the gallantry in his veins would not allow him to refuse. "*Sí*," he answered, and got up to fall in step beside her. "So, we will walk, and perhaps your Rodrigo will not shoot Varjona, eh?"

She opened her eyes wide. "He wouldn't." She shook her head at him. "He isn't that sort . . . You mistake him."

"No, Lady Jessica. I do not. Rodrigo and I . . . go back many years. He would tolerate much from me because of that. But if I really came between him and his *china* . . . his woman . . ." He shook his head. "It would mean bloodshed. Now, shall we still walk together?"

She stopped. "Still, I think you are wrong, and I am not his *china*. I belong to no one but myself. Varjona, I mean to return to England, to my family. I am not here by choice. If you will see me to Buenos Aires and help me find a ship returning to England, I will pay you."

He stopped and looked down at her lovely face. "What is this? Do you tell me Don Rodrigo . . . stole you from your family?" His accent was heavy with his shock. "I don't believe it."

"No, no, of course he did not do that." She looked away from him. "It doesn't matter how it happened, but somehow I found myself on his vessel in the middle of a storm and . . . and he felt it would be better if I stayed with him, came to his home, and married him. He thinks he is being quite the gentleman, and indeed, he is, but I cannot allow him to throw away his life because of some notion of honor. Var, he does not love me. . . ." Her voice trailed off.

Varjona thought about Rodrigo's disdain for most of the females he had chosen to align himself with over the years. True, he had never really loved any of them. He thought of Rodrigo's behavior in regard to the English girl, and his dark shaggy brow went up. "I dunno. Maybe you are wrong."

"Will you take me to Buenos Aires . . . tomorrow . . . please?"

"And if I do this thing, he will try to kill me and I will defend myself, maybe kill him. . . ."

"He won't know, will he? How would he know? That is the whole idea, Varjona. We must plan this thing so he will have no idea where I have gone," she answered him on a breathless note.

He touched his forehead thoughtfully. "Me, I know better. You see, I know Rodrigo. If you have it in your pretty little head to run away, run back to England, *he will know*." Varjona shook his head, and there was a frown drawing his thick brows together. "What will he do then, eh? He will come after me. Not that I am afraid. No, but with all our angry words, still I have no wish to kill Don Rodrigo."

"Kill Rodrigo? What are you saying? Don't be absurd." Jessie's violet eyes went wide.

"He will be much upset," Varjona offered in way of explanation.

"Nonsense. He will be pleased to be rid of me—once his pride has weathered the blow." She was scarcely audible now, but drew on air, and with a swish of her hand she did away with this thought. "So all we have to do is make certain he doesn't know who helped me get away."

"*Sí*, so you will leave it to me. First, a ship bound for your England must be found, then we will see." He touched her chin and the flirtatious gleam was back in his dark eyes. "And for my trouble, what shall you give?"

She smiled. "As much gold as I can spare, sir. What else could a lady give?"

He made her a mock bow. "What else, señorita? I have the answer to that and, being a gaucho, there is no shame in giving it to you, but we will leave it for now. . . ."

On this they both laughed, only to draw up short as they rounded the bend on the flagstone path, for there, leaning against the barn with his arms across his chest, was Don Rodrigo, and his black eyes were glinting up a storm!

Quickwittedly Jessie moved to extricate herself and Varjona from the rush of temper she could see on Rodrigo's countenance. She turned to Var, and, giving him her hand in formal style, she said lightly, "Thank you, sir, for giving me the tour and helping me find my wayward fiancé. It was most kind of you."

Varjona's dark eyes twinkled as he backed off with a flourishing bow. "It was my great pleasure to do so." A moment later he had vanished into the darkness and Jessie was smiling up at Rodrigo.

She moved herself to please and went to take up his arm. "And was your trip to Buenos Aires successful?" It wasn't hard to smile at him. Faith, she found she could do naught else as she looked up at his face and found her heart beating wildly.

He was angry and jealous. He wouldn't have her walking with Varjona. He wouldn't have it, but damn, she looked beautiful with her golden hair dressed high and in curls all around her piquant face and her eyes.

Certes, they tore through his anger. Still, he would teach her now, from the start. "Jessica." He said her name stiffly, almost coldly. "You know how I feel about you spending time with Varjona."

She curbed her hot blood and held back the retort that sprang to her lips. "I know, Rodrigo, but I wanted to find you and he was sure he had seen you."

He relented. What else could he do with her looking the child, the repentant child. He didn't stop at that moment to consider how out of character this was for Jess. "Very well, come on, then, and I will tell you what is in store for you tomorrow!"

Chapter 12

Uruguay's coastline faded as darkness set. Deep blue water lapped at the anchored ship and a soft breeze played with Pauly's light brown hair. He frowned, sighed, and scanned the ship's deck. What in thunder was he doing here? Had everyone lost sight of their original purpose? Just what in hell was going on?

Lady Jessica was now only two days away, just within reach, but were they proceeding to Buenos Aires? No, they were not! Below, war games were being discussed, and though the young viscount did not consider himself pudding-hearted, he certainly could not condone a sneak attack on a friendly nation. It was unthinkable. Well, he had better get below and see just how far the admiral had allowed Popham to go.

No one looked his way as he opened the admiral's stateroom door and entered. How could they? Four men were deep in the heart of argument, and each felt strongly that only he was right. Popham, incensed that he was being encumbered by what his comrades thought rational, jumped to his feet. "What is it? Why can't I get through?" Almost helpless, he turned to the viscount Beresford. "Surely you, Beresford, you see that we must strike immediately."

Viscount Beresford represented sanity at the table, so

Pauly folded his arms and leaned against the corner wall to watch the proceedings. Indeed, he could see that Beresford was taking his time with his answer, tempering his thoughts and his words. He was, after all, a man of discipline. He had not had an easy life growing up as the illegitimate son of the Marquis of Waterford and then going forward to become the hero who commanded the Connaught Rangers in the reconquest of the West Indies. Right, then, so Pauly watched with keen interest to see what line Beresford would take.

"Actually, Popham, I don't see that at all," he answered quietly. "And I am at a loss to understand your reasoning."

"Damn it! I am sitting with fifteen hundred men! What the devil do you think the Argentines will do when they get wind of it?"

"Do? What should they do?" the admiral stuck in. "We are here to pick up supplies."

"They are not so stupid," returned Popham.

"Precisely why I do not think this maneuver of a sneak attack through the River Plate will hit its mark," answered Beresford. He shook his head. "We haven't enough men yet. I say we are to wait for word from the home office."

"Right, then, but I am sailing into Buenos Aires to retrieve my niece. It is settled." The admiral stood up.

"No, it is not settled!" Popham was shouting now and thoroughly enraged. "Here is the golden continent, ripe for the taking. Gentlemen, *we owe it to England*!"

Sir Warren had been sitting back, contemplating both Beresford and Popham thoughtfully. His blue eyes were lit with excitement. They were very near his purpose. He would make a name for himself, return a trumpeted hero, and have Jessie by his side. It had been the fantasy of this that had carried him over the long and tedious sea voyage. He wasn't about to allow this fool Popham to lose it for him by acting too rashly.

"We are all, I think, looking toward England," Sir

Warren said quietly. "But in order to achieve for England, we must temper our actions, pull out the wisest course."

Popham was near spluttering as he turned on Sir Warren. "What do you know of it? You are some political figure, nothing more!"

Sir Warren got to his feet. The admiral stayed him with a hand to his arm, and Pauly in his corner grinned at the show.

"And you, sir, are a warmonger without thought!" snapped Sir Warren. The two men glared into each other's eyes, but the admiral called their attention.

"Enough! This bickering gets us nowhere. We have been anchored long enough. My purpose here is to retrieve my niece and see her safely home, and I will not be detained from that any longer."

"Indeed, Admiral," answered Sir Warren slowly, "but perhaps we may yet achieve both goals."

Pauly's grin vanished, and he dropped his arms to his sides. "Lady Jessica has naught to do with England's designs on Argentina."

The admiral nodded. "That's right. I won't have her name linked with this business." He wasn't about to have any battles fought with Jess's name as their cause. The very idea!

"No, no, of course not," Sir Warren hurriedly assured him. "That is not what I meant."

"No? Then what did you mean?" Pauly was not about to let it drop.

"Hold a moment!" This time Beresford was putting up a hand. "We are all agreed that the lady Jessica's name is to be protected. Now, if we may, a decision must be made regarding our position and our plans as a unit."

"You know how I feel," answered Popham. "I am for striking, now, from the River Plate!"

"Yes, and I have carried through with the orders I

received from the home office, which were to meet the admiral here and await further word. It has always been a dictum of mine to tread warily in strange waters," Beresford said quietly.

"What then? How can a decision be made when we ride different roads?"

"Popham, ol' friend. You are after glory, as each of us is in our own way, but a good soldier picks his time; he doesn't allow others to pick it for him," Beresford answered.

Popham's eyelids flickered. He considered Beresford for a long moment before he was able to collect himself and his reply. "So it would appear that *you* have made a decision for us."

The viscount Beresford had been ordered to sail for Argentina with Popham and fifteen hundred men. More than that had in effect been left in his hands. Popham was directly responsible to him, but it would appear that the gentleman wished to strike out on his own. That was fine, but he wasn't about to let the man drag him with him.

"I have, in fact, made a decision," said Beresford easily.

The admiral frowned. "Have you, by God! Do you mean to share it with us or keep us on tenterhooks?"

Beresford laughed and clapped the older man on the shoulder. "My lord, be calm in this, for you shall have your niece and perhaps, just perhaps, we may have Buenos Aires!"

Maria's dark eyes snapped as she put a hand between the bold gaucho, Varjona, and herself.

"I have seen you with my own eyes, devil! You—you want that pale witch he has brought from England! You always want what Rodrigo has." She was in a cold rage.

He laughed out loud and took her shoulders, but she

257

shook herself free and stamped her foot. "No, do not touch me!"

He did not answer her, and this time he did not laugh. Instead, he allowed instinct to handle the situation, and when he took hold of her, there was no letting go. She struggled in his arms, but he held her firmly, and when his mouth found hers, the kiss was one that conquered, not seduced.

When he let her go it was to turn his back and without a word start to walk off toward the stables. She couldn't believe it, but when she called his name and he would not turn, she ran after him and caught his bare arm, for his shirt-sleeves had been folded back and above his elbow. "Varjona?"

He looked haughtily down at her. *"Sí."*

"You—you can't just leave." The doubt was in her voice, in her eyes, and he almost lost sight of his purpose as he felt the need to reassure her, but he was too experienced to do that.

"No, and why not? You accuse me of things that hurt my pride. Me, I do not allow this from my *china*!"

"I am not your *china*." She put up her chin.

He softened and stroked her cheek. "Are you not? Well, then, you give your kisses lightly, little one, and I must look to another."

She was no match for him. Fear filled her dark eyes, and she threw her arms around him. "Varjona, don't . . ."

"Ah, you would have me faithful? But you have said you are not my woman. How, then, can I be your man?"

"Beast! Go on, then, do what you please, for I tell you plainly, Varjona, I am not a gaucho woman. I am a Cesares, and you will treat me with respect and kindness . . . or . . . or I shall have to let you go, though it would break my heart." Was that honesty she heard from her lips? How had she come to this? What was she doing? Her mother would go into a convulsion to hear her give herself away to this gaucho. What was she doing? There was Rodrigo, yes, but he had eyes for no one save the English wench, and here was Varjona, who made her heart pound and her knees weak.

He was touched. His Maria, his love, was actually growing up, committing herself to him, and he—was he worthy? He frowned over the thought. She was a Cesares, a pureblood. Would Don José, would Doña Julia, allow the match? *Never!* He touched her nose, ran a gentle finger over her lips. "You would be better off without me, little one."

"Yes, I know, but one cannot stop one's thoughts, and mine are all of you," she answered in a small voice, scarcely audible.

He bent and kissed her lips lightly. "Go now, before your mother misses you."

"Varjona?" The insecurity was there in her eyes.

He saw it and laughed, not willing to say more now. "Go on, little one. We all have our dreams. Perhaps yours and mine . . . may meet."

Inside the hacienda a buxom dressmaker fussed around Lady Jessica, who stood balanced on a narrow wooden stool. Rolls of material in various shades of ivory, white, and soft pink had been produced and lay negligently about the furniture. Patterns and their accompanying drawings lay scattered over these rolls and the sewing room was a scene of gay bustling as the señora Rosa sent her two girls to and fro to do her bidding.

Jess stood in abject misery, lifting her arms when told, turning on command and silently giving herself to the *señora*'s pushes and pulls. Her unhappiness stemmed from two convictions. One, that she was behaving like a "back-stabbing wench" to accept this trousseau, which Don José and Rodrigo were bestowing on her in good faith, and the other being the fact that she was fairly certain Don Rodrigo would be the only man she would ever love. There, once again she admitted this to herself, even as she made plans to escape him and the marriage he designed.

She had no choice. He was marrying her out of a sense of duty. She thought, in fact, that he was behaving in a noble fashion, for her observations had led her to believe that he was in love with his young cousin, Maria. Sad, unrequited love, but she had to leave him, allow him his freedom. It was the only way if she really loved him, wasn't it? No, you fool. You could marry him, teach him to love you. Couldn't you do that? No, she was certain this was no way to start a marriage. He would forever feel she had captured him by force, and she would always feel he married her to save honor.

Don José wheeled himself to the sewing room, a ready smile on his thin lips. A wedding was just what the hacienda needed, and this English maid was just the girl to tame his wild son. He had observed them last night at dinner and then afterward. They both had a fire in their eyes, a dangerous fire should it get out of hand, but he rather thought Jessica had enough sense to school the flames and wield them into something good. He stopped at the sewing room's large arched double doorway and a frown drew his graying brows together. Why should the lady Jessica look so sad. Here she was with all this finery about. . . .

Odd. He had observed these last days that she was a bubbly sort, that laughter sprang easily to her lips, a smile to her eyes, yet here she stood, looking as though she were about to cry. What the devil was wrong? Perhaps he was wrong. Perhaps she did not love Rodrigo. Was his son forcing her to the altar? Could that be it? Damnation! This was a tangle.

Quietly he made his way into the room and stopped short of the darkly colored carpet. "Have you no smile for an old man?" He teased Jess to get her attention.

She turned around and blushed. "Don José, I did not see you there."

"No, you were in another world," he answered gently. "In England, perhaps, missing your family?"

She was too wise to fall for his game, and her eyes twinkled at him. "Indeed. I would imagine such thoughts would trouble any girl about to be married far from home."

"Very good, Jessica, but witty replies will not solve the problem," he answered in a tone of fatherly rebuke.

"Problem? I did not say there was a problem," she returned, "though I am heartily weary of all this. . . ." She made a wide gesture with her hands.

Don Rodrigo appeared in the doorway. "Then you shall have done with it!" he said in a tone that indicated he was in the best of spirits.

She smiled in spite of herself. His presence had the power to dissolve all fears, all doubts and unhappiness. Don José noted this between his knit brows. What was it, then? He couldn't discover what was wrong, and it irritated him. However, it was at this moment that one of the *señora*'s girls pulled at a roll of material, which caught at the wide ribbon near Jessica's ankles. It caught Jess around the ankles and cost her her balance. With a startled cry she went toppling over and landed on her hands and knees.

Rodrigo was beside her in a moment, taking her arms, righting her, cursing the poor young girl who was crying her apologies, and all this commotion brought Don José's eyebrows up with wonder. Surely his son was in love. Look at him! His concern was genuine, his handling of Lady Jess was tender, and his eyes . . . hell and brimstone, they spoke volumes to the girl! What was it, then?

Jessie's violet eyes were dark with the emotions she was experiencing. Her cheeks were aflame and her lips were pursed in embarrassment over the awkwardness of her fall and the fuss going on all around her. She swished such considerations away with a wave of her hand. "Please, it is nothing."

He was helping her to her feet and his hand was tightly clasped to her small waist. He had an absurd urge to hold her to him, to whisper words he wasn't sure he was feeling. What was it he was feeling for her? He was very nearly frightened of the answer, so he quickly put aside this silent question and asked, "Are you hurt, Jess?"

"I am fine. Really. Now, what was it you were saying about leaving these women to their silks and brocades and taking me off somewhere?" She was smiling at him, but there was restraint in her voice.

"Indeed. I have to ride to the south pampas and thought you might like to join me."

She brightened like a child receiving a rare treat and clapped her hands before she realized what she was about. "Oh, Rodrigo, I would love to."

"Good!" He laughed, pleased with her enthusiasm. "But you will ride sidesaddle, my girl, and you will behave yourself."

She stiffened but controlled herself. "Oh?"

He was surprised by the meekness of her reply. He had expected to meet with an argument, for which he was totally prepared. "That's right, for I mean to stop by the Madryn Rancho and introduce you to some friends of ours, and it would not do for them to see you at your rough-and-tumble antics." In part he was goading, only teasing her in his wish to play.

He had very nearly succeeded in his efforts, for she felt her temper bristle, and the flitting expression of anger could be seen in the fire of her violet eyes. She managed to curb her tongue. After all, she told herself, she would soon be leaving him for England's shore. He would be but a memory, as she would be to him, and as she was very certain that his memory would linger in her heart, she would have hers touch his soul; hence, she must be pleasant.

"If I promise not to gallop off and land my horse and

myself in some hole or ditch, may I ride astride?'' she attempted gently to compromise.

Again, he was taken aback. What was this new docile behavior? What was his spitfire up to, behaving the angel? This was unlike her. He attempted to ruffle her feathers. ''Does this mean the lady Jessica does not feel she can manage the skill of riding sidesaddle?''

She very astutely surmised what he was about, and even so, she had to restrain her foot, which itched to stomp on his.

''Oh, as to that, the lady Jessica was wont to ride sidesaddle whenever the need arose. Is that what would impress your friends? Doing what any woman of breeding is taught to do? So be it. Sidesaddle it is, though in truth I thought you had more spirit.''

He held her wrist. ''And what is that supposed to mean?''

''Rodrigo, I rather thought *you* of all people would flaunt your future wife's unconventionality and dare them all to criticize!'' she answered, her chin up.

He eyed her in some amusement. ''You are, of course, quite right, but I find that while I invite anyone who chances it to criticize *me*, I will not tolerate anyone thinking you one ounce less than you are.'' So saying, he had her hand and was placing a kiss upon her knuckles.

''Touché, Rodrigo!'' Don José laughed from his wheelchair as he slapped his thin thigh. He had been sitting in the background, forgotten while the two volatile youths had been battling it out, and he had enjoyed himself immensely. Here indeed was just the woman his wild son needed.

There was nothing left to be said. Rodrigo had won this round, and though Jessie's cheeks were flushed with her chagrin over the defeat, there was something inside of her that was pleased, quite pleased, that he had managed her. Also, the fact that she would be spending an entire afternoon in his company was enough to depress the sadness in her heart at the thought that soon, very soon, she would be leaving him forever.

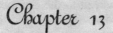

The young viscount, Paul Bellamy looked around himself with some show of enthusiasm. Damn! Here he was in Buenos Aires and there was even a festival of sorts. This was the first piece of good luck he had had in more than three weeks! And the chits! Lord, but they were wondrous, with those large dark eyes and those swaying hips.

"Pauly, I say, Pauly!" He was called to order by the admiral. "Ask him if he knows of a Don Rodrigo Cesares. Ask him if he could give us the scoundrel's direction."

The viscount's Spanish was dusty. He hadn't used it since his days at the University, but he pieced the words together in his mind and in halting but clear Spanish he managed to make the shopkeeper of the men's clothing store understand.

The little round tailor nodded his head vigorously and ripped off a protracted rendition, all on the subject of the Cesareses and their long satisfaction with his work. The viscount followed bits and pieces and with his hands asked the shopkeeper to slow down. He smiled and continued to question the man about Don Rodrigo's whereabouts.

This was easily understood by the Argentine fellow, who whipped up a map of sorts with his feather quill and a slab of yellowed writing paper. When he had done, he attempted to make it understood that he wished his regards to be conveyed to the Cesares family.

Pauly nodded and, backing off, took the admiral's arm. They both smiled and gave their thanks and made good their escape, as the shopkeeper seemed inclined to conversation. Once outside, the admiral took over the map and frowned over its drawing.

"According to this, we should take the main road from where we stand and follow it out of town. . . ." He paused to consider. "Aye, here"—he pointed with his finger—"we fork to the left, is that it, Pauly lad?"

"Yes, from what I managed to understand as he went over the thing with me, that is it precisely. He says that on horseback 'tis no more than two hours' ride. So, all we have to do is hire a couple of hacks and be off. . . ."

"No, lad. I don't mean to go charging into Cesares territory demanding the return of my niece. If the man had the audacity to abduct a Stafford, he might be inclined to keep her!"

"What, then? For I tell you to your head, Admiral, I think there is more to this than meets the eye. I don't think you have got Don Rodrigo right in this."

"So, you have been saying. Yet the facts are that Jessie is in his company. That much we gleaned when we stopped for supplies and inquired after his ship. Damn it, boy, he was seen buying clothing for an English wench!" He shook his head. "To think of my Jess . . . talked about in such a fashion."

"Yes, but do you think he and his family would keep her from us if we rode up to his hacienda and demanded her release? Admiral, we are not dealing with an outlaw. Don Rodrigo is a nobleman."

"He is a Spaniard!" replied the admiral, staunch to the belief that if not English, then not civilized.

"Yes, but admiral, think. He would have to murder us to keep us from taking Jess. Honestly, I don't think we are dealing with that sort of gentleman. I am certain that there will be a logical reason for all of this," Pauly argued reasonably.

"Yes, and while we are demanding her release Popham will be waging war on the Argentines. What then, sir?"

"All the more reason to attend to this now, without waiting for Sir Warren and his unscrupulous plans."

"What galls me beyond endurance is that this Don Rodrigo Cesares, who you say is a nobleman, has paraded my niece . . . as his mistress. Such was the information . . . the picture we received in that dress shop. I tend to agree with Sir Warren. He should be cut down, I say! Cut down. Lady Jessica is a Stafford! She is my niece, and damn it, lad, if I don't call him out on this, Sir Warren will!"

"Neither of you will have to. Something tells me Jess is safe and sound and that we shall have no trouble when we go up to the hacienda."

Some feet away, yet well within hearing, a colorful and bold-looking gaucho leaned against the corner of the brick shop and watched the two Englishmen. Varjona was filled with excitement and concern. He had heard enough to know that somehow Rodrigo had abducted his English bride. An unpardonable act. She was not, after all, some peasant, but a noblewoman. He wanted to slap his leg and laugh out loud.

Something inside of him was moved to admiration of Rodrigo. They had grown up together, and this was the boy he had remembered. Passionate, impulsive, wild! That had been Rodrigo. He had taken the woman he wanted, just as any gaucho might do. Indeed, there was much of the gaucho in Rodrigo's hungry heart, thought Varjona with a grin.

He sighed as he took up the reins of his horse and slid his bare foot into the wooden stirrup. It was too bad that he was going to have to betray Rodrigo in this, but he had given his word to the English girl. And then it dawned on him. Wait, now, he wouldn't have to do very much, not with her people right here in Buenos Aires. All he would have to do is see her safely to the city—tonight. He couldn't be blamed for that. He would be back by morning with none the wiser. No one would suspect him. *Sí, sí.* That was the answer. He would see her to her people. She would have what she wanted. He would have fulfilled his promise. Her people would go off and not make trouble for the Cesareses and only Rodrigo would suffer in this—but such is life. Not everyone can win always. Such was Varjona's way of thinking.

Maria's dark eyes flashed as her mother spoke. Her small hands went to her slim hips and then moved to swish the blue satin of her full-skirted gown.

"Enough, Mama!" was her hard reply. "You have said enough. It is obvious that Rodrigo sees no one but that pale-cheeked wench! I am his little cousin, nothing more—and besides, I want Varjona!"

Her mother put a hand to her heart. "What are you saying? A common gaucho? You cannot mean it!"

"He is not common, and a gaucho is a man worth the having!" Maria snapped. "But thanks to you, he became impatient with me. His interest has been turned to this wonderful English creature Rodrigo displays!"

"Ha!" Her mother snapped her fingers in the air, forgetting for the moment her palpitating heart. "He makes you jealous; that is all. He knows well how to play his cards."

"No, you are wrong. I have heard him whispering to her—something about going off to Buenos Aires, and, Mama, I could not bear it. Do you hear me? I—I will never forgive you, for it was you . . . you who said I could have them both. *Sí,* you said I could win Rodrigo and still keep my pet gaucho. Isn't that how you educated me?"

Her mother turned away. Indeed. It was what she had learned as a woman in a hard world. One married for convenience and comfort. One took on a lover for heart and soul solace. It was not something she was ashamed of admitting, yet under her daughter's accusing eyes, she winced, and said quietly, "I had only *your* interests in my mind. I wanted you to be mistress of this rancho, to bear children proudly and have a husband who could see to their worldly needs. Never mind. It is Varjona you wish to wed, so be it. You will have some very fine nights together, then youth will pass, and what then, daughter? You will have hungry children and a man who has left you a memory!" So saying, she left her daughter's room.

Maria stared after her for a while and then at herself in the looking glass. She was an ambitious girl, and her mother was correct. In taking Varjona for a husband she was throwing away much, for if not Rodrigo, there were others just as wealthy that she could set her sights on. This was something she would have to think about later; for now she would make it clear to the English wench that Varjona was taken. After all, she could promise Varjona much and still not walk down the aisle with him.

Rodrigo stopped outside Jessie's door and touched her cheek as he bent to place a tender kiss on her full cherry lips. "Thank you, pet, for a lovely afternoon."

"Do you leave me now?" she whispered on a husky note. All she wanted, had been wanting for hours, was to go into his arms. Didn't he feel that way? Wasn't the need shared? Something inside of her moved to tease him further. Tantalizingly she gazed deep into his dark eyes, touching his chest as she brought herself closer still.

"Rodrigo, can't you come into my room for just a moment? There is something I want to show you."

"Impudent she-devil." He grinned as he allowed himself to be pulled along. However, he mitigated the words by closing and bolting the door at his back. "What, then, do you want to show me?"

"This," she whispered, rising to her toes, spreading her hands up and over his hard, lean chest, tentatively touching his lips with her own. She could feel him withhold himself, and it fevered her into further action. She took his hand and placed it over her breast, and this time no further prompting was needed. With something of a groan he caught her up with his free hand, and when his mouth met her hers, she felt the excitement she had generated in him take strong hold of them both.

"Jessie girl," he whispered as he covered her face with his kisses and then lifted her cradlelike into his arms and carried her to the bed. "I have been wanting you."

"Have you, Rodrigo?" Her voice was scarcely audible. "Show me, love, show me." Were the words emanating from *her* lips? How could she be talking in such a manner? It didn't matter. This would be the last time they would be together, and she wanted him to remember her always.

She engendered a passion in him and he felt swept away by the sound in her voice. He couldn't believe what he was feeling, for sensations flooded through him, engulfing his heart, rendering him ravished with desire and something more, something he knew he had never felt before. All he knew was that nothing mattered but this woman and how she made him feel.

He was burning with the steady flow of the hot blood she had ignited. He was trembling from the overwhelming reverberating beating of his heart and the pounding in his head. He had to have her now. It didn't matter that he shouldn't be here, in her room, with his family not so very far off. All that mattered was his need of her and the sudden knowledge that he wanted her body, yes, but also, he wanted her soul!

"Mine, Jessie, you will always be only mine." It was very nearly a growl as he pulled away at her clothing. Damn! She felt so good, so firm and supple.

It was exciting knowing that he could be moved to

such hunger, but it was strangely irritating to be told she belonged to him. After all, he had never even said he loved her. She felt him loosening his britches and she managed to pull away slightly. "I never wanted to be anyone's property, Rodrigo."

"Not my property, Jess." His lips discovered and touched hers gently as he drew her back into his arms, pulled her with him to the bed. "Not my property, but my precious woman, my wife."

To some extent this mollified her. He had still not said he loved her, but it was sweet thinking of herself as his wife. Bittersweet. She had never really understood the meaning of that word until now and, oh, his hands felt so good roaming her body as they were now, touching her pleasure points with a skill enough to make her groan for more.

There was so much he wanted to teach her. He wanted to please her, and as he parted her legs he started gently with his first new instruction by kissing her sweetly just at the apex of her thighs. Then he was nibbling, moving his lips higher, parting her honeyed opening until she gasped with both shock and pleasure.

Somehow, she wasn't quite sure how, he managed to place himself so that she found her cheek against his hip and she heard his voice as it came in soft tones. All the while he took her to a new height never before explored. She discovered the hardness of his manhood and proceeded to attempt to satisfy him. Encouraged by him, she pursued this course, using her hands with a new-found skill.

This time he groaned and, no longer able to control himself, he pulled himself away from her touch. "Not yet, babe, not just yet." He wasn't about to allow himself to climax, not until he had her, all of her. So saying, he took her beneath him, and with a thrust that left them both gasping, he found her tight, soft, and hot. It thrilled him to know that he was pleasing her, that he could bring her into a wanton show of desire, and he sought with all the expertise at his disposal to display that she belonged to him, only him.

Jessie held him and knew she never wanted to let him go. At that moment all thought of going home had been banished. That was a nightmare she didn't want to step into, not now, while she was dreaming so sweetly.

"Rodrigo, I . . ." She wanted to tell him she loved him, but something kept the words deep in her throat.

"I know, babe, I—it's good between us," was the response she received.

It kept her silent still.

An hour later she heard his words again. "It's good between us." That was all. No words of love or devotion. No promise to the future, only a statement of his physical satisfaction. Abstractedly she drew her hairbrush through her long flaxen curls and set them at the top of her head, pinning them in place. She wore an aqua gown of silk that displayed her charms alluringly in its simple lines.

Varjona. She expected him to take her to Buenos Aires, put her on a ship, and . . . and . . . and she would never see Rodrigo again. Oh, God, the thought of that frenzied her. It was, of course, the only answer, but such an answer.

Earlier, when she lay in his arms, she had been on the verge of confessing her feelings to Rodrigo, telling him how very much she loved him, but she had stopped herself. She didn't want to entrap him into repeating the same only because she was marrying him. She wanted him to love her freely. There was no real intimacy between them. In spite of the fact that they had made love together, something was lacking.

A tapping at her terraced door brought her head around. Her maid had drawn all the hangings earlier, so carefully, warily, she drew a corner aside. Her delicate brows went up to find Varjona impatiently awaiting her on the other side. Quickly she opened the door wide and stepped out. "Varjona, what is it?"

"Tonight, little one. I shall take you to your people tonight."

"My people? What do you mean?"

"They are in Buenos Aires. They came in the big ship to take you home. Me, I think it would be better if I took you to them. The Cesareses are good people." He thought a moment. "Rodrigo too. I should not like your men to find trouble here and ruin the name. No. It would be better if I took you to them, for I think if they came, Rodrigo would not give you over, and that would be trouble." He shook his head. "In any case. We go tonight. You will take very little and be ready to ride hard. *Sí?*"

She should be pleased. Her uncle, or certainly a ship sent by her uncle, was here to take her safely home. Indeed, what more could she want. Dully she nodded her head. "Yes, I will be ready. I—I suppose I can retire early after dinner and be ready to ride by midnight. Does that suit you, Varjona?"

"Nothing suits me, for I don't doubt that somehow Rodrigo may find reason to blame me in this." He shrugged. "We shall see. So, you will be ready to ride at midnight. This, I suppose, is good."

She watched him turn and go. This, she supposed, was the only way. Good? No, probably it was the worst thing that could ever happen to her.

Chapter 14

It was late, the sky was a mass of thickening clouds, and Varjona sighed over the fact that he was fairly certain it would rain before the night was out. He sat at his uncovered wooden table within the walls of his one-room adobe and pushed his mbaipoi away in some dejection. Leaning forward onto his elbows, he pressed his full lips into his clenched fists and stared at the bowl of unfinished cornmeal.

Who was he fooling? How dare he dream of wedding Maria. What right had he to think that he, a poor gaucho, could wed a wealthy Cesares? He thought of Maria. Petite, dark, pert, and haughty. He thought of the way she would twinkle up at him, her eyes glaring her demands, her lips soft as he conquered her will. Could he do without her? Yes, damn it! He was a man, a gaucho. He would find another to take her place.

Another? Damn it! He couldn't think of that now. There was a knock at his door and he looked up in irritation. "*Sí?*" he called.

The door opened and a small, cloaked figure stood on the threshold, her eyes not meeting his own. In some surprise he stood up.

"*Maria?*"

She moved toward him, her step hesitant. "Varjona, I

had to come." She was annoyed with herself. Why was she intimidated? Usually she was in control of herself, but she felt suddenly on unsteady ground.

What was this? he asked himself as he scanned her features in the dim candlelight. Why was she here? What was she up to? Maria was forever up to something. This would not do. It would ruin her reputation, and if he meant to take her for a wife, he would not allow her name to be bandied about. Indeed, she must leave his adobe at once. Sternly his features drew together as he went toward her.

"Maria, what are you doing here?"

She felt her cheeks go hot. She had taken her pride and shelved it by coming here, but she hadn't been able to stop herself. He was, it seemed, always avoiding her these days. She wanted to be alone with him, tempt him, make certain he still wanted her.

"Are—are you not pleased?" she asked hopefully, her piquant face raised to his.

There was no answering smile in his eyes. His expression was grave, disapproving. There was too much on his mind. Her timing was all wrong, but of course, she could not know that, and he did not take the space to reason it out or give her some understanding.

"Pleased? How could I be? What sort of behavior is this from a lady?"

She was hurt to the quick. It slashed through her sharply, and her chin went up in defiance. "I *am* a lady, Varjona, and, as such, I have my own rules!"

"As always, you think the world revolves around you! It doesn't, little one," he answered her, surprising himself that he had not lost his temper. He had to get her out of here before someone discovered she was missing from the hacienda. That was all that mattered. She was a child, and what she was saying didn't matter. He would attend to her feelings at another time. "Now, I think you had better return to your room."

"Do you?" She was near screeching, so incensed was

she at his rejection, and her cheeks were full with fire. "Oh, but I do not think so." She put out her hand as though to stop him, though he made no move toward her. "No, but you needn't concern yourself, Varjona. I shan't bother you with my company any longer. However . . . there are others whom I might find entertaining." She knew she was being spiteful. She knew that he knew it, but at that moment she just couldn't stop the words from flowing.

Varjona was not the man to bluff in such a way. With an expression of utter disgust he took her arm and roughly yanked her to the door.

"Here, then, shall I call the men to order so that you may inspect them for your pleasure?"

She cringed and pulled away. He sneered and came on, his tone hard, his voice devoid of all feeling but contempt. "No? Ah, perhaps you would prefer to go to their beds and survey the merchandise."

"Varjona!" She was near tears, and then she let go an anguished cry, broke loose, and ran toward the hacienda. She hadn't gone far when she stopped and turned suddenly. She saw him standing in his doorway and imagined his grin, whereupon she stamped her foot and in guttural Spanish yelled, "*Pig! Gaucho pig!*" Then to herself as she turned once more and ran toward the hacienda, "Worse than an animal . . . *darle a uno en la mera . . .*" for indeed, he had struck home.

Jessie stuffed her long flaxen hair under her wide-brimmed leather gaucho hat. She stuck her riding crop into the insides of her boot until she felt its tip rest against her ankle, and quietly made her way down the long corridor to the servants' wing, where she stepped out into the cool night air. "Whew." It was an audible sigh of relief to have gotten that far undetected, and she waited a moment, listening. Satisfied that no one was up and about, she hurried down the gravel path's winding route toward the courtyard. There, she stood a long while, her eyes peering through the darkness, her ears on the alert. No one. All seemed safe enough.

She stayed close to the ornamental fence line, and then with her heart pounding she cut the courtyard diagonally and hurried down the wide lane to the barn. Her breath came in short, jagged spurts, because she knew that if Rodrigo discovered her, she would be guarded from then on, and there would be no other chance for escape. She had to be careful. In the excitement of her undertaking she was able to put aside the thought that she would never see Rodrigo again. At that moment all that mattered was getting away, going to her uncle who had come all this way in search of her.

It was nearly midnight; the sky was overcast and very little of the moon could be seen. Varjona. Where are you? She paced in her space, her brows drawn together in some concern. He was supposed to have been here already, horses saddled. Where was he? She made her way cautiously inside the long, stone-floored barn and stopped. Should she call his name? Dangerous. Better just to wait. She carefully picked her way outside and searched the darkness for him. What if he didn't come for her? Could she make the trip to Buenos Aires alone?

She took a moment to breathe, to steady herself, and that was a mistake. Rodrigo. The memory of his body brought a rush of sensation to her heart, jingled her nerves, centered her thoughts—and they were all for him. Rodrigo. What will you do when you wake in the morning and find me gone? Pick up your life, get on with it, and forget me? Yes. You are a man, and you will move on to others . . . forgetting me. What will I do when there is no hope of seeing you again? The answer to that was the ache she was experiencing now, the emptiness she knew she would be facing.

Must not think about it. That was all there was to it. Cope. Don't think. Don't feel. Cope, manage, get by! She had to leave. There was no other way. She had that firmly planted in her mind. It would be better when she was gone and no longer heard his voice, saw his face, fell beneath the charm of his smile.

Maria was crying out loud, pulling at her long black hair and having something of a heartfelt tantrum, when the hacienda door loomed up before her. She stopped. Unwilling to return to her room, she wavered with indecision, unsure what to do, where to go. Her dark eyes narrowed with the spite of her sudden thoughts and her small arms folded themselves across her middle. "So," she said out loud, "you do not care if I play in the stables, eh?" And then with much derision, as though he could hear, "Ha! We will see." So saying, she marched in bold fashion toward the barn, lost her nerve halfway there, and stopped once more.

Her cowardice in this regard so upset her that she kicked at the turf with her dainty foot, hit a stone, stubbed her toe, and with a yelp of frustration planted herself on the ground. She was a child with a woman's desires. So she sat, thwarted and fitful. The hacienda's sharp dark lines cut into the night sky at her back. Before her lay the stable courtyard, quiet but for the occasional whinny of a restless horse. She picked at the damp grass, cursing Varjona softly. She had too long been used to getting her own way, and this irritation was nearly more than she could handle, for it was tinged with humiliation.

Varjona had watched Maria stamp at him across the way, and a slow grin curved his sensuous lips. She was a babe caught in a woman's body, and one day he would have the training of her! He was a gaucho, but Cesares or no, one day she would be his. *Sí*, but that was for another time. Now he had to get to the stables and prepare the horses. His adobe allowed him access to the stable's rear entrance, and within a short space of time he was saddling his roan criollo and the gray gelding Lady Jessica had been using.

He clicked to them softly as he led them down the

barn's main corridor, wincing at the loudness of the clopping sound of their shoes over the stone floor. There was no doubt that a price would have to be paid for this night's work, he thought sourly, and in the end Rodrigo and he might have to face each other. Ah, well, perhaps not. If he were lucky.

Ah, there the lady Jess stood in the double-doored arched entrance, her hand extended forward to take one of the horses. So, it is begun, he thought. "No one has seen you?" he then asked on a low note.

"I don't think so," she answered, amazed to find herself so short of breath. Surely she was in control of herself by now.

"Softly then, woman." He was already bending to give her a leg up.

She allowed him to assist her, and as she settled herself into the ornate saddle, so different from her small English saddle, she remarked lightly. "How clever of you not to have bothered me with a lady's saddle." She was already adjusting the stirrup leathers to her length. The gray began to fidget, and she steadied him with one free hand, cooing to him sweetly until his ears flickered at the sound.

"*Sí*, but me, I have seen you ride. Besides, you will move faster astride." He grinned as he swung himself up onto his horse, and he could not help notice the look of fascination that came over her face as she watched him collect his stirrups. He, of course, as always, rode shoeless. Then he was gently urging his horse forward and looking around with some satisfaction to find Jessie jog her horse abreast.

"Are you really comfortable without the benefit of boots?" Jessie could not refrain from asking.

He shrugged. "It is a natural thing. Me, I do not understand how it is anyone can bear so much leather between him and his earth."

Jessie laughed and turned to take a long look at the home she was leaving behind. Oddly enough, she realized how very attached she had become to the setting and its people. Silently she said good-bye. Varjona watched her. "Me," he announced gently, "I think you are not happy to leave."

She had no answer to this, and so it was they rode on for a bit in silence, and neither one noticed the small figure crouching inside the green canopy of the *parral*, an arbored vineyard that ran adjacent to the long, wide drive.

Maria stood in some stupefaction as she watched the two riders jog down the drive, obviously on their way out of the estate. She couldn't believe it. She had watched Varjona come out of the barn with two horses, and she had carefully, deftly, slunk along the edge of the courtyard, making her way to the family's covered arbor. There, hidden by the green grapevines, she watched Varjona help Jessie onto the horse. Her jealousy threatened, but something kept her cool and watchful. There was something so very odd about all this. What were they doing? Surely, if they were lovers, they would have met in Varjona's adobe. No, perhaps they were afraid Rodrigo would find them there.

Oh, God! She wanted to kill. That was why Varjona had sent her away. He had this white, this lily-white-and-gold, English slut to please him. Still, she waited and watched. Odd. Varjona did not seem very loving. There was no caressing, no touching. Yet they were going off together. Where? Were they running away together?

They were nearly out of sight now, and still she stood looking after them. What to do? Her heart . . . oh, God, her heart was breaking. This was more than mind and soul could bear, and under such a weight she sank to her knees and started to cry. What else could she do? She was a child and she was growing up all in one night.

Chapter 15

Rodrigo moved restlessly in his bed. He set his pillows, buried his head, and stared through the darkness at the ornately styled stucco ceiling. Softly, shades of Jessie came to mind. The feel of her bright, nearly white hair. When the sun gleamed upon it he was too often mesmerized by its color. Then he would tear his gaze away only to discover her eyes. Damn, but there he would lose himself. It was not only the deep violet hue but the depth of feeling he would discover whenever he chanced to look too closely.

What was he doing here in this bed without her? Damnation! He couldn't wait until she was his wife and beside him. He wanted to reach out and hold her, touch her. Ah, Jess, what have you done to my soul? This was no good. Allow a woman to take hold and you were lost. Never! Not he! Oh, no. He knew better. His father had given his heart to his English mother and she had broken it . . . as well as his own. He would keep Jess as he would a fine horse. He would care for her, make certain she was not wanting, make certain she was happy . . . yes, that mattered. He wanted her smiling the way he had first known her to smile. He had too often these days looked to find a sadness about her lips, and it troubled him.

Jess, ah, Jess, how wildly she had given herself to him. It had been like that first time on board his boat. That first time when they had not even realized the boat had disembarked. Tonight she had been wantonly his, and how she had pleased him! Then suddenly he was frowning. There was something gnawing at him. Something that had intruded upon his thoughts all evening and had kept him on the edge, a certain foreboding, but what?

He found himself pushing up against the dark oak of his headboard and folding his arms across his hard, lightly haired chest. There had been something he could not name in Jessie's manner, and that something was at the heart of his concern, but what? Her lovemaking had been all-giving, all-accepting. . . .

That was it. There was something in the way she had held him, as though she might never do so again. Nonsense. Why would she feel that way? Yet the more this idea formulated, the more his brain centered on the notion. Desperation. She had been touched with a sure desperation, and it had translated itself to him. Of course that was it, but why? He remembered now the way she had clung to him afterward and then again when he had left her at her door. Suddenly he was swinging his legs over the bed and getting to his bare feet.

Damnation! This might just be an absurd fancy, but he suddenly felt he had to go to Jessica, hold her, make certain she was still in his house. Still in his house—he stopped and scoffed at himself. Where else would she be? Even as the preposterous question chided him, he felt prompted by an instinct that had no rational base. He was pulling on his britches, crossing the room, slipping on his stockings and then his gleaming black boots. He looked around for his shirt, and with only one arm through its sleeve he was already out of his room and taking long, hard strides down the main corridor, across the central hall, to the wing that housed Jessica's chambers.

Rodrigo pushed open Jessica's door. Her name came softly to his lips, but even as he heard himself, he knew she would not answer. He knew she was not in the room. Even so, he felt stunned as he looked to the bed and found it untouched. He looked around the room in the darkness of the night and said her name again, this time in total disbelief. *"Jessica?"*

This was impossible. A suspicion, a fear, had brought him hither, and even so, he found it incredible that she was not in her room, not in her bed. Where could she be? What could she be doing? Two hard strides took him to her wardrobe. The clothes he had recently purchased for her were there still. What then?

He attempted to calm himself with rational answers. Perhaps she could not sleep. Perhaps she had decided to go for a walk about the grounds. A forbidden thing at this hour—but then, Jessie was forever doing what she should not. That was it. Of course. She had gone for a walk. Damn the woman! How dare she? He was buttoning his white linen shirt and stuffing its tails into his britches as he made his way out of her room, down the long corridor, and outdoors.

His irritation heightened fullscore as he toured the immediate grounds of the hacienda and did not find her. Damnation to hell! Where had she gone? For a ride on the gray perhaps? Insane! Would she attempt such a thing alone at night? Why? Why?

He moved in the direction of the stables and there halted as he saw the outline of a female form on the wide lawns before him. She was running away from the hacienda and he could hear her sobbing. Jessica? He called her name out loud. *"Jess!"*

Maria did not hear Rodrigo at her back. Hurting does much to wrap one in its pain and in so doing shuts out the world. She had sat on the lawn and watched Varjona ride off with Lady Jessica. She was still a child and thought life was struck from her in one blow. She had grieved and in her grief knew no one she could turn to, so she ran. She had no clear idea where she was running, but the aching in her heart was such that she could no longer be still.

Rodrigo moved into pursuit. Something, perhaps the style of her outline in the dark or the sound of her crying, told him this was not his Jessie, but who, then, could it be? It had to be Jess, so he charged after her. "Jess! *Certes*, woman, will you stop!" He was lunging for her now, and, taking hold of her arm, he was swinging her around to face him.

"Maria!" This in shocked resonance.

"Let me go!" she bellowed between sobs of rage.

"What the devil are you doing out here alone?" he asked in Spanish with parental concern.

"Ah, you may ask why I am *alone*. Indeed, why not with Varjona, eh, Rodrigo?" Her hands went to her hips, and her dark eyes flashed at him. "Perhaps if you were to watch that English slut better, I would not have been alone." Again the constriction of her throat brought on a welter of tears.

"Listen to me, young lady," he started on a stern note.

She cut him off. "No! Why should I? You were the one who brought her here . . . just like your father. You are no better at holding an English bride!" Then, realizing what she had said by the look on his face, she gasped and put her hand over her mouth, taking a step backward. "I—I am sorry, Rodrigo, I . . ."

"Never mind," he said coldly, "explain yourself."

It suddenly occurred to her that if she told him that Varjona had taken the lady Jessica off into the night, Rodrigo would ride after Var and avenge his honor. He would kill Var! No . . . yes, Var needed to be killed for his betrayal, but . . . but she wanted to do it herself! She looked away. "There is nothing to explain," she answered on a quieter note. "I—I am tired. I want to go to my rooms."

He stopped her. "Maria. Where is Jessica? You know, don't you?"

"Jessica? Isn't she in bed?" She couldn't meet his penetrating gaze.

"*Hell and fire!* Where is she?" It dawned on him suddenly, and he felt a cold knife plunge into his heart. Not with Varjona. She wouldn't . . . couldn't be with another man! He took up Maria's shoulders and he shook her hard. "Maria! Tell me this moment. Where is she?"

Maria was frightened. He would go after Varjona and only Varjona would be destroyed. That English doxy would probably not even suffer through all this. Well, she wouldn't have it, even if it meant allowing them their night together. "How should I know where your bride is? I don't have any interest in her."

"Don't you? Then why do you resent her? Why did you say I should keep better watch over her?"

"Leave me alone!" was all she could answer. "Isn't it enough that—" She stopped herself.

"Isn't it enough that what?" he persecuted her.

"Nothing! Nothing!" She didn't want to stand here with him while her heart was breaking. She tried to move away, but he held her fast.

"Maria! Answer me. What have you seen tonight? What is going on?"

"Nothing. Do you hear me? Nothing. I have seen nothing. I—I was supposed to meet Varjona, but he forgets me, probably to meet with his amigos in town. That is all."

Rodrigo stood for a moment and considered her. "Go to your room, Maria. We will speak of this in the morning."

Thankful for the reprieve, she turned and ran. He watched for a long moment, but he wasn't seeing her. All he could see, all he could feel, was Jessica, and the way they had been in each other's arms. He couldn't be wrong about Jessica. She wouldn't be with Varjona, would she?

Damn it all to hell! What to do now? He started off in

the direction of Varjona's adobe, and, once there, he stood at its weathered door, taking in a long breath of air. He knocked. Nothing. Well, of course not. Maria had said Varjona was not there. He opened the gray wooden door and peered through the darkness. Nothing. No one. Right, then, what now?

Suddenly—he couldn't answer his own question as to why—he was running at a clip toward the stables. He rounded the open double doorway and lit an oil lantern before taking the corridor to the gray's stall. The gelding was not there. Further search told him the gray was nowhere in the barn. He stood and considered this as a sleepy young stable boy climbed down the loft steps.

"Don Rodrigo, you wish me to saddle your horse?" the youth asked as he rubbed his eyes.

"No, no, go back to bed, *muchacho*," Rodrigo answered absently. What was he going to do? Where was Jessica? If she were with Var . . . He felt a sharp pain twist in his gut. No, but if she were . . . What then? Damn it all to hell, he would erase Varjona from this earth and make Jess sorry that she ever looked at another man, but let her go? No. That was something he couldn't contemplate. Jessica was his. Only his . . .

So it was in this frame of mind he took up his stance at the stable door and waited. Sooner or later one of them would return, and then? He had no ready answer for that question, because his heart just couldn't accept the possibility of Jess with someone else. He loved her. The words flowed from his heart to his brain and demanded attention at last. He loved her. Ah, Jess!

Chapter 16

Varjona leaned his shoulder into the cabin door and watched the admiral, the young viscount, and Sir Warren embrace Lady Jessica. She was in tears and they were much elated, but was this a good thing? He wasn't quite certain. Pauly quietly withdrew from Jessie's circle and came to shake his hand once more.

"Thank you," the viscount said with much felt sincerity.

"You will marry the lady Jessica now?" asked the gaucho protectively. He didn't know why, but he suddenly felt responsible for Jessie. She would have to be married or ruined.

Pauly blushed. "If she will have me"—he turned to Jess—"will you, love?"

"Will I what?" She was smiling, but inside she was falling apart.

"Will you marry me?" he pursued.

She went white, but before she could answer, Sir Warren had her arm in his grip. "She will marry, and the admiral will perform the service, but the groom will be me."

"Stop it!" she returned, and without bothering to explain her intentions she went to Varjona and took him out into the companionway.

"Var, when you see Rodrigo will you tell him . . . tell him . . ." She was wringing her hands.

"I should tell him something? Don't you remember, I was not supposed to know anything about your . . . escape," he answered, but his eyes had already penetrated hers and told her that he would tell Rodrigo anything she wished.

"Var, tell him I loved him too deeply to allow him to throw his life away on a marriage of . . . honor. Tell him . . . there was no other man for me."

He squeezed her hand. "Come, I will return you to the rancho. That is your home, my lady."

"No, no." She turned and found Pauly watching them thoughtfully. "Pauly, Var has been most kind to me. I have much to thank him for."

"Indeed, we all do," he answered her gravely.

"I must go." This from the gaucho. He had been paid mightily by the admiral. He had seen the lady Jessica with her people, and though he knew in his heart she was suffering, there was naught he could do about it.

Jessie reached out and held him fast for a moment, then she was watching his retreating form. Well, it had begun. The emptiness of spirit filled her, and she knew a heartache never before experienced. She turned and found Pauly, and, diving full into his arms, she released a cry.

Rodrigo took to his horse. He couldn't sit and wait her return any longer. Where he could look for her, he didn't quite know, but he had to do something. The moon was obscured by masses of swiftly moving clouds, and there was little opportunity to track, but small piles of manure told him that someone had left the Cesares main drive for the pike. He took that direction.

He had been traveling for nearly an hour when he realized that he would soon be reaching Buenos Aires. Absurd. Why would Varjona take Jessie there? Turn back. By now she would no doubt be in her bed with a more than reasonable explanation. Of course. What was the matter with him? He turned his horse around and started for home.

The gaucho Varjona put the city at his back and moved his horse at a swift pace. He had a long day ahead of him and in a few hours' time it would begin. There was a cattle herd that had to be moved in for the slaughter, and there were . . . What was that? Someone on the road? *Si,* a man. He reined in his horse. One could never be too careful on the main road. Bandits had not hit this area in some months, but . . . He fingered his saddle pistol, and as the man ahead was moving at a brisk trot, he was not able to shorten the distance between them.

Rodrigo felt someone at his back before he heard him. Carefully, and keeping the tilted brim of his leather hat angled so that he could have a look without appearing to do so, he glanced over his shoulder. Indeed. There was a rider at his back. There was not enough light to be able to tell more than that. It was not comfortable having a stranger at his back, so he slowed his pace to allow the rider to come abreast.

Ah-ha! thought Varjona, watching this maneuver. Who is this fellow? There was something familiar in the man's style, and as he approached he felt a sinking feeling in the pit of his stomach. It is Rodrigo. Rodrigo is here looking for me. No doubt one of us will be dead in no time. With a heavy sigh he took the initiative. "Well, Don Rodrigo?" He felt a trickle of rain and sighed again. "It seems we will be soaked before we reach home."

Rodrigo's elation at finding the gaucho alone brought out a smile of greeting. "Var! Well, well, where have you been?" She was home. His Jessie was safely home. It was as Maria had said. Var had been out carousing with his mates. That was all.

"And you, Rodrigo? What brings you so far from the rancho at this hour?" Var answered the question with one of his own. Was it safe to tell him Jessie's message? Were they too close to the city? Was this the time?

Had God sent Rodrigo here to save Lady Jessie from herself?

Rodrigo was immediately on guard. Why had Var avoided answering him? A frown descended. "I couldn't sleep," was his quiet reply. "And you, Var?"

"Me, I am forever at something. Sleep on a night like this?" He raised a hand heavenward. "When one can be rained on?" There was a touch of the old amusement in his tone. "*Sí*, why would Var bother with sleep when he can aid those he has learned to care about?"

"Indeed, but who would Varjona be speaking of?" Rodrigo was sharp with his reply.

"One, though, is not sure that one has done the right thing," Var answered.

"No? What has one done? Perhaps I may help to answer the doubt," returned Rodrigo.

"Ah, but there is Var's problem. One helps a friend, but another may be moved to great anger. . . ."

Rodrigo felt a chill take hold of his spine. "Varjona. A man may often find himself caught between two friends, but *this* friend will not hold you accountable if you display a true friendship and discuss this matter."

Varjona grinned. "You are wise. So shall I be." He thought a moment. "Listen to me, Rodrigo. Your bride has joined her family in Buenos Aires." He put a hand up to stop Rodrigo. "Hear me out. She had asked me some days ago to help her get passage back to England. When I went to the city I discovered that her uncle and his ship had already come for her. So I did as the lady asked, *not*, do listen, *not* as the lady wished. You understand?"

Don Rodrigo received the blow full force. Jessie had run away from him. Willingly she had left him. Without a word, without a letter. She had plotted behind his back and off she went. So be it! Damn the woman, damn all women to hell! His pride felt battered and his heart torn. After this afternoon . . . after the way she had touched him? She had known then that she would be leaving him. Why?

Varjona frowned. "You do not wish to know where the ship is? You do not wish to know?"

"I know that she has returned to her uncle . . . to her young man, Pauly. No, I don't need to know anything else."

"Then, my old friend, you are much a fool! Me, I would not allow another to have what is mine! You wanted to fight *me* for even talking to Lady Jess, but you let these English nothings have her?"

"It is what she wants," he answered dully.

"No, it is what she thinks *you* want. She said to give you a message. I see now that it is necessary I do."

"Message? She had a message for me?" In spite of himself he felt heartened.

"*Sí*, her words"—he broke off into English—"were: 'Tell him I loved him too, er, deeply—*sí*, deeply—to allow him to throw his life away on a marriage of . . . honor.' She said also, 'Tell him there was no other man.' "

Rodrigo reached out and held Varjona's shoulders. "I don't know whether to kiss you or punch you!"

"Why punch me?"

"For waiting so long to tell me that last!" Rodrigo was already turning his steed about and taking off.

"Eh, Rodrigo, they are docked in the east harbor. You will need to be rowed there," Var shouted after him, laughed, and then, thinking all would be better now, started off for home.

"We are for home. Immediately," the admiral announced, "so off with you my Jess; you must be exhausted."

She had sat with them for more than an hour, describing to some extent her experiences over the last six weeks. She had excused Don Rodrigo his part by fibbing and saying that she had gone on board his ship to discuss a certain matter with him and was locked by mistake in the hold. She then told of the storm and that no one had discovered her presence until the next day. They were too far from England to return, so, promising to make an honest woman of her, Don Rodrigo sailed for home. At worst her story sounded lame, but it seemed to satisfy the party at large.

Thus they were left to discuss what next was to be done. Sir Warren took strong exception. They had Jess, and now he needed a war to distinguish himself. "Home? We have to stand behind Popham. We have to move to the River Plate for the attack."

Jessie stopped at the doorway and turned around. "Popham? Attack? What do you mean?"

The admiral frowned at Sir Warren. "Nothing, my girl. It doesn't concern us. We are for home."

"Now, just a minute," stuck in Sir Warren. "We have been commissioned . . ."

"You hold right there!" The admiral was on his feet. "*We* have certainly not been commissioned. I accepted one thing and one thing only. I had promised to look into the situation while I was here collecting my niece. That is precisely what I have done. It is my strong recommendation that our home office give up the notion of attacking Argentina!"

Jessie's hands went to her mouth, and she breathed on a low note, "War? Oh, my God, why?"

"Never mind that now, Jess." This from the young viscount. "Your uncle is right. We have nothing to do with it. We sent a message to Popham today that we would not stand by him in his decision, which he seems to have made without the benefit of your uncle's vast experience." He sighed. "All that is left for you to worry about is whether *you* will have *me*."

She turned to her friend. "Oh, Pauly, best of my friends, how can I?"

"By saying yes. Your uncle will perform the ceremony."

"She cannot marry you, puppy, not when she has me begging for her hand," stuck in Sir Warren, breaking

292

away from his argument with the admiral lest he be beaten out with Lady Jessie.

"Oh, please, stop, both of you," she begged. "I don't mean to take out my mistake on you."

Sir Warren took her hands. "Jess, beloved, I want you to be my wife."

"He isn't for you, Jess," Pauly went at them. "He'll make you miserable. He is a climber and means to use you along the way."

"Stop it, Pauly," Jess shouted at him, staying Sir Warren with her hand to his chest. "Sir Warren honors me with his proposal, as you do. Both of you propose for the wrong reasons, and I do not accept, for the right ones."

"Jessica," the admiral said softly, "you must marry, and I believe that either one of these men will make you an excellent husband."

"She certainly must marry," said a strong male voice at their backs, "but I must differ with you, Admiral. There is only one male here that can make her happy, and I intend to."

Jessie's heart leaped to her eyes as she spun around and found Don Rodrigo standing there, so tall, handsome, and powerful. He was all things to her. Wasn't he here now? Wasn't he here for her? She almost dived into his arms.

The admiral frowned. How much had the Latin heard? It wouldn't do. Had he heard about Popham's intentions? This was a damned sticky business. "How the devil did *you* get here?" he demanded in a blustery voice.

"An easy thing to have one of my people row me out to your ship. He awaits me and my lady now."

"Then he may take you right off!" snapped Sir Warren, and Lady Jessica is not *your* lady!"

"Isn't she?" He stepped forward, took up both of Jessie's hands, and bent and kissed them. "I have it on good authority that she belongs to no other man."

"Rodrigo," she whispered. She could say no more.

"I believe you would like your family at our wedding, so I mean to have the ceremony performed, here and now, by your uncle," he said in a low, emotion-filled voice.

"No, no, 'tis impossible," she cried in a feeble voice, and heard her cry picked up by Sir Warren. Pauly, she noted, had retreated with a smile to a corner of the room.

"Impossible? That word has little meaning for me where you are concerned, my own dearest, most adorable vixen."

"It isn't necessary. You needn't sacrifice your life—" she started.

"Precisely why you must marry me immediately, to prevent me from sacrificing my life to loneliness, which is what would happen if you left me," he answered, kissing her fingers again.

"Rodrigo, I can't . . . we can't . . . what of your family?"

"We will marry twice, once for yours, once for mine. What better way to seal our fates?" He was grinning broadly.

"But you can't," she protested still.

"Oh, but I can . . . and I will." Then for all the world to hear, "I love you, Jess. Am I wrong in believing you love me?"

She could withhold herself no more. Without even realizing it she laid her cheek against his hard chest. "No, you are not wrong. I have loved you for so long . . . and wanted to hear you say the same."

He kissed her forehead and then looked toward the admiral.

"My lord, I believe a wedding is in order."

Epilogue

There is always time enough for questions and answers in the aftermath of passion, and so it was for Jessie and Rodrigo. There was Pauly's note. It had sent Jessie running to Don Rodrigo aboard the *Amistad,* and between Paul and Jessie this was explained and understood by all three. Then there was the problem of June Keenen and Sir Warren, but again, the young viscount came to the rescue with the answers he had obtained when he had accidentally overheard the two in conversation.

So it was that a wedding, modest, but quite legal, was performed on the English warship by the admiral Thomas Stafford, Earl of Redcliff. Some days later, much to the viscount Paul Bellamy's relief, they set sail for England, leaving Jessica and Don Rodrigo to repeat their vows at the Cesares ranch.

The harmony of their love was, however, disturbed shortly thereafter by the sudden outbreak of war. Sir Warren had remained behind to join the viscount Beresford and Sir Home Popham on the River Plate, where they launched a surprise attack upon the Spaniards.

This was both bold and successful in its initial battle. Elated with the victory, the viscount Beresford made haste to trumpet his success to England, announcing that the whole of the golden continent, from which England had always been exluded, was now open to trade.

Their glee was short-lived. Before the first ship could sail from England in response to this, the inhabitants (including one particular regiment under Don Rodrigo's leadership) and a force of French militaries crossed the broad river in a thick mist and captured the entire British garrison.

Sir Home Popham blockaded the river and battered at Buenos Aires for some time, but unsuccessfully. He was commanded to halt such operations and return home, which he finally did. He faced a court martial, and it was supposed that it was Popham's fault in raiding a river instead of planning the conquest of a continent.

Jessie's loyalty throughout was to her husband and she was able to put aside her politics as a separate entity. Theirs was a deep, unquenchable passion protected by a mutual respect for each other. Even so, their personalities dictated that their relationship would be a stormy one. It produced a daughter much like her parents, but then, that is another tale altogether!

Love...
Romance...
Passion...

CLAUDETTE
WILLIAMS